I0761013

THE LAZARUS MEN

A LAZARUS MEN AGENDA #1

CHRISTIAN WARREN FREED

This is a work of fiction. Names, characters, businesses, places, events, locales, and incidents are either the products of the author's imagination or used in a fictitious manner. Any resemblance to actual persons, living or dead, or actual events is purely coincidental.

Excerpt from *Repercussions* 2022 Christian Warren Freed
Cover design by Warren Design
Author Photograph by Anicie Freed

Warfighter Books
Holly Springs, North Carolina 27540
https://www.christianwfreed.com

Third Edition: August 2022

Library of Congress Cataloging-in-Publication Data
Name: Freed, Christian Warren, 1973- author.
Title: The Lazarus Men/ Christian Warren Freed
Description: Second Edition | Holly Springs, NC: Warfighter Books, 2021.
Identifiers: LCCN 2021922761 | ISBN 978 1957326115 (hardcover) | 9781735700021 (trade paperback) Subjects: Science Fiction Noir | Suspense |Thriller

Printed in the United States of America

10 9 8 7 6 5 4 3 2 1

ACCLAIM FOR CHRISTIAN WARREN FREED

THE LAZARUS MEN AGENDA

'Reminiscent of Tom Clancy or Stephen King, where you can envision everything happening in an era that don't yet exist but feels as familiar as the room you're reading in at the time.'

'It's a sometimes violent, yet often entertaining, off-world adventure.'

'The author draws us into a world full of conspiracy in which those who have everything want even more because human greed for power is too great.'

HAMMERS IN THE WIND: BOOK I OF THE NORTHERN CRUSADE

'Freed is without a doubt an amazing storyteller. His execution of writing descriptive and full on battle scenes is second to none, the writers ability in that area is unquestionable. He also drags you into the world he has created with ease and panache. I couldn't put it down.'

'Gripping! Hammers in the Wind is an excellent start to a new fantasy series. Christian Warren Freed has created an exciting storyline with credible characters, and an effectively created fantasy world that just draws you in.'

DREAMS OF WINTER
A FORGOTTEN GODS TALE #1

'Dreams of Winter is a strong introduction to a new fantasy series that follows slightly in the footsteps of George R.R. Martin in scope.' Entrada Publishing

"Steven Erickson meets George R.R. Martin!"

"THIS IS IT. If you like fantasy and sci-fi, you must read this series."

Law of the Heretic
Immortality Shattered Book I

'If you're looking for a fun and exciting fantasy adventure, spend a few hours in the Free Lands with the Law of the Heretic.'

Where Have All the Elves Gone?

'Sometimes funny and other times a little dark, Where Have The Elves Gone? brings something fresh and new to fantasy mysteries. Whether you want to curl up with a mystery or read more about elves this book has something for everyone. Spend a few hours solving a mystery with a human and a couple of dwarves - you'll be glad you did.'

Other Books by Christian Warren Freed

The Northern Crusade
Hammers in the Wind
Tides of Blood and Steel
A Whisper After Midnight
Empire of Bones
The Madness of Gods and Kings
Even Gods Must Fall

The Histories of Malweir
Armies of the Silver Mage
The Dragon Hunters
Beyond the Edge of Dawn

Forgotten Gods
Dreams of Winter
The Madman on the Rocks
Anguish Once Possessed
Through Darkness Besieged
Under Tattered Banners*

Where Have All the Elves Gone?
One of Our Elves is Missing*
Tomorrow's Demise: The Extinction Campaign
Tomorrow's Demise: Salvation
Coward's Truth*
The Lazarus Men
Repercussions: A Lazarus Men Agenda*

A Long Way From Home+

Immortality Shattered
Law of the Heretic
The Bitter War of Always
Land of Wicked Shadows

Storm Upon the Dawn

<u>War Priests of Andrak Saga</u>
The Children of Never

SO, You Want to Write a Book? +
SO, You Wrote a Book. Now What? +

*Forthcoming + Nonfiction

Dedication

It takes an army to create a good story. I would like to thank mine for moving the characters in the right direction, kicking me in the behind when I started to lag, and for giving their support when I continued to ramble on about this scenario or that. Specifically I wish to thank Lee Heinrich and Raven Eckman for slashing this story to ribbons with their red pens, and to my wife, Annie, for all of her love and support over the years.

PROLOGUE

"Once you agree to this you can never go back. Your life will change forever and not necessarily for the best," Mr. Shine said, his thin hands clasped behind his back.

Carter Gaetis paused to glance at the odd man, doubts plaguing him. It had been months since their first meeting and he still didn't wholly trust Mr. Shine. Several qualities making him human were missing in Carter's opinion. Shine was tall, lightly built and possessed a permanent sneer. His pale complexion and dark hair lent a cadaverous presence Carter found acutely disturbing. When he spoke it was a thin rasp.

"Are you prepared to commit yourself, your life, and your dedication, to our cause, Mr. Gaetis?"

Carter tensed. Born to believe there was no escaping the past, he spent years languishing as a convicted murderer. Penniless and branded a villain by the rigid constrictors of society, he contemplated suicide. Darkness crept into all corners of his life, everyone left– except for his wife and daughter. They'd stood beside him through the worst of it, but even that wasn't enough. The longer he failed to act the more they suffered …

"Once you say the word all of your pain will be erased. Your debts to society will be paid in full and you will be free. Born again into a new life, a new purpose."

For a price. Nothing comes without a price.

The real question was he willing to pay it so blindly? There must be another way. And yet, there wasn't. All of his options were exhausted. He'd tried finding work, but convicts were mostly shunned. Mr. Shine offered him an escape but the cost … the cost threatened the security of his very soul. Carter wasn't a violent man, or so he told himself. He'd tried to live a good life, to matter in the eyes of God and his peers. A drunken moment of indecision stripped it all away and brought him to this point.

Carter clenched his jaw, staying silent.

Mr. Shine, for his part, had done this innumerable times before. Each situation was unique, but the candidates all acted similarly. He'd come expecting Carter's indecisiveness. After all, it was no easy thing to accept the forceful removal of one's past life without grave concerns.

Shine rolled the stiffness from his right shoulder, the lingering effects of an old injury, and viewed the street. The sleepy village along the Hudson River would have gone unnoticed if not for human expansionism. Linking Canada to old New York City via the major train hubs, the Hudson River maintained the prominence it once held during the colonization of the New World some six hundred years earlier.

Inhaling the early autumn smells of changing foliage and the dampness of the river, Shine briefly considered retiring to this part of the world. This forgotten stretch of the world was one of the few peaceful places he'd ever been.

Carter finally asked, "Will they suffer?"

There was no way a man like Shine could ever retire in any fashion save one: an assassin's kiss. He exhaled before smiling and turning to face Carter. "No. Their part in this sad tale will finally be over. They will be free, Mr. Gaetis, much as you will be."

Carter sighed. He wished there were another way. Anything but this. He was as much a victim of circumstance as his family.

With grave reluctance, Carter nodded curtly.

There was no other option.

"Mr. Gaetis, I need to hear you say it," Shine insisted. His eyes took on a wicked glow.

"Yes, Mr. Shine. I accept your offer." His words lacked the conviction with which they were meant. Carter was a strong man but even the severity of the moment left him weak in more ways than he was willing to admit to any man, especially Shine. He didn't like the thin man at all.

Carter imagined there'd come a time for reckoning before the end. He only had to wait until that day.

Shine clapped his hands, twice. "Good! I knew you'd make the logical decision. Very smart of you, Mr. Gaetis. Now, if you'd please follow me inside, we can conclude tonight's business and be off."

"You can't be serious!" Carter all but exploded. Making the decision was one matter, having to participate entirely was another. He wasn't prepared to endure the endless stream of nightmares from what came next. No man should.

Shine fixed him with a withering glare. "Oh but I am. This is not a game, Carter. The only way I can be assured of your commitment is by having you participate. Anything less is inexcusable. Our employers demand unconditional obedience." He paused. "Perhaps I was mistaken. Perhaps you are not the proper candidate for this position. Good night, Mr. Gaetis. I wish you the best of fortune in the future."

Shine turned to leave.

"No, wait. I'll do it. It's just going to be …"

"Hard? I understand. We have all gone through similar." Shine patted him gently on the back. "Consider it being part of a brotherhood."

***

Shine peeled the bloodstained, leather gloves off and tossed them down on the flower pattern comforter. He wasn't smiling but lacked the seriousness Carter expected after murdering two people in their sleep. Instead he wore the look of grim satisfaction that only a man trapped in such a profession could produce. And professional he was. Only a single speck of blood escaped the bed, landing squarely on his right cheek.

Shine looked down to where Carter had collapsed in a pile of vomit and tears. "It's done, Mr. Gaetis," he announced quietly. "As far as anyone knows you and your family died here tonight in a regrettable gas fire. Welcome to the Lazarus Men."

Carter failed to see the thin smile creep across Shine's face.

ONE

2273 A.D.
Old New York City Spaceport

The interstellar liner drifted down through the perpetual blanket of pollution and clouds concealing the open skies from the people grinding out their lives in what had once been the most populated city in the world. The firing roars of landing jets drowned out any sound the busy city could muster in response. Ground crews streamed from maintenance sheds as the sleek, grey skinned vessel inched closer to the ground. Steam and exhaust billowed out from its belly, spreading across the partially empty landing strip and north across Flushing Bay.

Touching down with the grace of an eagle, the passenger liner groaned as the landing gear absorbed its weight. Un-loaders lumbered out of the hangar bays to pick up baggage while the gangway slowly extended from the terminal to clamp with the docking doors. Metal scrapped against metal with a hideous scream. Crowds of civilian onlookers gawked at the newly designed liner built by McMaster's Enterprises. Earlier designs were bulky, squared brutes lacking grace. The latest models were sleek, elongated machines inspiring dreams and passion alike. as it was still a relatively unfamiliar sight, people were eager to get a glimpse of the new liner created from the imagination of Roland McMasters.

Earth had seen great changes over the last hundred years. The discovery of the interstellar drive ushered in a new age of expansionism. With Earth already overpopulated, the human race fled to the stars and, while there were a few disasters along the way, soon humans had colonized and occupied more than a score of habitable worlds stretching across the heavens. And for a time humanity prospered. Considering Old Earth was dying slowly from the combined effects of overpopulation and a dwindling supply of natural resources, it was all anyone could do to flee to a new world.

There had been a strange sort of peace between the worlds for five decades, but even the dreamers knew it wouldn't last much longer. Brush wars were springing up here and there as various Earth governments tried to establish dominance. Colonists were resisting living under rulers from their former home. Old Earth politics had never really gained a foothold on the majority of the colonized worlds. Desperate for power, the Old Earth governments banded to form the first Earth Alliance. They created subversive groups designed to halt the development and independence of the Outer Worlds.

No one from the Outer Worlds traveled back to Old Earth unless it was absolutely necessary. The majority of the indigenous Old Earth population was unable to leave, to move on to a better world and an easier life. They got through each day with grim determination, knowing there was no promise of a golden future. Life was life.

Lost in the throngs of people waiting for transport were two men who normally wouldn't have been with each other. The taller loomed over the shorter by almost a foot. He was lean but muscled under his dull grey suit. Keen eyes partially hidden beneath thick, black eyebrows endlessly scanned the crowds, like a tiger on the hunt. His hair was neat and well groomed, lending him the appearance of general civility. His sharp-edged features suggested a hard life. A thick moustache curled over his upper lip. People glanced his way and immediately moved away. The unspoken consensus was this was a dangerous man.

The shorter man was frail by comparison. His demeanor suggested he'd be more comfortable working in a library or a bank. Short and stocky, the hat he wore concealed his growing bald spot and shadowed his business-like face. Round wire framed glasses made him look as if he were constantly trying to peer into secret. His dark blue suit added little flavor to the odd couple. While he possessed the intuitive intelligence necessary for his line of work, he lacked his companion's sense of security. The briefcase in his hands was much lighter than it seemed and he was unarmed. That's what the taller man was here for.

Together they scanned the masses. Their target remained elusive, however, prompting the taller man to grind his teeth in frustration. A disappointed scowl soon darkened his face. He was a man unused to waiting.

"This is useless," the shorter man complained in a painfully thin voice. "He might not even be in the spaceport."

His counterpart grunted in reply and continued his search. Finding one man in a crowd of hundreds of vague, faceless civilians took time and, more often than not, proved to be highly frustrating. But he was a professional. Finding the impossible target was his specialty.

He would find who he'd been hired to find.

Keeping his disdain for the shorter man private, he briefly considered removing the man but knew their employer would be most displeased if he did. So he'd have to deal with this man always complaining about matters beyond his control — this man who never should have left Cestus III.

The crowd slowly started to thin, curiosity over the new liner now satisfied. The taller man nudged the shorter man, and both began to follow the flow of the crowd. They soon rounded a corner leading down the narrow corridor to the entrance of Terminal A.

Hints of desperation clouded the shorter man's face. Returning to Cestus in failure wasn't an option. Lost in thought, he failed to see the hands stretch out and jerk him into a dimly lit alcove. His glasses slid down his nose and he gave a startled squawk.

The taller man moved with incredible speed, roughly shoving his counterpart aside and crushing his forearm into the assailant's throat, driving him back into the wall. His free hand now held a snub nose blaster pressed against the man's ribs.

"Heeey, be easy man," the assailant cooed as his brief life flashed before his eyes. "Gholson, call off your pet. We've got business to discuss."

Jonas Gholson pushed his glasses back up his nose and flattened his ruffled jacket. "That was most unwise. Why should I have Mr. Edgemeyer stand down?"

"I have the information you need," the now frightened man replied.

Edgemeyer growled and pressed harder on the man's ribs.

Gholson smiled tightly. "I'm sure you have. Who doesn't when confronted with death? First, we must know where the Eye is. Our employer is most anxious to reap his rewards. As I'm sure you are."

Forearm almost crushing his throat, the once confident man stuttered, "Y-yeah, well I-I don't have it yet."

The blaster in his ribs dug deeper.

"I see. It was my understanding you were contracted to have the key in your possession by this time. Perhaps you didn't understand the technicalities of your contract concerning failure to produce?"

Wild fear filled the man's eyes. His mind raced over the different possibilities awaiting him, none of them good. Maybe he'd made a mistake taking this job in the first place. "No, wait, man. I can explain. Just give me a little more time and I can get your key and you can have your damned Eye."

Gholson shook his head, removing his glasses to clean them with a small white cloth. "I am quite afraid it has gone well beyond your ineptitude, Mr. Zilke. You see, in our business there is little room for error. You have failed quite miserably. Our employer doesn't look kindly on mistakes. The time has come for us to sever our relationship." He sighed. "Edgemeyer, escort Zilke to a quite place outside where we can conclude this matter. I will get in contact with the Fat Man." He turned back to Zilke. "It is most unfortunate that our dealing didn't work out. Most unfortunate indeed. Farewell, Mr. Zilke."

Gholson turned his back on the captive Zilke as his partner forcibly lead him out the main doors and into the steadily emptying parking docks. While Gholson had no compunction about the tactical side of their business, he lacked the stomach for the dirty work. Besides, he was merely the median.

Silently wondering just what to tell the Fat Man, Gholson wandered back down the corridor to the concierge desk. They didn't have the key and he didn't dare return to Cestus III without it. Not unless he wanted to suffer the same fate as Zilke.

Zilke watched the diminutive man amble away before Edgemeyer dragged him outside. He panicked and tried to escape, but Edgemeyer was stronger than he anticipated. His feet seemed lighter as he was dragged away. The cold blast of night air slapped his face, bringing a tear to his eyes. His unkempt hair danced across his shoulders. Zilke considered crying out but his experience with the city was enough to ensure no one would bother looking. He only had one chance to live, and it was slim.

"Mr. Edgemeyer, please," he begged. Death ticked closer like the great clock erected in Times Square after the 2140 terror attack. A tiny trickle of blood spilled from his lip where he'd bitten it. "Can't we talk about this? You don't have to do this."

Edgemeyer smiled. "No more talk. Gholson didn't want to hear it and neither do I." He dragged Zilke into the shadows behind the main terminal taxi stand and shoved him against the cold metal dumpster.

A scream pierced the night.

TWO

2273 A.D.
Old New York City Spaceport Taxi Stand

Edgemeyer stood over Zilke's body. The pistol felt light in his hand and his smile was wicked, harsh. He was a man who enjoyed his work. For Zilke there had ever only been one way out. Failing the Fat Man wasn't an option, not with the stakes raised so high. Decades of waiting and searching were drawing to a close and Zilke hadn't fulfilled his part of the arrangement. Edgemeyer felt no sympathy. Such emotions were beneath him.

Writhing and bleeding, the thief didn't have long to live. A gut shot was the worst way to die. Capable of perforating multiple organs and producing extraordinary pain, this had become Edgemeyer's signature method of execution.

"Terribly unfortunate, Mr. Zilke, but business and all," Gholson said as he approached the scene. "Mr. Edgemeyer, it is time to go."

He glanced up to see Gholson impatiently tapping his wrist chrono.

Edgemeyer gave a crisp nod and crouched down to stare into Zilke's eyes. Or at least the one that could still open. "Well, my friend, I am sorry to say that we no longer require your services. Goodbye."

Leveling his blaster at the thief, Edgemeyer fired four times. Blood blossomed across Zilke's chest and neck as the glass bullets ruptured vital organs. Zilke died in extreme agony. Rising Edgemeyer surveyed his work. The wounds were wild and poorly aimed. His hope was to make the murder look like a drug deal gone wrong, playing into Zilke's criminal past. It was one of the Fat Man's requirements for local talent. When the police discovered the body there would be nothing to connect Zilke to Edgemeyer or the Eye.

"That was crude," Gholson said without passion.

Edgemeyer shrugged. "And?"

Gholson was about to reply when two distinct sights caught his attention. The first was a seemingly empty car parked just down the road to his right. That in itself wasn't peculiar, given they were at one of the busiest metro hubs on the American continent. What bothered him was his inability to see through the dark-enhanced windows. He got the impression they were being watched.

The notion of confronting whoever was in the car almost formed until he spied a shower of tiny red sparks striking the pavement. Gholson squinted and caught a cloud of bluish smoke. He and Edgemeyer smelled the cigarette at the same time and wordlessly moved toward the spot. A witness. Discovery now threatened to bring their endeavors to a screeching halt.

Gholson scowled and shook his head with a worrying gaze as they reached the spot. Edgemeyer crushed the dying butt beneath his shoes. With the skill of a serpent, the lanky assassin swept the area nearby. He found nothing.

Gholson scanned their surroundings with disdain. Dozens of people now filled the street. Most wore Trans Stellar uniforms, the irony of it not lost on him, considering who their employer was. Many more were businessmen or last moment travelers. There was no way to determine who the smoker was. Frustrated, he resisted the urge to clean his glasses.

"What do we do now?" Edgemeyer asked, leaving the planning to Gholson. "We can't search the entire city."

Staring down at the cigarette butt again, Gholson almost smiled. "Oh, I don't believe it will be too difficult." He reached down and snatched the slightly used wallet off the ground. "It seems Zilke was hedging his bets. I suspect he planted the Eye on a dupe with the intent of returning to collect after he threw us off." He flipped open the wallet. "Mr. Gerald LaPlant shouldn't be too hard to find at all."

Life in the city was hard. Those not strong enough to handle it fled to the countryside or off world in the quest for more lucrative opportunities. Most of those who remained were hardcore men and women proud to call the city home.

Gerald LaPlant didn't much care for Old New York one way or the other. He'd read the histories as a child. They all proclaimed it as the *greatest* city in the world. He didn't understand why. Piles of trash lined the streets as far as he could see. Crime was rampant in certain areas. There were nice places, but those were heavily guarded and all but inaccessible to the general population. Common people like Gerald.

He'd just finished his shift at the spaceport and was looking forward to making his weekend rounds at the local bars. Trans Stellar wasn't the best employer, but it paid his bills and kept a wet drink in his hands when he needed it. Already middle aged, Gerald was slowly getting on with life and the dreams of youth started losing their effervescence. Divorced and with nothing to look forward to, he took each day as it came. It comforted him to think he was just an average man living an average life.

Little fields of grey were sprouting up across the roof of his head. His face and hands were getting lines now. He smoked too much and drank far more than he should, but when life continues to crap on you, you tend to hide behind things. His vices often kept him company into the lonely hours of the morning when the misery became unbearable.

Halfway through the main terminal and Gerald's thoughts were already focused on the future. It wasn't much of a life, but it was all he had. He was content with hoping for a better future, choosing to wait for that one spectacular moment to arrive and change his life forever.

Crowds were thicker than usual. Gerald never cared for the hustle of big city living. Too many people in small spaces left him feeling uneasy. Unfortunately, the only way out through what he called 'the herd' was twisting and dodging as they moved ever closer, and increasingly slower, to the front doors.

Then it happened. He knew it would. It was an inevitable fact of walking around the terminal.

A young man slammed into him, nearly jarring Gerald's bag out of his hands.

"Hey! Watch it buddy!"

The man scurried away, leaving Gerald glaring at his back. Faced with two options, one of which would result in both of them being arrested, Gerald took the higher road and continued on. Rude was too common and chances were he'd get bumped again before gaining the freedom of exit.

Once free from the tides of humanity, Gerald headed toward the taxi stand. Living in New York had plenty of perks, but transportation wasn't one of them.

The city was still overpopulated, forcing the government to ban private transportation of any sort. Gerald didn't mind. Having a vehicle proved an additional expense he didn't and couldn't afford.

Gerald plopped a cigarette between his lips and buttoned up his thick overcoat against the fierce winds blowing in off the Atlantic. It was the last day of April and still too close to winter for his liking. Living in the city usually protected him from the worst of winter though the cold never seemed to leave. He looked skyward, hardly noticing the full moon looming overhead. Taking a quick drag, Gerald instantly felt some of the tension fall away. He'd been working almost nonstop for weeks in the hopes of scraping together enough cash for a vacation. The strain was taking its toll. He needed a drink.

The winds blew harder as he headed toward the taxis. Trash flit across the pavement. Gerald rummaged through his pockets in search of enough loose change for a quick drink before heading home. Days like this shouldn't end any other way, or so he'd always imagined. He came to the end of the terminal building and was about to round the corner when strange sounds brought him to a halt.

No stranger to the crisp sounds of urban violence, Gerald recognized gunfire. He glanced down the alley in time to see a tall, slender man dressed in black fire four rounds into an already injured man. The very same man who had slammed into him inside. The smell of gunpowder and blood sickened Gerald almost immediately. It took a second longer than necessary for his mind and body to arrive at the same conclusion.

His cigarette slipped from his lips as he turned and ran. The only sounds he heard were his hurried footfalls and the thunder of every breath. A thin film of sweat quickly coated his face and hands. Gerald found a little luck as a crowd of returning passengers filed out of the terminal. He pulled his collar tighter around his neck and face and slowed to a walk, hoping to blend in as he redoubled back to the taxi stand.

He jumped in the first available.

The driver adjusted the meter. "Where to?"

"Just drive."

The perceived empty car rumbled to life the moment Gholson and Edgemeyer stalked off. Having overheard everything, the driver behind the darkened windows shook his head. Everything about the situation was rank amateur.

Frowning, he drove beside Zilke's body. The idiots should have at least disposed of any evidence of their presence, but their need to remove the potential threat of Gerald LaPlant overrode common sense.

The driver turned and sped off into the night with renewed purpose. Another important piece to the puzzle had been introduced this night and he was one step closer to fulfilling his purpose.

After all, how many Gerald LaPlant's could there be in the city?

THREE

2273 A.D.
Queens, New York

And endless stream of drab orange lights lined the roads as the taxi motored through the largely empty streets. Gerald resisted the urge to keep looking back over his shoulder. Cursing his luck, he wished he'd stayed at work just a little longer. His heart was pounding.

Murder.

He'd just witnessed a murder. And of a man he'd encountered mere moments before.

He lied to himself, telling him it was pure coincidence and nothing more. He knew he should go to the authorities, but …

His mind replayed the scene a hundred times. Splinter images took shape. The agonized look on the victim's face. The impassive stare of the killer. Blood. He'd never seen anyone actually shot to death. There was so much blood. Dark red and thick, it spilled out from the body to form a pool. Gerald had read stories about the frontlines of the border wars. Sure, it was horrible to see or read but that was the past. He had witnessed death firsthand and it was much, much worse.

A host of impossible questions sprang to mind. Who were the killers? What possible crime could the victim have committed to warrant execution? Gerald decided he didn't need to know. He needed to put as much distance as he possibly could between them and himself. The rest would either fall into place, or it wouldn't.

He reached into his pocket for his wallet— it was gone. A fresh wave of fear clutched him.

The taxi rolled up in front of his apartment hab.

"Thirty-seven credits, Mac," the driver called as he dropped the vehicle into park. Magnetic drive engines locked and the almost egg-shaped vehicle hovered inches above the street.

Panicking, Gerald found a crumbled pair of twenty credit bills in the bottom of his jacket pocket. Paying the driver, he exited as fast as he could. The very real possibility of the killers catching him produced raw terror. If they had his wallet …

With the taxi no more than fading taillights in the distance, Gerald was confronted with emptiness. The street was clear. Few lights were on in his building. Still, he glanced up and down the street for telltale signs of being discovered. A sigh of relief escaped his trembling lips when he didn't see anyone. Perhaps he had more luck than he thought.

Gerald entered his access code and slid through the automatic sealing doors.

Instinctively he knew that slowing down or stopping was a death sentence. Safety was as far away as his apartment, and then it was hit or miss. The murderer's cold eyes haunted him as he hurried up the stairs to the third floor. Gerald fumbled with his code, typing the wrong numbers twice before he was rewarded with the familiar hiss of his door opening. Gerald scanned the hallway one last time before slipping inside.

The door hissed shut behind him.

"What the hell have I gotten myself into?"

Lights, programmed to the sound of his voice, dropped down from concealed ceiling panels and brightened the room. Gerald stared at his meager belongings, trying to determine if anyone had beaten him here. Not generally an organized man, it was no easy task. Clothes were strewn over the furniture. Dirty plates and dishes piled up around the sink. The scent of old cigarettes was practically permanent now.

Gerald grabbed an old vase, a relic from his failed marriage, and staked around the rest of the apartment. The vase wouldn't do much, but it was the heaviest thing he could think to grab. The apartment being only three rooms, Gerald finished quickly. The bathroom was small, as was the single bedroom. Once he was satisfied nothing looked out of place, he set the vase down on the nearest table and began pacing.

"This is madness," he said. "I just watched a man get killed. What are the odds?"

Gerald liked to think he was a practical man. He kept his head down and minded his own business. The only real drama had been his divorce, which had started out civilly and went downhill fast. Now he stared bankruptcy in the face. He was in over his head and sinking quickly. Witnessing the murder tonight confirmed that suspicion.

He paced the room, arms folded, and brows knitted in thought. Who would he call? It wasn't like Gerald had an abundance of close friends. Should he go to the authorities? The New York police wouldn't be much help. Sure, they'd clean up the body, but they'd never find the killers and certainly wouldn't waste any time or effort with protecting a concerned citizen. Most of his friends were really his wife's, automatically ruling them out. They left when she did, and he knew he couldn't rely on the ones who stuck around. These days folks just wanted to look after their own affairs and pretend to care.

That seemed an end to his option, which was scary because, while the taxi hadn't been followed, he couldn't shake the feeling the killers were a step behind. Waiting for him to make a critical mistake.

Gerald thought of sliding his furniture to block the door but found the notion troubling and futile. The automatic doors would still open, and he'd wind up just as dead. He could try reasoning with the killers but doubted they'd fall for it. There was no escaping the fact he was a liability. From what little he knew, or assumed, killers seldom left loose ends.

Gerald didn't like the fact he had been reduced to a loose end.

Pacing the width of his living room, he desperately tried finding a way out of his predicament. He wasn't made for this sort of situation. Life had always been hard, but simple. The feeling of being hunted left him feeling hollow. Every shadow suddenly took on life. Behind every closed door lurked someone trying to kill him.

Frustrated, Gerald sat down. His mind was spinning, going in no particular direction. He attributed his condition to exhaustion from a twelve-hour shift and then being forced to flee across the city. The gentle hum of power generators attached to the outer walls lulled him to sleep. Fatigue settled in. His eyelids fluttered.

Yawning, Gerald rolled the tension from his shoulders and rose, heading to the kitchen to stir himself awake. Sleep was now as much of an enemy as those men from the alley.

"Think, damn it. I can't have much time left before they find me."

Cold reality suddenly reached out to slap his face. Stunned, Gerald felt his strength dissolve. None of his thoughts or feeble planning meant anything now. His wallet. If they had his wallet … He couldn't think where he'd lost it and that left him with profound dread. The only reasonable possibility was the dead man had lifted it from him when they collided.

Hurrying to the self-dimming windows, he stood just far enough back so as not to be noticed by anyone on the street. He stared out. Nerves twisted his stomach. Gerald never considered himself a brave man, though he seldom gave in to cowardice or fear. Despite the hard nature his life had developed, he maintained a neutral yet guarded attitude.

The normally insignificant pale orange glow from the streetlights took on a haunting aspect. Every shadow or tree became a killer waiting to strike. Gerald's heart beat faster again. The horror of his situation truly began sinking in. Shuffling in the hallway startled him. Gerald spun, reaching for the vase again.

A cough joined the shuffling; nasty and wet. Gerald felt instant relief. It was only Mrs. Vargas. She'd been battling a cold for weeks now and couldn't shake her cough.

"Either I need a drink or I'm losing my mind. One of the two," he muttered and went back to the window, looking at the empty street below.

Deciding his mind was playing tricks, Gerald returned to the couch and slumped down. He began laughing. Everything about the situation was weird. Part of him refused to believe it. An ordinary life didn't sound like much to ask for and, up until now, he'd led nothing if not an ordinary life.

Yet as much as he wanted to forget this incident and move on, he couldn't. He pictured the tall man in black hunting him down and slitting his throat.

He needed to get off world, and fast.

"Call Creeps," he told his house automated response system.

A series of high-pitched beeps filled the space as the computer made the call.

"Do you have any idea what time it is?" a gravelly voice asked.

Gerald almost grinned. Creeps never had been one for idle conversation, even back in their school days. "That's no way to speak to an old friend."

"LaPlant? Holy hell, what do you want? I haven't heard from you in a long time."

What did he want? Gerald wasn't sure but he needed to act fast. "I have some time off and was thinking about heading your way."

"You mean off Earth? I never thought you'd see the light, man. Where did you scrape up enough to make it to Mars?"

Gerald winced and pinched the bridge of his nose. What if his line was already tapped? "You know me, I've been working my tail off since the divorce. Figured it was time to take you up on your offer. I need a break."

Silence filled the space between them just long enough to rouse Gerald's suspicion. He shook the feeling away, dismissing the notion of the killers getting to Creeps. Hundreds of millions of miles away, there was no way they could have gotten to his friend … not yet at least.

"Yeah, come on up. I'm sure we can get into enough trouble up here to keep you content for a while."

Gerald snorted. As if he needed help in that department. "Great. I'll book a flight and send you the data." He paused. "And Creeps?"

"Yeah?"

"Thanks, buddy. I owe you one."

"Forget about it. What are friends for?"

"End transmission," Gerald said, and the line dropped.

Alone again, he leaned his head back on the couch and started to think. No matter how hard he tried, he couldn't shake the image of the man's face as he took four rounds to the chest.

FOUR

2273 A.D.
Queen, New York

Gerald didn't remember falling asleep. His adrenaline had been pumping so hard he was sure he would not be able to rest. But when the excitement of the moment passed, he collapsed. Nightmares plagued his dreams. Faceless killers stalked him through mist shrouded streets. Bloodstains discolored his face and hands. He felt the violent puncture of a dozen bullets plunging into his stomach. He wanted to scream but no sound escaped. The sensations left him in a cold sweat.

Jerking awake, he sat up from his slumped position on the couch and hurried to the window.

Nothing.

The street was empty.

Gerald relaxed, if only just. A glance at the wall chrono told him dawn was still some time away. He wanted to think the worst was over and his worries had all been creations of an overactive imagination. There was no killer hurrying to find him to keep him silent. More than likely his wallet was at his workstation, and he hadn't really seen what he thought he saw. He almost laughed at his ignorance.

Yawning, he stretched the kinks from his back and thighs. His stomach growled, reminding him that he hadn't eaten much since lunch. Turning, Gerald ambled into the small kitchen and fixed a cup of coffee. The scent was a childhood favorite, reminding him of his grandmother's house. Despite admonishments from his mother, his grandmother often snuck him sips of her straight black coffee and shared bites of her burned toast. He could pass on the charcoal taste of what little remained of the bread, but the acidic taste of the coffee hooked him.

Mug in hand, he opened the refrigerator and rummaged around for something to eat. There wasn't much. Bachelor life wasn't the party he thought it would be, yet Gerald took to it with what enjoyment he could find. He'd gotten married at an early age, against his parent's wishes, and came to regret it. Youth did foolish things.

Grinning at the memory, he ambled through his kitchen—

His world suddenly exploded.

Heavy pounding at his door startled him. The ceramic mug smashed to pieces on the floor. Hot coffee splashed across the faded white tile and his lower pants. Cursing, Gerald bit his lip and shook the scalding liquid from his hand. He began to shake and his heart beat wildly. He froze as the infant feeling of safety evaporated.

He'd been tracked down.

He was a dead man.

His apartment had one way in or out, effectively trapping him.

Finally moving, Gerald grabbed the same vase from earlier with sweaty hands. Another round of banging had him creeping toward the door.

"Mr. LaPlant? Mr. LaPlant, are you in there?"

He froze again. Instant recognition robbed his adrenaline— a woman. Not the silent murderer from the night before. He opened his mouth, but no words came forth.

"Mr. LaPlant, please open the door," she persisted.

Sweat beaded on his brow. Gerald struggled with confusion. There was the very real possibility that he was being set up. Led into an elaborate scheme with one inescapable conclusion: his cold, lifeless body rotting at the bottom of the East River.

The fine line between paranoia and caution played havoc with him. He wanted to scream. To vent frustrations to the heavens and everyone caught in-between. Gerald drew a deep, shuddering breath and hit the button. The door hissed open, revealing an old woman, alone, staring back at him.

"M … Mrs. M-moorhead?"

Perplexed, she folded her thin arms while attempting to peer around his shoulders. "Is everything all right?"

Gerald took a quick glance down both sides of the hallway. "Well enough. What can I do for you?"

"Are you sure you're fine?" she pressed.

"Yes, Mrs. Moorhead. Nothing's wrong. Now, if you please, I'm going to be late for work."

She pursed her lips. Untrusting. "There's word going around that strange men have been seen looking to get inside. No doubt with nefarious intent. The community watch is meeting tonight at 8 p.m. Will you be there?"

Community watch? As if that will help. If nothing else though, his fears were at least confirmed. The killers from the airport might not have found him last night, but the vultures were circling.

He feigned calm while feeling anything but. If she noticed his smile was false, she didn't say. "If I am home, yes I will."

Satisfied, the old woman gave a curt nod and headed on to the next apartment. "Thank you, Mr. LaPlant. 8 p.m. sharp. Don't be late."

"Have a good day, Mrs. Moorhead."

The door hissed shut.

Gerald exhaled, leaning back against the cold wall. A look down at the vase he held produced a laugh. He could hope Mrs. Moorhead, who's reputation as the building's resident conspiracy theorist was well documented, hadn't noticed. That chance, however, was unlikely. She may be in her late seventies, but she was every bit as sharp minded as she was decades ago. No doubt more than a few laughs would be had at his expanse tonight. Too bad for them he did not plan on attending.

If any of what she'd said was true, he needed to leave sooner than he'd planned. Gerald set the vase down and hurried to pack a small bag. Taking only the absolute necessities, he finished in moments before realizing the time. If he didn't leave now, he was going to be late for work and, in all likelihood, fired on the spot. His employers lacked empathy, regardless of the purported situation. Gerald couldn't take the chance of being fired should his apprehensions prove to be baseless. It wasn't much of a job, but it was all he had.

Slipping into his jacket, he was thankful that working for Trans Stellar require uniforms, thus alleviating him of the responsibility of making daily clothing decisions. Two important things happened then. He automatically reached for his wallet, normally kept on the counter beside the refrigerator wall unit, only to discover it wasn't there. He next reached into his jacket pockets, praying he had missed it the night prior.

When his fingers brushed against a foreign object he froze. Puzzled, he produced a small, cylindrical object and studied it closely: it was the color of cold granite and dense; easily heavier than anything that small should be. Odd, he didn't recall having anything like this and should have noticed it yesterday. Chalking it up to the situation, Gerald set the thought aside for the moment.

"What the …?"

Aside from it being completely alien to him, Gerald found nothing special or significant about the cylinder. Frowning at his recent string of bad luck, Gerald dropped the cylinder back into his pocket and prayed his wallet was at the terminal.

"Hey man, you're acting kind of funny today. What's going on?"

Gerald frowned. Maybe it would do to ease his troubled mind if he got what he saw off his chest. He set the last bag on the conveyer truck and pulled his gloves off.

"Earl, can you keep something to yourself?"

The younger man nodded, his dark complexion a contrast to Gerald's paler skin. "Sure. What's going on?"

Without realizing it, Gerald looked around. Suspicion glazed his eyes before he whispered, "I saw a murder last night."

Earl jerked back; disbelief stitched across his face. "Come on, man. A murder?"

"I know what I saw. It was by the taxi stand. This tall guy went and shot another man four times."

"What did you do?"

Gerald snorted. "I ran. What else could I do? The guy had a gun."

Earl stepped closer, genuine concern in his eyes as he laid a hand on Gerald's forearm. "Tell me you at least went to the police?"

"I … I didn't," Gerald admitted as a lump formed in his throat.

"Shit man! That makes you an accessory," Earl almost shouted. "You gotta go to the cops, Ger."

"I don't have any proof. You can't expect me to believe the body is still there and no one has noticed it? I bet there's not a drop of blood."

Earl shook his head. "Doesn't matter. Go tell the police what you saw. At least that way you'll be off the hook when they find anything bad. My cousin Jimmy in Upstate had the same thing happen. Wound up getting a nickel for it."

While he doubted the accuracy of Earl's story, Gerald knew going to the authorities was the right thing to do. It was just getting there that might prove a problem.

"Promise me you'll do it," Earl almost pleaded.

There was a hint of … of what?

Seeing Gerald's hesitancy, Earl joked, "I can't do this crappy job by myself. Go tell the cops what you know and get back here. My knees are already killing me."

Gerald threw his hands up. "All right, all right. I'll go ask for an extra break and take care of it. Happy?"

Before Earl could answer, a young woman in clothes too smart to be out on the flight line approached. The soft click of her heels stole their attention. Their gazes traveled from her calves to her blue eyes, taking in every line and curve on the way up. Gerald noticed with bemusement that she rolled her eyes in false disdain.

"Mr. LaPlant? The director wishes to speak with you," she said in a voice almost as golden as her hair.

Gerald shivered.

"Oh shit," Earl whispered.

FIVE

2273 A.D.
Old New York City Spaceport

Gerald managed to walk beside his escort rather than a step behind. Any other day he might have reveled in walking next to a good-looking woman. Just not this one. His fear resurfaced; he resisted the urge to ask her what was going on. He'd already judged she was the tight-lipped sort. Staying silent, he marched along feeling very much like a condemned man going to the gallows.

A handful of passersby offered odd stares, heightening his discomfort. Gerald was thankful he managed to make it to the director's office without seeing any familiar faces. Directing him to a row of empty leather chairs, the women disappeared into a private office.

She returned quickly, pausing to smooth her pleated skirt before taking her seat at the small, cherry desk. "He will be ready for you in a moment."

Gerald tried to smile to show her he was calm and unconcerned but failed miserably. He began to think about the last couple of days, trying to decipher why his boss would want to see him. Aside from the incident last night, he couldn't think of anything worthy of either praise or reprimand.

The office door opened.

Gerald looked up, impressed the antique door still worked. It was the only one he had ever seen with an actual knob that required physical manipulation. A gray-haired man in an impeccably tailored navy blue suit and red tie stepped out. Wise eyes stared at Gerald, silently assessing him. Wordlessly, the director beckoned then went back into his office.

Must be nice to have so much power, Gerald thought as he rose and followed. A brief and final glance at the assistant left him more puzzled than before—she mouthed 'good luck' as he passed by. Confused, Gerald made sure to close the door behind him.

"Sit, Gerald," the director ordered, gesturing to the empty chair on the near side of a desk that easily could have fit a family of four at dinner.

Gerald looked around, obeying. This was his first experience in the director's office, and it was impressive as the situation was intimidating. Ornate wooden paneling covered three of the four walls, the fourth being windows from ceiling to floor and overlooking the main runway. Old style books, something Gerald had only seen in historical records, lined three rows behind the director. A small table with different liquor bottles sat off to the right beside a waist high globe. Even the cushions on the chair felt opulent.

"Gerald LaPlant, employee number 1023345. It's come to my attention that you've had an excellent record with us for nearly ten years," the director began. "Are you happy here?"

Gerald paused, thrown off his train of thought. *Has the whole world gone mad while I was asleep?* Swallowing, he said, "Well enough I suppose."

"Explain." The director interlaced his fingers and patiently waited.

"Well sir, the work is hard, but fulfilling. I'm on a good crew, which makes coming to work easier."

"But?"

Gerald ran his tongue over his last wisdom tooth. “The hours are long, and the pay could be better. Aside from that I really don’t have any complaints.”

Calculating eyes searched Gerald for signs of subterfuge. “Pay and hours. I see. What would you say if I offered a solution for your particular dilemma? One I assume the others feel as well?”

“Sir, its not my place to speak for the others,” he said.

“No, I suppose not. Gerald, your record speaks well for you. You have made yourself an extremely valuable member of this team and I feel it is time to reward you for it.”

Gerald tensed. The hammer had to drop at some point.

“I am promoting you to shift supervisor. I need quality people in positions I know they can handle. You can handle it, can’t you?”

It was all he could do to keep from grinning. “Yes … yes sir. I can handle it.”

The director clapped once. “Excellent. Report at once to personnel to turn in your old badge and receive a new one. You begin immediately.”

“Thank you, sir. You won’t regret this,” Gerald said.

“I pray you’re right. Good day, Gerald.”

The door clicked shut as he returned to the reception room. Beaming, Gerald looked at the assistant. Any thought he had of being congratulated by her were dashed when she looked at him from behind the she glasses she was now wearing with a stack of paperwork in her hand.

“Take these with you. Make sure you fill in everything correctly or they won’t be able to process your new pay grade,” she told him. “Oh and you’ll need to trade in your uniforms. Supervisors need to look sharp."

Gerald accepted the paperwork and strode from the office whistling. Perhaps his luck wasn't so bad after all.

Paperwork filed, new badge issued, Gerald officially took on his new role. He'd given up thoughts of a promotion or a new job a long time ago. The economic pressures of the city and the atrocious labor market meant there weren't any new jobs, and no one seemed interested in creating any. All big corporations were now focused on the stars. New planets were being developed with surprising regularity, creating a wealth of potential profit. Earth was being left behind.

Gerald accepted his new position with the enthusiasm of a man recently granted parole. The promotion was entirely unexpected and, for the moment, almost enough to distract him from his worries. Almost. His thoughts kept returning to his missing wallet and the strange object that had somehow found its way into his pocket.

He tried to retrace his steps but couldn't figure out where he had lost his wallet. Nerves frayed, Gerald hurried back to his new office and shut the door. He was exhausted. His muscles were rubbery and his eyes raw from lack of sleep. It was all he could do not to let his forehead crash against the faux maple desk.

Gerald jumped at the unexpected knock. He panicked. Once again, he was trapped with only one way in or out.

"Come in," he finally said, strangely wishing for a proper tie to lend him a more professional appearance.

He only relaxed when he saw Earl's smiling face.

"Man, they messed up for sure," Earl said. "You belong down there on the line with rest of us goons, not hiding behind a desk."

"Are you kidding? At least I can take naps up here," Gerald replied. "Who let you up here?"

Earl feigned a hurt look. "What? I can't come up to congratulate my friend on his undeserved promotion?"

"Undeserved? I busted my ass for years in the same position. It's not my fault the big boss recognized true potential."

"Whatever, man," Earl waved him off. "Hey, I heard you lost your wallet."

Gerald was instantly suspicious. "Where did you hear that?"

Earl shrugged. "Word around the terminal … Any luck finding it?"

Alarms screamed in his mind. Without thinking, Gerald gave his jacket pocket a quick pat. The smooth object within was oddly comforting, making the act almost natural. "Right here in my pocket. I never lost it, buddy."

"Just making sure. I can't have my new boss walking around without proper identification," Earl said, offering a weak laugh. "All right, Ger. I'm going to leave you to it. I wouldn't want to get written up on your first day as supervisor."

"And I don't want to get fired," Gerald agreed.

"Maybe we can go out for a drink later."

Gerald wasn't sure what game his friend was playing. They were friends at work but had never socialized outside of that. Earl was a nice enough sort, but there was something that set Gerald on edge ever since he had told Earl about last night.

"Yeah," he said. "Maybe."

SIX

2273 A.D.
Queens, New York

The rest of his day sped by. Gerald successfully managed to avoid both Earl and Mrs. Moorhead as he returned to his apartment. He still hadn't booked a flight off world. Despite nothing more happening, he wasn't able to shake the hunted feeling. Every stranger was a potential killer searching for him. He scanned every face, jerked at every hint of suspicious movement on his way home. The longer he sat alone, the more his mind concocted wild thoughts. He had been sure he had run before anyone could see him last night, but now he wasn't so certain.

Gerald rubbed the back of his head in frustration. There was work and home. He didn't need much else. Certainly not finding himself a witness to murder. Earl's advice about going to the police was sounding better and better. Tired of thinking about it, Gerald headed for the shower. He hoped getting clean and then getting some food in his belly might calm his nerves and allow for clearer thought.

The warmth of the shower threatened to put him to sleep the moment he stepped under the water. Until now he hadn't realized just how wired he'd been. His stomach growled. There was no way he'd be able to drink his dinner, not tonight. He sighed. *Rest and relaxation. That's all I need.*

Dried off and dressed, Gerald stumbled into the kitchen. The days old leftovers he found in the refrigerator weren't enticing but would have to do. He was already too tired to actually cook, so a quick warm up in the microwave sufficed. He was half finished when his automated system announced an incoming call.

Fork hallway to his mouth, Gerald frowned. The chime repeated until he couldn't help but answer. He'd expected Mrs. Moorhead's voice on the end—

"Ger, I thought we were meeting for drinks?"

Earl. Damn it. What does he want? "Yeah, I'm sorry but my stomach isn't feeling good. I left work a little early."

The pause on the other end was long enough to feel unnatural. Gerald began to suspect Earl was more than just the good work friend he was pretending to be. "I'm sorry to hear that. Anything I can do to help?"

Gerald decided to play his hand. "What's going on, Earl? We're not even that close. Why the sudden concern into my wellbeing?"

"I was hoping you wouldn't catch on so fast," Earl said. His voice abruptly changed. "You're not safe."

"What are you talking about? Not safe from what?"

"This is no joke, Gerald. Forces so powerful you can't begin to imagine are converging on your position. We've been tracking certain individuals, major players, coming in and out of the spaceport for months now."

The sheer incredulousness of the admission was almost too much for Gerald. Until now he'd managed to get through life without intrigue or controversy, aside from a nasty divorce. His mind refused to accept what Earl, or whoever was pretending to be Earl, was telling him.

"What are you talking about? Major players? Who is we?" he demanded. "Earl, what in the hell is going on?"

"Gerald, I need you to be calm and listen closely," Earl said and waited a few seconds for his words to sink in. "I'm not really Earl. I can't tell you who I am but know that I am looking after you best interests."

"Bullshit! We've known each other for a long time. Who or what exactly are you if you aren't Earl?"

There was no sound of agitation in Earl's voice. "There never was an Earl. I was planted by the government to uncover wrongdoing by Roland McMasters. He's a very dangerous man linked to numerous missing persons cases on several worlds. My job is to find proof that McMasters was involved."

Gerald hesitated. He knew the name. "The same McMasters who owns Trans Stellar?"

"The same."

"What the fuck have you gotten me involved in?" he asked, defeat lacing the words. His only solace stemmed from finally knowing he wasn't going crazy.

"None of this was intentional. Trust me. We much prefer not to get civilians caught in the line of fire."

Civilians? Only then did Gerald realize Earl hadn't answered all of his questions. "Who are you? Give me a reason to trust you."

"I am … on your side."

The line went dead.

Gerald's fork clanged as it fell to the table. Food spilled. He didn't know what to do. Discovering Earl was an imposter left him feeling unexpectedly hollow. In truth, he didn't know the man that well, but knowing he was false was worse than being gut punched. Who was he? Who were these power players the man pretending to be Earl hinted at? Did all of this have to do with the murder he'd witnessed? Without admitting it out loud, Gerald knew it was all connected.

So what was his role in all of this?

His hand dropped to the cylinder in his pocket. Gerald carefully withdrew it to study it again. He failed to find anything special about it. In fact, if he'd seen it lying on the street, he would have walked right past. The surface was entirely smooth, without so much as a nick or gouge. He was no expert but somehow got the impression that the cylinder, or artifact as he decided to call it, was older than he first guessed. Old meant valuable to the right circles.

Circles that might well be hunting him now for what he has and what he saw … All because of his missing wallet. There was no other explanation. Somehow, someway, the killers had found his wallet and were undoubtedly using it to hunt him down. The cold realization that a man with a gun could be lurking anywhere left him rocked. He needed to take his mind off it lest he fall prey to madness.

Gerald held the artifact between his thumb and index finger, eyeing it appraisingly. Now that he took the time to admire it, it did have an almost mesmerizing quality. The flawless craftsmanship was captivating. He'd never seen anything like it.

Reluctantly pulling his gaze from the artifact, he closed his eyes. Using the serenity of the imperfect darkness, he started to retrace his steps from the moment he witnessed the murder. But no. There'd been no interaction with anyone, except for a limited conversation with the taxi driver. No one since … that man who bumped into him in the terminal! Gerald's eyes flew open with revelation. The man, the murder victim, must have slipped the artifact into his pocket when they made contact.

But why? Gerald's only conclusion was the man knew he was about to get into trouble and took advantage of the small collision to drop the artifact into Gerald's pocket in the hopes of finding it later. Gerald was just a man at the wrong place and wrong time. There was a conspiracy in play, one he had been involuntarily drawn into.

He needed to board a shuttle and get off world as soon as possible. He doubted giving up the artifact would do much to secure him a longer life. The man by the taxi stand had been all business and didn't seem the type to leave loose ends.

The travel bag by the door drew his attention, unmoved since he dropped it there on his way to work. His thoughts whirling, he focused on one: *if I leave maybe no one will find me.*

All he had to do was make it to the Lunar Transfer Station and disappear among the stars. But then there was the Earl imposter. The more he gave it thought the more Gerald started to believe the Earl imposter was either on McMasters' payroll or, worse, actually a government agent. Neither possibility seemed to hold a good outcome for him.

Nor did getting drunk when he needed his wits the most. Gerald wiped the sudden wave of perspiration from his face and made up his mind. Earth had become too small for his comfort. It was time to go.

After taking a few bites from his now cold dinner, he hurried to his small bedroom to change for what he hoped was going to be along, uneventful flight. Only when he was dressed and ready to go did his thoughts return to his missing wallet. He'd never get off world without it.

The frenzy of knocks on his door startled him. Mrs. Moorhead's voice was almost welcome. "Mr. LaPlant, please open the door!"

He glanced at the wall chrono, surprised to find it only a few minutes past nine. Tenant meetings normally drudged on for hours. Especially when she was the speaker. Then again, and refusing to chalk everything up to random conspiracies, Gerald figured that she had been most adamant about his attendance. Perhaps the others had sent her to come get him. He decided to take a chance and opened the door.

Mrs. Moorhead collided with him. Her wild eyes searched his for a split second before blood exploded from her back. She died in his arms with a strangled gurgle. Gerald, horrified, jerked back.

The body hit the floor.

SEVEN

2273 A.D.
Queen, New York

The killer entered the apartment as if it were his own. He took delight in seeing Gerald back away, hands helplessly held up as if that was enough to protect him. Humans were such predictable creatures there almost wasn't any sport in hunting them. Reaching into his pocket, the killer waved a battered wallet.

"Mr. Gerald LaPlant. You've been a careless man of late," he teased.

"Please take what you want. Just go. I won't tell anyone."

The killer paused. Lending the illusion of considering the act.

Both men knew it was a ruse.

This was the same man who'd killed the victim at the terminal. The same man Gerald had spent the last day looking over his shoulder for. And now the same man who'd murdered Mrs. Moorhead. The gun in his hands, pointed at Gerald's face, told him what was coming next.

Quietly, a second, shorter man entered. The newcomer paused to remove his glasses and clean them before focusing on Gerald. "Ah, much better. You would think after all the advances we've made as a race we'd be able to finally get rid of these contraptions."

"Who are you?" Gerald asked, his mind racing. He needed to find a way out of the apartment.

The taller man gave the shorter a sharp look that went ignored.

"Since you are about to die, and you truly are, I don't see the harm in a name. I am Gholson. This wiry fellow beside me is Edgemeyer. Not one for words, or the sort you'd cross lightly. I can assure you he is the most remorseless man in his profession."

Gerald sickened at the way Gholson beamed about Edgemeyer's work. The pool of blood oozing from Mrs. Moorhead's corpse reached his toes. "What profession is that?"

Gholson's eyebrow, obnoxiously thin, arched. "Stalling, Mr. LaPlant? That's not very becoming. We've come a long way and you are the only obstacle preventing us from accomplishing our task. If you would be so kind, hand over the key."

Key? That's what this is? Key to what? Out loud he said, "What key? Look, you guys have got the wrong man. I'm just a shift supervisor at the terminal."

"Indeed. Congratulations on your promotion by the way." Gholson snorted. "Oh, don't look stunned. We all work for the same employer. Finding your personnel records wasn't exceedingly difficult." He shrugged. "Now, the key. I would hate to unleash Mr. Edgemeyer on your building just to prove a point."

"You wouldn't," Gerald protested.

"I can assure you it is no bluff. Few men in the galaxy are as resolute as my friend. Test us and the blood of scores will rest on your hands," Gholson said, calling his bluff.

Gerald raised his hands higher. "Look, I told you, I don't know anything about a key."

Gholson surveyed the apartment, crinkling his nose. "Going somewhere? Not many people I know keep a packed travel bag by the door."

"I-I have sick family on the west coast."

Gholson clicked his tongue against his teeth. "You don't expect me to believe that do you? Stuttering is a telltale sign of deception. Gerald, may I call you Gerald?"

Gerald shrugged. "What difference does it make if you're going to kill me anyway?"

"Very perceptive. I like that in a man. The realization of one's fate is a remarkable experience, don't you think?" Gholson theorized.

Edgemeyer took a step forward with a grunt. "Enough talking. We're wasting time."

Frowning, Gholson put his glasses back on. "My colleague of few words is right. Tell us where the key is. I promise he'll make your death as painless as possible."

Gerald wasn't sure what kept him from just digging into his pocket and giving Gholson the artifact—the key. His brain screamed to do it. To save his life at least for a few moments longer. Rather than producing the key, he kept his hands at chest level.

A sudden commotion in the hall distracted Gholson. The short man turned and Edgemeyer's eyes darted to his companion, giving Gerald a chance. Snatching the nearby vase, Gerald smashed it hard against the side of Edgemeyer's head. The slender man dropped, blood splattering from his cheek to forehead. Ceramic bits were embedded in his flesh. The immediate threat was subdued, but there was still Gholson—

Gerald leapt on him.

"Wha …" Gholson managed before Gerald spun him around and slammed him face first into the nearest wall.

One of the lenses of his glasses fell out and there was a crunch. Gholson whimpered, a man unused to pain. Gerald jerked him back, ignoring the smaller man's flailing arms and dropped a left hook to his temple. Gholson crumpled and Gerald let him fall.

Heart racing as his mind struggled to catch up with his actions, Gerald reached for his travel bag, stopping halfway out the door to rush back and grab his wallet from the prone Edgemeyer. He knew he should at least call the police, if not dispose of both men permanently, but he wasn't a killer.

Gerald grabbed his bag and ran for his life.

The cab sped through the winding streets of Queens, dodging traffic with remarkable deftness. Gerald held on as the cabbie drove like they were being chased. Ironic, as he considered what had just happened. He found himself looking through the rear window every few seconds, betraying that nervousness permeating his core. The vase had been thick and sturdy, but not enough to incapacitate Edgemeyer for long. Hopefully he managed to rattle the killer's brain enough to give Gerald time to board the next flight off world and put Earth behind him.

On edge, Gerald rubbed his knuckles. It had been a long time since he punched anyone, almost back to his grade school days. He noticed skin torn in places and the blood had lost its luster, already starting to clot. The worst part was how much it ached, leading him to suspect a broken bone. He couldn't afford an injury.

His free hand remained jammed in his jacket pocket; fingers curled around the key. Gerald found it oddly comforting. The tip of his thumb ran the length with almost loving precision. If he closed his eyes and listened closely, he was almost certain he heard soft voices whispering words of confidence in a hypnotic lullaby.

Blinking rapidly, he dissolved the effects the key had on him. Did he really hear voices? Provided he got off world, there'd be plenty of time to explore this new gift. And gift it was. The more he felt the alien smoothness the more he became convinced the key was not made by human hands. In so far as he knew, there was no technology capable of transferring thought into objects. Researchers had tried and failed for generations. That much he recalled from the news and holo-recordings.

Arguments sprang up between church and science, arguments managing to transcend centuries of ignorance and firebrand rhetoric. Gerald was neither a scientist nor overly religious but was wise enough to know when something just didn't sit well with his conscience. Whoever was responsible for the key's creation, and whatever it unlocked, was clearly superior to modern human evolution. The prospect frightened him beyond measure while leaving him wanting to know more. Knowledge was power, but it was also the most dangerous aspect in the world.

"Hey buddy, you plan on paying or do you want to drive for the rest of the night?"

Gerald looked up. The bright lights of the taxi stand were blinding. His head ached, pounding in sync with his heartbeat. He hadn't noticed until now how dry his mouth and throat were. Or that they'd arrived.

Fumbling in his pocket, he paid the driver and hurried inside.

Any sense of normalcy was gone. Every face in the crowd was a potential villain. Fear compounded his list of enemies. Fear, debilitating and ignoble, threatened to send him over the edge. Knowing that his would-be killers worked for Roland McMasters only made the situation worse. Anyone in the terminal might be looking for him.

And then there was the Earl imposter …

Gerald hadn't had the chance to give it much thought. Nor had he spared the time to consider who Earl really was, or even what he was. He frowned thinking of all the time he and Earl had shared on the flight line. All of the stories, the history. It was all cast in doubt as the warped truth slowly eased into the open. Gerald now figured the Earl story was fragile at best. Gerald went cold with the thought that the Earl imposter knew far too much about him and what he had seen.

Ticket lines were thankfully short and, using his work pass, he was able to go behind the counter and book his own flight—one of the few perks of the job. That and no one questioned him.

Ticket in hand, Gerald hurried off to security. The flight didn't board for another hour but the closer he got to the gate the closer he got to freedom.

It wasn't until he neared the security checkpoint that his fear rose again. What if the Earl imposter had already gone ahead and alerted security? Gerald might well be a wanted man. A recent string of sabotage attacks on major shipping had increased security measures exponentially. Armed government patrols were now common at all of the major spaceports in North America. Rumors among the work crews was that Trans Stellar was being targeted by rival shippers. Now, Gerald wasn't so sure. Roland McMasters was clearly in a position to get what he wanted and wasn't afraid to take losses. It wasn't difficult to imagine that the attacks were in response to McMasters' aggressions elsewhere.

Gerald passed a pair of government soldiers. Their dark camouflage pattern uniforms were overtly threatening in this setting. He didn't like the idea of living in a police state—which the current government promised wouldn't happen. An actual war hadn't been fought on Earth in decades. Now battles took place on random moons and lifeless chunks of rock. Not here in New York City.

Neither soldier so much as acknowledged him. Gerald continued moving up the line until his turn came. Blockish metallic scanners prohibited pedestrian traffic from avoiding official screening points. A pair of disinterested local security manned each of the seven positions. None were familiar.

Gerald took a deep breath and advanced when called. He stepped into the full body scanner, nervous about the artifact in his pocket. Without knowing what it was or what it did, there was every chance it might set alarms off, ending his escape bid. A green light flashed and he was waved through. Filled with relief, Gerald stepped up to the security guard manning an outdated desk.

"Tickets, identification, and passport. Where are you headed?" the guard asked.

Gerald paused for split-second to dig out the required documentation. "I'm visiting sick relatives."

The guard took his eyes off the ticket and passport. "Relatives?"

Swallowing a curse, Gerald shrugged. "That's what I was told. Would you argue with your grandmother?"

Noncommittal, the guard handed Gerald's paperwork back. "I never knew my grandmother. Next."

Feeling his confidence growing, Gerald gave a curt nod and hurried on. The last hurdle was cleared. All he had to do now was wait for the boarding call. His shoulders sagged. The unsustainable pace he'd been thrust upon finally slowed, leaving him both mentally and physically exhausted. He selected a seat in an empty row against the wall separating gates and waited.

EIGHT

2273 A.D.
Absolution, Cestus III

Powerful. Wealthy. A man of extreme influence on a dozen worlds. His name was synonymous with success. Few in the modern age had carved out an empire as extensive as Roland McMasters. The equivalent of Carnegie or Rockefeller, McMasters was both revered and despised. World leaders bent ears when he beckoned.

Born into moderate wealth, he took his family nest egg and multiplied it exponentially. He threw all of his considerable resources into the fledgling Trans Stellar space lines, transforming it into a premier company in the galaxy and making him wealthy beyond imagining. Rivals were driven under through manipulation and other, less savory means.

Monopolies were supposed to be a thing of the past, broken by the old United States government three hundred years earlier. Expansionism helped revert that. The colonization of outer space reopened old ideals. McMasters jumped at the opportunity. He waged a ruthless campaign across a dozen worlds, securing contracts and rights to future shipping lanes. His influence drove smaller competition out of business or well out of his market niche. By the end of a ten year span he controlled one of the largest shipping conglomerates in human history.

In the end, there could only be Trans Stellar.

And yet, it wasn't enough.

McMasters was a man of impressive appetites. Excess became a creed. Health issues arose at a relatively early age as a result. Obese and covered with liver spots, McMasters hated all he'd become. Hated the way his body betrayed his mind. He felt his health slipping daily, carrying him closer to the end he so desperately sought to avoid.

He'd secretly spent a small fortune on doctors to no avail. By fifty he was one of the richest men in the galaxy. Sixty came and went and he realized that the sum of his success meant little. Greed consumed his thoughts. Being rich was one thing, a very important factor helping shape his dwindling days to be sure, but it wasn't enough to propel him into the offices of power he brazenly craved.

Cestus III was a gorgeous world by all accounts, made up of massive continents of forests and rivers divided by oceans reminiscent of Old Earth. Tourists flocked to the colony in the hopes of escaping back to what their home world once was. McMasters owned much of the new world, but the provincial government was so small it lacked the resources to give him the powerbase he craved. He'd bought the major moon, one of three, out of spite and transformed it into the largest shipyard in existence. Using it as a base of operations, he branched out to the stars. No one would ever guess his true motives—that was a secret he kept closely guarded.

He scowled out the bay window of his private sanctuary. Nature never meant much to the man. He much preferred the cold steel of a ship's interior. A flock of red ibis soared far below his mountaintop retreat, mingling with wisps of cloud. McMasters swirled the single malt in the glass in his right hand before draining the last of it.

"Tell me again why I don't have the key in my possession," he demanded, turning to face the holo-screen on the far wall.

McMasters watched Gholson fidget, focusing on his twisted nose and blackened eye. The short man was easily manipulated, which was why he hired him. McMasters knew there was deviousness deep within Gholson's heart waiting for exploitation. It was but a matter of prodding hard enough to get the desired results. Having a man like that on his payroll was dangerous, but ultimately necessary.

Edgemeyer, who stood beside Gholson on the screen, was decidedly more stoic. The killer was motionless, his face impassive. McMasters had no doubt Edgemeyer harbored no such deep resentment over being used. Indeed, he almost carelessly entertained the idea of allowing Edgemeyer to seek out a counteroffer from competitors. That would prove interesting should it fall out that way.

Gholson, as usual, did the talking, "Mr. McMasters, we are pursuing the quarry as we speak. He has proven most difficult to—"

"I don't recall asking your problems, Gholson," McMasters interrupted. "The key should be in your case, enroute back to me."

"Please, Mr. McMasters. Let me explain."

"I am not a man fond of excuses, Gholson."

Edgemeyer, frowning at his counterpart, looked back at their boss. "We had the rat, but he managed to slip the key to someone else."

"Where is Zilke? I wish to speak with him."

"Dead."

McMasters concealed his surprise. "Dead. That's it? Care to elaborate? Perhaps I should take your reticence for broader ignorance?"

If Edgemeyer was disturbed, he hid it well. "I killed him and dumped the body at the spaceport terminal."

"I am … most disappointed with that result," McMasters scolded. Edgemeyer's nonchalance infuriated him. "Gholson, seeing as how my thief has been … decommissioned, where is my key?"

Twin beads of sweat rolled down Gholson's right temple. "Sir, we believe it is with one of your employees."

"That's not an overly surprising fact. Who is he and where did he go?"

"We … ah …"

"Gone," Edgemeyer supplied.

McMasters hurled his now empty glass against the wall. Pieces sliced through the air upon impact. "Gholson, remove this man from my sight before I order both of you evaporated!"

Holding up his hands in a gesture of compliance, Edgemeyer casually strode out of the picture. McMasters was fairly certain he spied a smirk twisting his favorite killer's lips.

"Sir, we are doing our best to locate him. His name is Gerald LaPlant, a minor flight line worker, or so we believe. He made the mistake of dropping his wal—"

"Spare me the details. This LaPlant will be dealt with from my end. I expect you to find him. A man who works at a space terminal will most likely attempt to board a shuttle elsewhere if he suspects he is being hunted. Check all departing flights. My techs on this end will scour all databases to find him."

"Yes, sir. Edgemeyer and I shall redouble our efforts. You won't be disappointed."

"For your sake I hope not. I don't treat kindly those who fail me repeatedly," he countered. "Oh, and Gholson …"

"Sir?"

"Do not let Mr. Edgemeyer speak to me again until he fixes the problem he created," McMasters warned. "I want a report from you in four hours. Do not disappoint me again."

McMasters pushed the button on his desk to kill the connection. His need for the key heightened with each passing day. The thought of finally wrapping his fingers around the small object sent ripples of excitement through him. And for good reason. The key was, in his opinion, one of the greatest finds in human history.

Suddenly concerned with his prospects for success, McMasters began to pace, his footsteps heavy across the hardwood floors.

Gholson and Edgemeyer, while highly competent assets, weren't going to retrieve the key for him, or so he concluded. McMasters had it on good authority Earth Alliance agents were also searching for the key.

It was, it seemed, to be a race.

The prize, the key.

***

Space was remarkably comforting for troubled souls. Soundless, the vacuum represented the eventual demise of everything humanity strove for. Satellites ranged across the atmospheres of dozens of worlds. Massive cargo liners and passenger transports trudged between fixed points. Stars collapsed in on themselves and died without so much as a gasp. All in pure silence. No finer symphony had ever been composed.

Space, Mr. Shine decided, was perfection.

It was also the logical place to construct and emplace his base of operations. Long ago, when men first took to the stars in earnest, Shine secured a private facility on the small moon of Io. He offered a one of a kind service to the galaxy, making him rarer than the finest gem. That sphere of influence also made him a wanted man. Shine delighted in the fact so many governments placed exorbitant prices on his head and those of his agents. It was through his diligence these agents remained faceless.

Shine was a man of little excess. He took enjoyment in walking his shipyards, funded, unbeknownst, by Roland McMasters and other conglomerate leaders. The sheer delight in effectively fleecing major companies seeking to eliminate him often sent him to sleep with a smile. Shine, his first name unused in so long not even he recalled it, lived in a harsh world with often bloody outcomes. But even a man in his position needed to smile every once in a while.

He was sought out by rich and poor, though unless one had the financial resources to make his efforts worthwhile, they seldom received Shine's services. His name was synonymous with terror laden shadows in children's nightmares. He was the boogeyman. A ghost. A vengeful spirit come to reap a grizzly harvest. Shine was the Grim Reaper.

Men and women, all hand selected over the course of generations, dressed in jet black uniforms nodded in passing. None bothered to stop. Nor were they expected to. Shine deplored wasting time in pointless conversation with those he had no emotional or intellectual connections to.

Each and every person in the Lazarus Men was expendable and knew it.

He wound through the sterile steel corridors circling the main construction hangar. Crews rotated shifts in a continuing effort to produce the latest frigate for their blossoming fleet. Showers of sparks rained down to the accompanying sound of welders, drills, and heavy machinery. Shine took great pride in the professionalism of his people. It showed in every aspect of his organization.

"Pardon me, Mr. Shine?"

He froze midstride, eyes narrowing to daggers. "You do remember this is the one part of my day where I do not wish to be disturbed?"

"Y … yes sir," the young blond man replied.

"Good. Then tell me why I shouldn't kill you now and tack your corpse to the wall as a reminder to the others?"

"My apologies, but Roland McMasters is on the line for you. He was most adamant about speaking only with you."

McMasters? What could the Fat Man possibly want? It would take more resources than he had at his disposal to discover the money siphoning. "Very well, inform him I shall be there shortly."

"But he …"

"Speaks with me at my discretion. Remind him of that. Now, leave me."

Shine resumed his walk. Much in life could wait. Roland McMasters was certainly on that list.

His office was empty by the time he finished his morning tour. A cup of hot tea sat on the desk, freshly brewed and, unless he missed his guess, only placed there moments before he entered. Rather than feeling pleased at not having to kill one of his favorite people for an avoidable mistake, Shine relaxed. What had begun as a promising day was marred by the earlier interruption. The tea helped salve the wound.

Patience already worn thin, Shine sank into the well worn cushions of his chair and clicked the intercom.

"Roland McMasters," he said flatly.

There was silence for a moment as McMasters suddenly realized his was connected. "Mr. Shine, you're not one to move with purpose to a summons, are you?"

"I will spare your insolent tone this time since I decided I am going to have a good day. Otherwise, I'd already have agents dispatched to … deal with you. What do you need from me?"

He caught the sigh, that slightest fraction of hesitation before the Fat Man divulged his needs and desires. Shine couldn't help but smile as he listened.

It was going to be a good day after all.

NINE

2273 A.D.
Enroute to Mars

The Trans Stellar passenger liner moved so quickly through the shipping lanes that Gerald couldn't even tell they were in space. Remarkable considering this was his first time off world. All of his childhood dreams of going to space, exploring the cosmos like an Eighteenth Century adventurer exploring Earth had finally come to fruition and, oddly enough, were mildly disappointing.

Gerald unbuckled from his seat once the flight crew gave the signal and set about inspecting a vessel he had only viewed from the outside. He knew the specs by heart. Each liner was a four thousand ton behemoth capable of traveling just below the speed of light. He read once that the research and development teams for Trans Stellar were busy trying to solve the faster than light principles but had yet to achieve a sustainable breakthrough. The thought of being able to travel faster than the speed of light thrilled him to no end.

The liner was three-quarters full, carrying over seven hundred passengers. Not unusual for the time of day he departed. Later flights would be overbooked just to ensure there were no empty seats. As the only major fleet in service, Trans Stellar could do as they pleased without suffering much customer backlash or government interference.

Twin cabins ran the length of the fuselage with common areas in between. The dining facility served basic meals designed to fill the stomach rather than please the palate. Considering the price of each ticket, Gerald assumed the food would be better, but he couldn't complain. It did the trick and left him lulled toward sleep. And sleep was a thing he could not afford. Just because he had not spotted the odd pair of killers who invaded his apartment didn't mean they or others weren't on board.

Gerald figured it was only a matter of time before they reported back to their boss. When they did, it wouldn't take long before they figured out he had bought a Trans Stellar off world travel chit.

So much for his new promotion. His contract would be terminated, and he'd likely become a wanted man. It made sense from his point of view. While he didn't know his employer, there were enough rumors and whispers circulating that Roland McMasters was as heartless as they came in business matters. At the end of the day, Gerald wasn't much more than a replaceable cog in the great machine.

He refused to let those kinds of thoughts debilitate him. Especially when he needed a clear head. Mars was nearly a day away by standard travel. If Gholson and Edgemeyer had not managed to find him in time to get on this liner or send someone in their place, he would have a little time to get the jump on them. He was mostly finished with his meal when a soft voice disturbed his thoughts.

"Do you mind if I sit here?"

Gerald nearly choked on a piece of steamed broccoli when he found himself staring up at a striking woman. Her smile, red framed glasses, and button nose made his heart beat faster. "N-no, please. B-be my guest."

It had been such a long time since he had last had dinner with a woman he'd almost forgotten how to behave.

Her smile widened as she slid into the seat opposite him. "Thank you. It seems my timing is always horrible. I always manage to get hungry at the same time everyone else does."

Gerald looked around the room, surprised to find most of the tables occupied. "It happens." He silently cursed himself the moment the words left his lips.

"Yes, I suppose it does. I'm Charlotte."

"Gerald."

She nodded. "It's a pleasure to meet you, Gerald. Is any of that good?"

The look on her face told him she'd already made up her mind, but he answered anyway. "That all depends on what you want it to be good for. I think too much of this will make your hair fall out."

She laughed, golden and warm—he melted at the sound.

"I'm not a gourmet woman, but I would like something better than army food when I make a trip across the stars," she said.

Gerald didn't know what army food tasted like, but if this was an indication, he was glad he never enlisted. "We have to eat, and they are contracted to feed us. They didn't bother promising it would be good though."

"You sound like you know about this subject."

He nodded. "I used to work on the flight line at the New York terminal. We loaded everything from bags to dinners."

"You're a brave man to be eating stuff you loaded."

Gerald wasn't sure if he was meant to laugh or take offense. "Work is work."

She sampled a little of everything on her plate, doing a double take at the browned meat smothered in gravy. "Aren't you going to ask me what I do?"

He winced. "I'm sorry, I …"

"It's quite all right. I understand. Getting tongue tied when a strange woman asks to join you for dinner is a perfectly reasonable reaction I think."

"Tongue tied? Not me, I've talked to plenty of strange women before," he tried, unsuccessfully, to recover. His face burned when she laughed again. It was a sound he could listen to forever.

"A man of the people I see. I'm just messing with you. You seem tense, distracted, and I was trying to lighten the mood."

"You're a psychiatrist?"

"Oh heavens no. I have enough of my own problems. I'd literally go crazy if my head was filled with everyone else's problems. I'm an archeological assistant," she said.

"So you play with rocks?"

"On a very basic level, I guess you could say that," she replied. "The group I work for is searching for pre-existing civilizations on other worlds. Quite fascinating stuff. It's just extremely unlikely that we are the only sentient beings in the universe capable of mastering all of this. I mean, the impossibility of that occurring naturally is almost one hundred percent."

He'd never paid much attention to the crackpots who insisted on the existence of alien life. It was pure fantasy for a man in his former position. Gerald worked long days in a dead end job. There wasn't any time to ponder the probability of alien species. Come to think of it, he didn't much care for the majority of the human race.

"I don't believe in aliens," he said.

She leaned forward, a conspiratorial look in her eyes. "You should. If you knew some of the things we've discovered …"

He was suddenly eager to know what those discoveries were. "You're messing with me again."

"No," she said around a mouthful of carrots crunching between her teeth. "We can't offer definitive proof yet, but there have been significant artifacts uncovered on almost a dozen worlds. Its almost as if there was a worlds spanning empire long before the human race crawled out of the oceans." She paused, "How can carrots be crunchy on the outside and mushy in the middle?"

Artifacts. Aliens. His hand dropped to his pocket. He hadn't seriously thought about the mysterious key being an alien artifact. Now he wondered. Gerald didn't know who this Charlotte was, but he decided he wanted to hear more about her work. It might help him figure out why those men were so anxious to get the key.

Dinner continued comfortably through mild conversation even as his mind struggled to put the pieces together. There were moments of subtle flirting, also genuine conversation. It was over much too soon.

Gerald laid his napkin on the plate. "That was …"

"Bad," she finished.

It was his turn to laugh. "Extraordinarily. Would you care to join me for a coffee in the lounge?"

The request surprised both of them. He'd never been bold or forward with women, as his ex-wife would attest. For some reason, he felt comfortable around Charlotte. Maybe it was because all the adrenaline was finally bleeding out of his system. He felt exhaustion creeping up on him, but he wasn't ready to end their conversation. Coffee was the only thing he could think of that might help.

Charlotte concealed her surprise before replying, "I think coffee would be nice. Much nicer than returning to my seat."

Grinning, and feeling foolish for it, Gerald rose and offered to pull her chair back. Charlotte excused herself to freshen up, vowing to meet him in the lounge area shortly. Warnings screamed in his head as the fear of being hunted once again resurfaced. She seemed harmless in a potentially deceptive way, but wouldn't that be exactly the sort McMaster would send to disarm him?

He struggled with his paranoia, his instincts urging caution. Gerald decided that if Charlotte was in league with the men actively trying to kill him, he would be better off keeping her close.

Fumbling with the key, he went to the restroom to wash his face and hands. Maybe the delay would give her time to arrive before he did. That way at least he'd have a little time to come up with a plan in the event she was another of McMasters' killers.

That first sip of coffee, burning as it slid down his throat, was pure bliss. The smell alone had been enough to revive Gerald. McMasters and Trans Stellar may have skimped on food quality, but the coffee was delicious. To his disappointment, Charlotte was already seated in a small booth just off to the side of the entrance. He slid into the bench across from her.

"I was beginning to think you'd changed your mind," she said after he set his coffee down.

Gerald just gave a noncommittal smile and wrapped both hands around his mug. He relished the feeling of the hot liquid traveling down his throat.

"Has it been a long time since your last cup of coffee?" Charlotte asked, noting his attachment to the mug.

"No, but the coffee we get at work isn't anything like this and you've no idea how much I need this right now," he replied. "What sort of artifacts have you found so far on your digs?"

Just like that. No build up. No prelude. He dove into the conversation and waited for her reaction.

"I don't think I should discuss that," she said. "Much of what we have found is still classified by several governments. Why would you even want to know?"

Gerald blew out a sharp breath. Shoving all his misgivings aside, he'd already decided what he wanted to do, but going through with it was suddenly much harder than he expected. Charlotte was far from being a friend, but he was almost certain she wasn't the enemy. Gerald needed people he could trust if he was going to escape McMasters' goons. Besides, she specialized in what he needed to know.

He pulled the key from his pocket. "Because of this."

Her eyes widened. "Where did you get that?"

It was his turn to be shocked. "You know what this is?"

Charlotte leaned closer. "Of course I do. It's the key to finding the Eye of Karakzaheim. Where did you get this? How?"

Gerald hesitated, knowing he was either going to sound crazy or send her running to the authorities.

It was a risk he needed to take. “You’re not going to believe this, but …”

TEN

2273 A.D.
Oberon City, Mars

The passenger liner docked in Oberon City shortly after dusk. Gerald's eyes were glued to the windows during the process. The Red Planet looked beautiful in the twilight. He never thought he would leave Old Earth, much less walk on Mars. There was a thrill of excitement and apprehension.

He and Charlotte deboarded the liner together and waited their turn in the customs line. Their conversation about how he came into possession of the key had been awkward, one he hurriedly brushed through to avoid further questioning. Just having the artifact was dangerous and he still wasn't sure if he could fully trust her. Choosing not to dwell on possible betrayal, he changed their conversation to a trivial one. He discovered her last name was Bailey and that she came from a modest family.

The line crawled forward. They were next. Gerald was relieved when none of the officials seemed remotely interested in either of them. The pair collected their bags and jumped on the first rail car heading into the city proper. Only when the doors closed and they were underway did Gerald relax enough to stop looking over his shoulder. Now he had a new worry. He may have escaped Old Earth, but he had no idea what to do next.

Charlotte reached over to squeeze his forearm. "Stay calm. Enjoy the view. Mars is a special place."

He took her advice and soon was taking in the rolling hills and endless sea of red soil. The gathering night sky took on a purple hue making the landscape almost magical. Gerald didn't notice he was smiling until they entered a tunnel and the ultra-neon lights along the walls sent his reflection back to him.

Oberon City, the government seat and planetary capital, was a sprawling complex of ornate domes and towers stabbing up into the manufactured cloud cover. Martian atmosphere still wasn't breathable, even after decades of attempted terraforming, but the local officials promised it was getting better.

Aptly named for the legendary figure in Merovingian tales dating back almost one thousand years, Oberon, king of the fairies and believed to have originated from the Germanic Alberich, meaning 'elf king', was the definition of majesty. Oberon City was no less spectacular. Gerald found no comparison between what New York had developed into and the impressiveness of the Martian capital. There were building of every color, though subtle purples and greens dominated the landscape.

Martian architecture owed nothing to Earth. Irregular but beautiful shapes dominated the skyline. Somehow the lack of vegetation didn't detract from the views. Dazed, Gerald looked around, trying to take in all the grandeur of this spectacular city that he could. After a lifetime of being trapped within a maze of rectangular buildings it was almost too much to take in.

"You get used to it quickly," Charlotte offered upon seeing his bewilderment. "Mars can be slightly overwhelming the first time. Especially coming from Earth."

"It's beautiful, but it doesn't make sense. Cities are supposed to be orderly, easy to navigate in a grid pattern. Not like this."

"The rumor is that the first Martian colonists wanted to start fresh and not cling to old traditions. For them that even meant new architecture styles to change how cities looked and functioned." Charlotte laughed. "For example, you'll find very few roads in Oberon City running in a straight line."

"Or normal buildings," he added.

Charlotte smiled. "Indeed. Mars is a special place in all aspects."

"What about the people?"

"Hard workers for the most part. You won't find a more honest bunch if that is what you're getting at."

It wasn't, but he couldn't say more without causing alarm. He'd only divulged the base facts of the key and left it at that. What he really needed to know was how to find someone he could trust and, if somehow, he could disappear underground to hide from McMasters. There were areas in New York he wouldn't go in the daylight, much less the dark of night. Thinking such places existed on Mars wasn't much of a stretch for his already overactive mind.

Their earlier conversation about the key and the Eye of Karakzaheim left him cold, troubled. The promise of what scholars and treasure hunted theorized it held went well beyond the limits of his imagination. According to Charlotte the artifact was the key to locating an untold treasure, amassed and hidden long ago by a powerful alien civilization. As far as Gerald knew, McMasters already had more money than anyone in the galaxy. Why would he go to such lengths just for more?

"These are good people, Gerald. Trust me."

Settling back in his chair, Gerald tried. He hoped Creeps was waiting for him at the end of the line. Maybe then things would start to make sense.

Charlotte watched Gerald, guessing what was going through his mind. Never in her wildest dreams did she think she would actually see the key. She'd spent years researching legends, myths and tall tales. Years in which she'd learned all there was of the mythos of Karakzaheim. Now the key was only a few feet away. In the pocket of a complete stranger. Her thoughts turned toward trying to wrest the key from Gerald or, at the very least, convincing him to help her. She didn't want the money. It was the fame that would come from finding the key that thrilled her.

Charlotte shook her head trying to dispel the thought of becoming the preeminent archaeologist in the galaxy. She needed to change the subject, if for no other reason than to clear her thoughts. "Tell me about this man we're supposed to meet."

"Creeps? He's a good sort," Gerald said. "I suppose."

"With a name like Creeps I can see that." Her tone suggested otherwise.

"Don't let the nickname fool you. Creeps and I grew up together back in Queens. While I tried to make a clean living he went a different route, sticking to the shadows doing odd jobs for what remained of the old New York mob families. That's where the 'creeps' part comes in."

"Is he a criminal?"

Gerald barked a laugh. "Not even if he wanted to be. Creeps does some petty work from time to time, but he's never had the stomach for hard crime. Still," he sighed, "I'm fairly certain he can get us in and out of places respectable folks won't go."

"Lovely. I can't wait to meet him," she said.

He didn't know if she was being facetious but decided not to press it. The more they spoke the more he discovered she was the reserved, quirky sort. His guard began to drop and he forced himself to maintain it. She was attractive and easy to get along with, which made it more difficult. Not that he harbored romantic illusion, but … *Oh, what the hell am I thinking? She could be waiting for me to relax just enough and stick a gun in my back just like those two on Earth.*

The railcar pulled in at Oberon City's central terminal, stuttering to a halt over the course of half a mile. With a pneumatic hiss, the doors opened and hundreds of passengers debarked. The terminal filled almost instantly. Noise drowned out his thoughts and he was filled with a sense of comfort. The terminal of Oberon City reminded him of the bustling streets of Earth.

Suddenly standing in the middle of the busy terminal, the realization of what he was attempting hit him. His time as a Trans Stellar employee was finished. He couldn't go home. He was on Mars, with no place to live and no resources of any kind. His chest tightened at the prospect of all he knew being stolen form him. Gerald had never felt more alone. The hint of a tear welling, he turned to his new partner.

There, lost in the depths of her eyes was the combination of curiosity and fear. He felt drawn to her in an inexplicable way. Charlotte seemed to be able to offer a way out of his nightmare.

"Me either," he murmured, offering to take her large bag. It was heavy. He was glad it had wheels.

"You'd think there'd be more ground support to help with baggage," she said.

"Like one would see I'm struggling with yours and offer to help?" he quipped.

She gave him a queer look. "Sure. Something like that."

"What have you got in this thing? Rocks?" he asked after an uncomfortable silence.

"Sorry, but you did offer."

"I was trying to be a gentleman," Gerald frowned.

Crowds began thinning the closer they got to the main entrance. Most of Oberon City was encased beneath a magnetic shield, providing the citizens the ability to roam about without the use of pressurized suits. Visitors found the illusion of being the masters of the planet most comforting, often forgetting the very real danger should any of the control systems malfunction.

Some of the worst disasters in space engineering occurred during construction of Oberon City, some ninety odd years ago. A memorial wall containing the names of seven hundred and three workers who'd perished in the construction stood at the terminal entrance in tribute.

"Where are we supposed to meet Mr. Creep?" Charlotte asked once they exited the building.

Gerald tapped his foot on the ferrocrete road. Martian soil was compacted and, with no rainfall, too brittle to support heavy traditional concrete. So the lighter weight ferrocrete was used for buildings and major roads. He'd heard of it but, until now, had never seen it.

"Gerald," she pressed.

"Eh, what?" He blushed. "Sorry, I was just checking out the road. I'm supposed to contact Creeps once I arrive."

"Good. We can go to my hotel room and wait there."

Finding no better idea, yet leery of the possibilities, Gerald flagged down the nearest taxi and they headed off.

ELEVEN

2273 A.D.
Waldorf-Astoria Hotel, Oberon City, Mars

Gerald could only whistle softly at the sheer opulence of his surroundings. Apparently, archeologist assistants made serious money. That or she was loaded. He didn't care either way. He never imagined he would spend the night in one of the premier hotel chains in the galaxy. Waldorf-Astoria had jumped at the prospect of going interplanetary and secured contracts before other elite chains. With limited competition, their profits soared.

Vases and urns from deep in Old Earth history lined the halls. Rich carpets and pots filled with exotic flowers were everywhere he looked. Gerald decided he could get used to this. Not that he was welcomed. Sneers in passing told him enough. He didn't care about that either. As long as Charlotte was offer, he was staying. For now. The rest could learn to deal with it.

Attendants dressed in gold and crimson escorted them to the room, going so far as to refuse Charlotte's offered tip. Gerald didn't understand that. He and his flight line crew gladly accepted any tips that came their way. He briefly tried to picture himself wearing the gold and crimson uniform but failed. Working around arrogant rich people wasn't very appealing.

"How did you score this?" he asked once they were alone.

Charlotte waved around. "What, this room? I only stay in the best."

His expression prompted a laugh. "I'm kidding. My benefactors put us up in these hotels almost every time we travel, at least on the inner worlds. You can consider it a perk of the job."

"Digging around in the ground is that lucrative?" he asked.

"Unfortunately no, but we are backed by very large government and private corporation investors. They spare no expense."

He set the bags down beside an excessively large leather couch and dropped down. His eyes fluttered closed as he felt his weight sinking into the plush cushions. "I could definitely get used to this."

"Don't. If this key is in fact the path to the Eye and your Mr. Creeps shows—"

"Just Creeps," Gerald interrupted.

She frowned. "Regardless, if he shows up I don't imagine we'll be staying here long. Roland McMasters is one of the most ruthless men in the galaxy. He gets what he wants. We either move faster than he does or he'll kill us."

"Right."

Now that he was on Mars he needed to slow down enough to start thinking ahead. His efforts thus far lacked direction and he didn't know which way to turn. McMasters would have his hands in every government pocket on all of the known worlds, automatically making Gerald an outlaw.

He was trapped.

"What are you proposing?" he finally asked, seeing the growing excitement in her eyes.

Charlotte hesitated, which Gerald took as a good sign of healthy caution. It made him feel better.

"We could go after the treasure," she whispered.

"Are you crazy? I was almost killed back on Earth, in case you forgot. This isn't a game, Charlotte. McMasters has men actively murdering people who get in his way."

"McMasters isn't the only power in the galaxy, Gerald. Right now we have the advantage. They think you have the key, but no one suspects you know what that key is. Why would the think you're going after the treasure? Think about it. We can do this before McMasters realizes what's happening."

"Just because we know what the key is doesn't mean we know where it leads or what to do with it. We don't even know where to start looking."

"Yes we do. You have the key and I have access to every archive in recent history. We stay here long enough to rest and then head out."

"Head out to where?"

"Creighton Colony, on the far side of the planet," she answered. "It has the largest database of archeological facts in the galaxy. I was supposed to go there anyway. That's what's in my bags. Data on important finds and some research to add to the archives."

He couldn't deny her trip provided the perfect cover story. For the first time since this sad affair began Gerald considered striking out to find the treasure before McMasters did. All he had to do now was convince Creeps to keep Charlotte safe and him out of sight.

"I need to get Creeps," he said.

She nodded. "All right. Go, but don't be long. I'll start researching."

Gerald was already at the door. "I'll try not to be."

He wasn't sure if he was ready for this unwanted adventure as he hurried off to call Creeps. What choice did he have? There was no going back to Earth. Moving ahead was his only viable option, even if it meant being hunted.

Life, Gerald decided, was a bitch.

When Gerald arrived at the small, out of the way café, Creeps was already seated by the window, his back to the wall. Thought Creeps was younger by a few months, Gerald spied the first hints of grey creeping into his full head of hair. He ran a hand over his own painfully thinning scalp. Though frustrating, going bald was the least of his present worries.

"There he is!" Creeps said and gestured to the server for another coffee. "I was starting to think you weren't going to show."

Gerald took the chair opposite. "Hello, Creeps. It's good to see you again."

"You too. What brings you to Mars? Last I heard you had some cushy job at LaGuardia."

"Yeah, I did, but it didn't work out." He paused, weighing his words.

Creeps, wearing a half unzipped brown leather jacket that had seen better days, slouched deeper in his seat. One hand disappeared under the table. Gerald knew from experience his friend had more than one concealed weapon on his person.

"Creeps, how well do you know Mars?"

"Better than most. Why?"

"Because I've got a wild story to tell you and I need your help."

Gerald sped through his tale, highlighting the important parts. He was going for just enough hook to lure Creeps into helping him and Charlotte move unseen across Mars. No need to tell him everything just yet.

"Creighton Colony? That's a long way from here. I thought you were just coming for a vacation?"

"I was, but things changed. This is something I have to do. Can I count on you to get us there?" Gerald asked, settling back in his chair to take a long drink of already cooling coffee. He winced. The quality was nowhere near as good as the passenger liner's.

By the look on Creeps' face Gerald could tell the man wasn't satisfied with what had been shared. They were casual friends over the years, growing apart after Creeps fled Earth. Neither had seen the other for a handful of years. Gerald nervously sipped his coffee and waited.

"Give me more, Gerald," Creeps demanded. "I have to know why before I leave my life here."

"You really don't want to know," Gerald mumbled, avoiding eye contact.

"I do want to know, because if I'm going to have to leave Oberon City myself, I'm not going without one hell of a good reason."

Gerald's head dropped. He hated feeling backed against the wall, especially by a man he had hoped to count on. Seeing no way around it, he decided to give just a little more. Anything to entice Creeps into jumping in with both feet.

"Come back to the hotel with me. I don't think it's safe to talk about it in the open."

Creeps finished his coffee in one swallow. "If I do this … *if* … what promise can you deliver that will make it worth my time?"

Gerald grinned. "It will be the adventure of a lifetime."

***

The private shuttle docked shortly after dawn on an unregistered flight plan. Local authorities hurried to clear the shuttle through customs. Once the boarding ramp dropped, a handful of officials fell into twin lines on either side. Two men dressed in black waited with hands folded in front of their waists. Dark glasses hid their eyes, lending severity to their appearance. A hint of danger swirled around them as their shadows blurred.

Gholson and Edgemeyer stalked down the ramp, one content to be on solid ground, the other bunched up like a predator on the hunt.

The two men in black stepped forward.

"Mr. McMasters sent us," the man on the left began. "We have located the man you seek."

"He's here?" Gholson asked. His quick glance around the dock for a body trussed up produced nothing.

"Confirmed. He arrived on the last liner yesterday."

"Where is he?" Edgemeyer cut in. His gruff tone set the rows of workers back a step.

"We've tracked him to the Waldorf-Astoria in Oberon City."

Edgemeyer edged forward, fist clenched. Gholson stopped him. "We cannot take him there. Not even McMasters has enough pull to get us out of trouble in the rich district—we must wait."

"For what?" Edgemeyer snorted. "McMasters has given us no time. I say we find LaPlant and drag him back to Cestus III. Unless you care to be the one to report our recent failure."

Gholson scowled. "That won't be necessary." He turned to the pair of men. "Gentlemen, return to the hotel and follow LaPlant. The moment he clears that district, we make our move. Gerald LaPlant will be in our custody by the end of the day."

Edgemeyer balled his fists, simmering with impotent rage.

TWELVE

2273 A.D.
Ramses, planet 123A (Borax)

The first settlers on planet 123A hastily named their discovery Borax after an obscure myth from Old Earth. It was one of those moments where a name sounded much better rattling around the confines of tired minds than written on paper. Regardless, the deed was filed and complete before euphoria wore off and those colonists realized their error. Borax sound more like a bad joke or the remnants of a pharmaceutical company than the lush, green paradise it was.

Three massive continents were surrounded by oceans and myriad islands each capable of sustaining life without harsh climates or difficulties. Seemingly endless forests and wide, clear rivers intermingled with rolling plains filled with herds of beasts numbering in the millions. Historians compared the wilderness of Bora to that of North America before it became the United States. Minus the native tribes of course. A fact Carter Gaetis was immensely thankful for as he drove around the capital city of Ramses.

He'd been on planet for almost a month, developing his cover story and embedding himself in the local culture. People knew him by sight and accepted him as one of their own. They would never suspect he was one of the most lethal men in the known galaxy.

His years in the Lazarus Men had been good to him. Bank accounts with more funds than he ever thought possible were in his name on every world. He was untouchable, though several governments and local military branches attempted, on numerous occasions, to stop his clandestine activities. Women thought they loved him. Men thought they befriended him.

It was all a lie.

Under any other circumstances Carter might have laughed. There was nothing special about him. He should have perished for his crimes long ago. And would have if not for the convenient appearance of Mr. Shine. Now that he'd been in the organization for some time, Carter suspected their meeting was far from coincidence. Men like Shine didn't depend on chance. Everything Shine did held purpose and reason. That hadn't mattered to Carter. He'd accepted the offer and entered a rewarding new life. What were those lives he'd taken in the line of duty but steppingstones along the path of advancement?

Crowds were thinning as the sun dropped low on the horizon. Life here on Borax wasn't as civilized or advanced as the earlier colonized planets, but it provided ample enough comforts to satisfy him. The weight upon his soul, he imagined, would be felt after his final breath. Carter's only concern was the idle wonder of how that end would come. It didn't take much to assume it would be from the barrel of a gun.

He deftly maneuvered the small hovercar down the main avenue and into a cut grass field that served as the largest parking area. Ramses was still a wild town with limited law enforcement. The perfect place for him to finish his assignment. Unlike contract killers or mercenaries, Mr. Shine's agents dug deep into the local culture before acting. They often spent weeks, months even, on assignment before the order to terminate came in. Carter was here long enough to think Mr. Shine had forgotten him.

Then he got the word.

Excitement coursed through him. He'd spent his day completing his work as a minor crofter apprentice before leaving early to collect his weapons and kit. Homeless for the most part, along with every other agent, Carter lived in each town and planet like he belonged. Shine claimed it was for the betterment of the operation. Carter had no reason to disbelieve him. Living among those he viewed as potential targets had proved problematic to his conscience in the very beginning. Those days were now long behind him.

His microfiber body armor, the most advanced and durable on the market, fit snugly like an old shirt. A standard issue Roltech snub nose blaster clung to his hip. The weapon was thin enough to go unnoticed to the untrained eye. A second weapon was strapped to his right ankle, along with a handful of thin knives tucked here and there. Carter didn't anticipate the need for all of this, but he knew better than to take chance. Only fools entered hostile situations unprepared.

Carter scratched his jaw as he watched the small storefront across the street. A flock of red and yellow storks as tall as a man sailed overhead. They provided pleasant distraction. Carter spent so much of his previous life going through each day with his head down he found enjoyment in the simplest things. Nature, he concluded, was a fascinating thing.

He checked his wrist chrono and frowned. The target was late. Carter was about to get out to investigate when the front door opened and a smallish, middle-aged man emerged. Recognizing his target, Steven Milburn, from Shine's intelligence packets, but also from buying merchandise from the store, Carter's adrenaline surged. Milburn was a good enough sort, but for some reason was targeted for immediate execution—Carter didn't care why. He only cared about mission success.

Pushing the embedded node in his neck, Carter's face shimmered before transforming into a different look. His dark hair and eyes turned into blonde hair and blue eyes. Using an unregistered vehicle stolen from one of the docks along the ocean front, Carter turned the engine over and backed into the street just as Milburn started to cross.

He waited until the target was halfway across the street before gunning the engine. It struck Milburn with a fleshy thud. Blood splashed across the front of his vehicle. Carter slammed on the brakes, reached into his jacket and fired two quick shots into Milburn's chest and face before driving away.

Operating in the daylight always bothered him. The risk of something going awry was too high, but Shine's orders were precise. Steven Milburn was to be executed in broad daylight and with witnesses.

Orders were orders.

By morning the entire city would be scoured for a blonde haired killed. No one had any reason to suspect the mild-mannered apprentice was responsible. An amateur might have tried to run immediately, thus giving away his cover. Carter knew better. He'd wait for a few days before the message would come that a death in the family required his attention. And that would be that.

He drove recklessly, lending the appearance of a wild man intent on fleeing the scene of a horrific crime. It felt wrong to have so many witnesses to his deed, but Shine was adamant. A laser round struck his windshield, melting a fist sized hole in the glass. Carter spared a glance over his shoulder and frowned when he spied a pair of sheriffs on fliers bearing down on him. Carter had no issue with law enforcement. They had a job to do just like he did, but that didn't mean he wouldn't kill them if he had to.

Carter cranked the steering column, juking the vehicle hard left down a tight alley. Dust, rocks, and shredded blades of grass spun up in his wake. More rounds sped by. Some struck the vehicles, others the ground or surrounding buildings squeezing him in. Carter searched for a secure position from which to return fire. He was not going to be able to shake the sheriffs. Mr. Shine was not going to be pleased. However, he'd be less pleased if Carter was caught.

The kilometer wide clearing surrounding Ramses loomed ahead. Forests had a habit of growing back exponentially, forcing the locals to prune the vegetation regularly. Carter knew he needed to reach the safety of the forest. He was fair game in the open.

He opened the throttle all the way. The abused vehicle lurched forward with a roar. Both of the chasing fliers, now single file to build momentum off each other, screamed in closer.

A handful of workers jumped out of the way seconds before all three vehicles roared toward the imposing wall of green. A glance in the mirror told Carter the sheriffs weren't letting up. This was the most excitement Ramses had seen in years. Carter gained the tree line first. He cut the engine and abandoned the vehicle with precious few seconds before the sheriffs arrived.

Grabbing his rifle bag from under the front seat, Carter sprinted into the trees, using the natural lay of the land for cover. He chose the thickest stands of trees to reduce the aerial advantage of his hunters.

Force the sheriffs to the ground and it was an even fight. Few were as skilled in marksmanship as he.

Two rounds and no wind. That's all he needed.

He ignored the fact they were just doing their jobs. That they were men with families. Carter crouched down into the soft ground and took aim as the sheriffs climbed out of their vehicles.

His plan worked flawlessly. Carter squeezed off two shots, each clipping a sheriff in the left breast. He watched through the scope long enough to see red stripes spreading down their shirts before breaking his rifle down and heading back to the vehicle. By his calculations he had just enough time to get back into Ramses and ditch the vehicle before others arrived. Knowing the two he'd just left for dead in the forest would have relayed their positions before leaving their aircraft, others would soon home in on the last known transponder position.

Carter planned on being long gone before they arrived.

Having reverted back to his normal self, Carter shouldered his kit bag and headed into the apartment house he shared with seven others. No one was the wiser as he nodded and waved in passing.

Once secure in his second floor room, Carter hit the frequency jammer in the drawer of his night table. The small device allowed him to call out while preventing all external detection devices.

"Mr. Gaetis, I trust you've accomplished your task adequately?" Shine asked as his wraith-like image blurred into view.

"The target has been eliminated," Carter replied.

Shine leaned forward, giving Carter his full attention. "I sense you're keeping vital information from me."

Bastard. "Sir, I was detected much sooner than anticipated. Two local sheriffs found me."

"Were they dealt with?"

"I had no choice. I tried losing them in the city proper but they were good enough to keep on my tail."

"Dead?"

Again Carter hesitated. Killing officials wasn't part of his objective. Mr. Shine didn't like his operatives deviating from the mission. Matters tended to get sloppy that way, threatening to expose their organization.

"Both confirmed kills," he answered.

Shine made a show of picking his teeth and flicking the prize away. "I am … disappointed. Mr. Gaetis, I expect better from you."

"I wouldn't have been forced to kill innocents if the kill had been done at a different time," Carter told him, knowing it might anger Shine.

Rather than bristle with hostility, Shine leaned back in his chair and grinned. "No, perhaps not. I am disappointed but willing to give you the opportunity to redeem yourself. There is a man recently arrived on Mars. He holds a very important object. Relevant files with be transferred to you once you are in orbit."

"Yes sir, what is the objective?" Carter asked.

Shine's smile inspired cold fear. "Retrieve an object and terminate the holder with extreme prejudice."

The line went dark.

Carter began packing.

THIRTEEN

2273 A.D.
Oberon City, Mars

Charlotte stared out the bay windows of her room, trying to enjoy the view of Oberon City. Legs propped on a cushioned stool; she couldn't stop her foot from twitching. Nerves and raw emotions collided in the quiet of her room. Lights from atmospheric fliers streamed back and forth, reminding her of clouds of insects. They weren't enough to distract her from the problem at hand, however.

She pursed her lips, feeling the weight as her mouth turned downward into a frown. Gerald LaPlant successfully managed to derail her momentum. She'd been assigned to deliver key documents and a handful of minor documents to the central museum warehouse and return to the dig in Central America. The task came with the promise of promotion and the opportunity to lead her own expedition deeper into previously undiscovered Mayan ruins deep in the jungles of Costa Rica. Her run in with Gerald threatened to undo all of it.

But how could she resist? He was likeable enough, but not enough to detract her from her work. The key, on the other hand, was more important than any small promotion, no matter how far it might advance her career. The key to finding the Eye … She was barely able to contain her excitement. Validation for all her years of hard work had finally dropped into her lap.

It didn't take much to imagine the looks of surprise on her co-workers faces when she appeared on every major network and newsfeed after discovering the treasure of Karakzaheim. She'd quite possibly become the most famous person in the galaxy. The thrill was intoxicating … Right up until she thought of Gerald again. He was running for his life and bringing all of that danger in his wake. More trouble than it was worth, in her opinion. Almost.

Charlotte had briefly considered using her charms to seduce the key from Gerald. Once she had the key in her possession, ditching Gerald and spiriting away long before any of his pursuers caught up wouldn't be that difficult. Her conscience got in the way, and she abandoned the thought. She wasn't that type of woman. Nor was she a thief.

Partnering with Gerald was her only viable option. They needed to leave immediately if they had any hopes of staying ahead of the hunt.

Having made up her mind, Charlotte was disturbed by the high-pitched chime of an incoming call. She made her way across the room to the large teak desk and accepted the call. Blanching as the voice on the other end began speaking, it was all she could do to keep her mouth shut and listen.

Gerald and Creeps walked side by side through the busy Martian streets. He tried listening as Creeps explained minute details of his adopted home—tried and failed. Gerald had far too much on his mind to enjoy the sights. He scanned the crowds for familiar faces as Creeps, seemingly oblivious to all Gerald confessed in the diner, droned on. A hundred million miles from Earth still wasn't far enough; nowhere near far enough to evade a man like McMasters' reach.

"Hey, what gives?" Creeps slapped him across the arm.

Gerald jerked away. "What?"

"I get it, at least I think I do," Creeps said. "But this disembodied shit you're doing is driving me nuts. Focus, buddy. Look. We're already at the hotel."

"Sorry," Gerald mumbled.

Guests and staff stared openly at the odd pair. Gerald ignored them all. He was already over his own feelings of not fitting in. God only knew what they thought when they saw Creeps. It wasn't until the elevator doors hissed closed that he exhaled.

"Hey, is she good looking?"

Gerald frowned. "Who?"

"This Charlotte dame? Is she cute?"

"You really want to go in thinking about that? This is serious, Creeps. I've got real killers looking for me."

Creeps shrugged. "A man has to have priorities."

Gerald shook his head as they exited the elevator and approached the room.

"Charlotte, I'm back," he announced upon entering. He heard Creep snicker.

"I'm in here," she answered.

Gerald gestured for Creeps to follow, and they found Charlotte sitting by the large windows. Creeps whistled, much to Gerald's embarrassment.

"Charlotte, this is Creeps. He's housebroken, at least I think he is. The rest I can't vouch for."

"Ouch," Creeps said, hands over his heart. He paused when her expression hardened. "Gerry tells me you've got some problems."

Charlotte feigned a smile. "Don't we all? Can you get us to Creighton Colony without being seen?"

"Sure I can. That's what I do. What's in it for me?"

Anger flushed Gerald's face. There'd been no mention of actual reciprocation until now.

Charlotte glanced sideways at Gerald, "I don't suppose the satisfaction of helping a friend and his colleague is enough for a man of your … quality?"

"Praise doesn't fill my stomach," Creeps replied. He folded his arms, leaning against the doorframe. "How much? He already told me about your troubles. Perhaps not all of them, but enough for me to figure out I can make a pretty sum off my time."

Charlotte ignored him. "Gerald, we need to leave immediately."

"Why, what happened?" he tensed, hand reflexively digging into his pocket.

Her face was pale. "McMasters has alerted the local police. They're looking for you. The sooner we get to Creighton Colony the better for both of us."

All of his carefully constructed walls collapsed down around him. Each step taken in the right direction resulted in equal or greater setbacks. Beating McMasters didn't seem possible. The overwhelming sense of defeat was almost enough to make him throw his hands up in surrender and turn himself in. No doubt McMasters had bribed enough law enforcement and government officials to make that option just as deadly as being caught on the run. He was in a hopeless situation.

"Is there any transport running this time of day?" he asked Creeps.

"A train leaves in about an hour for the CC," Creeps confirmed. "Tickets aren't much, but there's going to be a problem boarding if you're a wanted man. We need to make you blend in."

"I'm not looking like you. No offense."

Creeps snorted. "That's not what I mean, dumbass. You need to change your clothes, hair, even the way you walk and talk. It's the only way we're going to get you on that train."

"I was hoping you were going to say a hat and dark glasses," Gerald tried to joke before Charlotte snatched him by the arm and dragged him into the bathroom.

Thirty minutes later they were packed and heading through the lobby. Feeling eyes on him, Gerald picked up the pace, hurrying out the front doors and into a waiting taxi. Gerald looked back to see a man climbing into a waiting air car and motion toward them.

"Quick," he urged the driver.

Roads not being what they were on Earth, the Martian driver could only go so fast without crashing or running over pedestrians. Two las rounds struck the back of the taxi, melting the left brake light. Charlotte clutched Gerald's arm. Creeps cursed.

"We're not going to make it," he snapped as a second volley struck the taxi.

Gerald thought the same thing. He was the one they wanted. Once he was gone, the killers had no reason to hunt down Charlotte or Creeps.

"Hold on!" the driver shouted and spun the taxi hard right.

All three in the back seat slammed together, eliciting shouts. Instead of following, the attacking vehicle continued ahead.

Gerald was confused. "Where'd they go?"

"We lost them!" the driver shouted back. "Who are you people? What's going on?"

"The less you know the better. How far is it to the train station?" Gerald asked.

"Half a kilometer."

Gerald grimaced. "Drop us off here. We can walk the rest of the way."

"Who's going to pay for the damage to my cab?" the driver demanded, indignant even as he accepted the payment chit Creeps handed over and the trio poured out.

"Your company has insurance," Creeps replied.

Following his lead, Gerald and Charlotte wound through the strange streets of Oberon City with racing hearts. Only once they thought they spied their pursuer and rushed into the nearest shadow bank to avoid being spotted. Ten minutes later they slunk into the train station, blending into the throngs of workers trying to depart the capital. Creeps purchased tickets, pausing every so often to look at Gerald's unnatural red hair with a frown.

"We need to split up," Gerald told them, eyes running over the crowd with growing unease.

"I don't thi—"

"We don't need to do anything," Creeps told him, interrupting Charlotte. "I got you here. Now pay up and I'll be on my merry way."

Familiar movement stole Gerald's attention and he stiffened. He caught sight of the top of Edgemeyer's head. Wherever he was, that toad Gholson was sure to follow.

"There's no merry way, Creeps. They're here," he muttered.

"What? Where?" Creeps started to look around before Gerald jerked him back.

"Stop it, you fool. They haven't seen us yet," Gerald hissed through clenched teeth. "Here's the plan, you take Charlotte and get her to Creighton

Colony a different way. I'll board another train and, hopefully, get those two to follow me."

"You'll never make it," Creeps told him.

"What about the key? If they catch you …" Charlotte didn't finish her thought.

Gerald offered a weak grin. "None of this will matter much then, will it?"

"Gerald, we're so close," she urged.

"Close enough to get killed," he retorted. "I'll meet you at the museum, or I'll be dead."

Gerald saw Edgemeyer was moving now, stalking through the crowd with inhuman precision toward them. "Time to go. Good luck and I'll see you soon."

He waited until Creeps dragged the reluctant Charlotte away before weaving through the crowds toward the waiting train.

Gerald was weaponless and alone. How could anyone follow him tens of millions of miles so unerringly? He'd managed to best Edgemeyer and Gholson once through blind luck. He wasn't likely to get that lucky a second time.

FOURTEEN

2273 A.D.
Enroute to Creighton Colony

Martian intercity travel was largely based on the old bullet trains of the 20th century. Fast and reliable, the trains offered a bit of nostalgia for those who managed to pay attention. For others, it was a simple conveyance to and from work.

Gerald fell into the first category. All of the metros on Earth ran off magnetic propulsion and a dozen other principles he didn't know anything about. His sense of wonder quickly rose the longer he went unmolested on the journey. It had been two hours and he hadn't seen a sign of the pale faced killer.

Escaping them was a minor victory, but that meant they had likely continued following Charlotte and Creeps. Now there was nothing to do but fret over their safety. He needed to find a quiet place to sit and think. To formulate at least some sort of plan that didn't end with them all getting killed.

The more time passed, the more he spiraled down into an abyss of self-pity. Gerald was trapped and lacked the skillset necessary to find a way out. He let him mind think about what life might have been if he hadn't seen that man get killed. A good job. A promotion. All wasted thoughts.

He let his head rest on the back of the navy blue cushions in the quiet of the empty compartment and closed his eyes. A sturdy female voice stirred him back to reality. Charlotte? How had she eluded the killers and found a way to reunite with him?

Gerald opened his eyes with a reluctant groan. *When was the last time I slept*? When his vision finally cleared, he was staring up at an attractive blonde. Her piercing blue eyes looked down on him with casual fondness, accented by the full pout of her lips.

All he could do was stare.

"You can sit there and gawk all night, but at least answer my question," she said.

Gerald cleared his throat. "I'm sorry. I was busy thinking. What did you ask?"

She gave him a stern looking over. "I asked if anyone else was sitting there."

His eyes flitted to the empty rows of seats surrounding him before he controlled himself. "Nope, they're all yours. I'm Gerald."

"Tianna," she replied, and took his offered hand before sitting in the seat opposite him.

"Nice to meet you."

She smiled. "You as well. Are you coming or going?"

His eyes crossed in mild confusion. Suspicion resurfaced at the question, only to be rationally countered by the thought that any enemy agent would already know everything about him. By that logic, her question made sense. Right now he needed to believe that not everyone had nefarious motives. That the galaxy was filled with more decent people than bad. It was all he had to cling to.

"Going," he said while attempting to come up with a viable cover story. His lack of knowledge of the red planet hampered him greatly. Then a thought struck. "I'm supposed to meet a colleague at the museum annex in Creighton Colony."

"Do you work there?" she asked with genuine interest.

Shit. I'm not going to be able to pull this off. "No, just temporary duty. I was on a dig site down in Central America back on Earth. Nothing fancy, just a lot of jungle and dirt. Still, its better than uncovering the history of the New York City subway system. How about you?"

She blinked once. Twice. "I've only been to Earth once. It wasn't a pleasant experience."

"Sorry to hear that. It can be that way sometimes. Where are you from?"

"Cestus III, but my work often takes me off world. I'm a procurement specialist for one of the larger banks. My employers have eccentric tastes at times."

He had no context for her comment. Life on Earth was hard, grueling even. He woke, went to work, and returned home only to repeat the process the next day. Permanently overcast skies drained hope away while reminding everyone there was but one inevitable conclusion to the whole drama.

"Never been, but maybe I should go," he offered.

"How's that?"

He grinned sheepishly. "If all the women on Cestus are as attractive as you, I think I might have been born on the wrong world."

She flashed a sultry grin. "You wouldn't be disappointed."

His nerves failed him then. Never a ladies man, he had no idea where this sudden gusto came from. Flirting was fun, entertaining at times, but he was never any good at it. Eventually, and it always happened, he wound up saying an offhand comment that led to offense. It happened with his wife and every girl since.

Tianna shifted, exposing part of her thigh as her dress slipped. He didn't know if she'd done it on purpose, but he also didn't care. She was a beautiful woman. The pearl white dress she wore was straight out of a holovid, right down to the strapped heels accentuating her legs. He wanted to sigh.

"If you stare much longer I might have to charge," Tianna teased.

"S-sorry," he stammered. "It's been a long time since I last saw pretty."

There it was. That awkward moment inviting disaster. He winced, bracing for the impact. It never came. Instead, Tianna cocked her head and pursed her lips.

"I'll take it," was all she said before nestling deeper into the cushions and falling asleep.

Gerald continued staring, but for different reasons.

"How long did I sleep?" Gerald asked, jumping awake only to be bombarded with neck and back pain from his uncomfortable position.

His body was sore, run down. Long hours of travel combined with fright had drained him. The whirlwind progression of the last few days was mind numbing in intensity. It left his thoughts fractured, and him terribly exposed. He no longer knew which way to turn or who to believe. Subconsciously he slid his hand down to the artifact.

"Not long," Tianna replied, batting her eyes twice. "You hum in your sleep."

"I do not," he replied, horrified. "Why, were you looking?"

She made a gesture of looking around the compartment before answering. “It’s not like there is a lot of conversation happening here. Embarrassed?”

“No,” he replied too hastily.

She smiled, but her eyes maintained a cautious edge he hadn’t noticed before. “Are you thirsty? Its still a long way to Creighton Colony and a lady could use a drink.”

“Especially if a man’s buying?”

“Most definitely,” she affirmed. Tianna rose in one fluid motion, smoothing the front of her dress in the act. Gerald’s eyes followed the trace of her hands, narrowly averting them before she caught him. She held out her hand, expecting him to take it.

Gerald’s arm snaked out before he could think. Up until now he hadn’t had much luck with women. His marriage was short and nothing significant had happened before or after. Now, in the span of a few days, he’d met two women who seemed interested in him. Charlotte was witty and attractive in her appearance, easy to get along with and a welcome distraction. Tianna, on the other hand, was so far out of his league he couldn’t begin to fathom why she was wasting her time with him.

She seemed the sort he always imagined hanging on the arms of celebrities or, perhaps, was one herself. Always going to the finer places in the galaxy. Definitely not slumming with men like Gerald. That raised suspicion. He hated admitting it even though he enjoyed the attention. Gerald snorted as an old saying came to mind: *The sun shines on a dog’s ass some days. Guess that makes today my day.*

“Is something wrong?” she asked after seeing his bemusement.

“No, nothing. Let’s go.”

They took their time heading down train. Gerald's mind swirled through the impossibility of his situation. Fears of being hunted for the object in his pocket diminished, if just. Guarded, he was starting to allow himself to relax just enough to appreciate the woman he was with. Even if he still had no idea who she was. Finding an empty table in the lounge car, Tianna insisted he sit while she got their drinks. Unused to such treatment, Gerald slid back into the plush seat. He was rewarded by Tianna returning a moment later with a drink in each hand.

"I figured you for a whisky man, Gerald," she said with a smile he returned.

"I'm a drink whatever is free man."

They spoke for some time, discussing nothing important and not learning much about each other. Whenever Tianna pressed on why he was on Mars, Gerald deflected. His vision started to swoon as he neared the bottom of his first drink, prompting him to stare into his glass.

He hadn't drank since witnessing the murder, and though he enjoyed drinking and had his share of days when he couldn't remember what happened the night before, there was something off with this one. Nothing he had had on Earth compared to the exotic flavors of Martian whisky. Tianna, for her part, took her time sipping hers without the same effects. Two drinks later and his head was swimming.

"You're a very guarded man, Mr. LaPlant," she said as the last swallow of his second drink burned down his throat.

Gerald tensed. "I never told you my last name."

Her smile was disarming. "Sure you did. When we first me."

He drew back and instantly regretted it as his head swooned. "No, I don't remember yours. How did you …?"

"Under different circumstances I might be offended, Gerald," she made a show of pouting. "I already told you, my last name is Everson. Try not to forget again."

He blinked in a futile attempt to regain sobriety. Eyes narrowed, Gerald raised a finger and pointed. He knew he should stop, think this through or protest in some manner, but the words failed. *Damned Martian drinks.*

"I don't feel good," he mumbled.

"You don't look well either. I think the local brew is a bit much for your Earthly tastes," Tianna chided. She was still on her first, sipping slowly. "We should get some food in your belly. That will make you feel better."

Gerald covered his mouth to burp. "Or make me vomit."

She shrugged. "Either or."

Tianna gestured for a server.

"So, Gerald LaPlant, tell me about yourself," Tianna said after setting her fork upside down across the corner of her plate.

"What would you like to know?" he replied, knowing he needed to be careful with the information he divulged. The hot food helped settle his stomach. His thoughts were not as muddled as before.

Tianna leaned forward, exposing the swell of her breasts. "What makes you, you?"

"That's a good question. These days I'm not sure I even know."

The train rattled on.

FIFTEEN

2273 A.D.
Oberon City, Mars

Crowds continued growing as the city workforce was released for the day. Charlotte was grateful for this one respite. She and Creeps slipped through the crowds, hoping to throw the killers off their trail long enough to hop on a train and join Gerald halfway around the world. Guilty by association, she knew they were in trouble should they be caught.

The logical portion of her mind demanded she turn and make a stand. After all, she wasn't their intended target, nor did she possess the key. She could easily claim ignorance telling the truth about how she and Gerald had come to be together. But she didn't and her burgeoning loyalty to Gerald surprised her. Perhaps it was all about the key in his pocket.

She needed to get back to Gerald.

Charlotte grabbed Creeps by the sleeve. "When does the next train leave?"

"Half an hour, but we had tickets for this one," he said, pointing at the departing train.

There was no way they'd be able to get aboard. Frustrated, Charlotte balled her free hand into a fist and struggled not to curse. Lashing out at Creeps for events beyond either of their control wouldn't solve anything. What they needed was a plan that didn't result in them getting killed.

She glanced back, trying to peer through the crowds in the hopes of finding either of the two men Gerald was terrified of. "We can't wait here."

"What else are we supposed to do? I don't have the funds to get more tickets and leaving the terminal now will only make us miss the next train."

"Leave the tickets to me."

"Are you sure those guys are after him? I've known Gerald for a long time. He's never been mixed up in anything like this," Creeps said.

Unlike her less than savory companion, Charlotte didn't know Gerald at all. What little she learned during the flight to Mars was all she knew. He could have been a killer himself … That uncertainty was oddly arousing. Charlotte hadn't realized her attraction to danger until this moment. Thrill aside, it didn't mean she should abandon all of the principles that had seen her through life to this point.

"He was quite adamant when he was telling me about these men while on the shuttle here," Charlotte said slowly. "He's also in possession of a very important archaeological find that I believe these men are willing to kill for." She paused as the color drained from his face.

Creeps had good reason to be afraid if what Gerald told her was remotely true. Two bodies were already rotting on Earth. Who knew how many more they were willing to sacrifice to get the key?

"We need to keep moving, Creeps," she said. "It's our only chance of getting away from these two and to Creighton Colony unnoticed."

"Sure, but what about the tickets? The booths are back that way," Creeps insisted.

Her smile was strained, too weak to appear convincing. "I'll take care of it. Trust me."

"If you say so." Creeps looked around, gauging the crowd without knowing what he was looking for. "Care to fill me in on who is after us? Or him?"

Charlotte wasn't sure who they were or what they looked like, only that they were employees of Roland McMasters.

"I'll let you know when we outrun them," she said then gestured for him to go.

Creeps lifted his shoulders, stuck his chin out. "You better not get me killed, lady," he warned and ducked down a small side street.

They tried moving at the same speed as the crowd, hoping not to draw attention. Charlotte's heart raced. Finding a small shop with the lights on a few meters off the main road, they huddled under the blue and white awning and waited.

Not more than a few heartbeats later Charlotte saw two men dressed in black moving through the crowd, scanning faces. The taller one wore a hard expression while the shorter man seemed out of breath. An odd couple to be sure, but one with obvious murderous intent. They passed the street and kept hunting.

"That was them?" Creeps asked.

"I think so," Charlotte whispered.

"The little guy doesn't seem like a problem, but I don't like the looks of that skinny one. He's got hard ass written all over his face."

Frowning at his word choice, Charlotte nodded. The tall man definitely had the look of a killer. Until now it had been little more than a fantasy she envisioned from conversations with Gerald. Seeing those two for the first time brought the danger into sharp focus.

"Come on, back to the booths. We can still make the next train," Creeps said and stepped back into the crowd without waiting.

Charlotte was forced to hurry after. It was a harrowing trip, those frantic hundred meters back to the main ticket booths. She looked over her shoulder repeatedly, praying not to see them again. She didn't want to die.

If Creeps was affected, he didn't show it. The local moved with the confidence inspired from having navigated such crowds countless times before. His actions suggested casual ease despite their situation. Charlotte had a suspicion all was not what it seemed with Creeps. A small detail failing to make her feel safer.

"If we can get on the train, there's a good chance we'll be home free," Creeps told her, though it was more to quell his troubled mind than hers. She was excess baggage as far as he was concerned. Unfortunately, he was honor bound to help Gerald—for now. Creeps had already made up his mind to ditch Charlotte the instant things got too hairy.

He wasn't far from that mark.

"Creeps! They're coming back," she hissed.

He refused the natural urge to turn around. He needed to run. To get away so his corpse would not be found in the back alley days from now. Charlotte could fend for herself. She was an attractive woman. They had no reason to kill her. On the other hand, he was expendable. Creeps walked faster, brushing past unsuspecting people in the process. Any thoughts of abandoning Charlotte evaporated when he couldn't shake her grip. Jets of pain shot down his forearm where her fingers dug in through the sleeve.

"Did you hear me?" she asked, more frantic.

Creeps skidded to a halt and pulled her close. "Listen lady, I don't know who you are or what any of this is about. Gerald told me a little, but not enough for me to go bouncing around all of Oberon City."

Disbelief registered on her face. "Wha … What are you saying?"

Creeps jerked her even closer and kissed her on the lips, holding her so tight she couldn't back away until he finally let her go. The slap came much quicker than he thought, stinging the right side of his face. He hadn't felt that particular touch in a very long time. Well, not that long.

"What in the hell are you doing?" she fumed.

Creeps rubbed at the soreness in his jaw. "Saving your life. Those two goons had spotted us. Kissing you was the only thing I could think of."

Indignant and breathing hard, Charlotte made a show of wiping her lips. "Don't ever do that again."

"Hey, I've been told I'm a pretty good kisser," he said in defense.

Creeps didn't like being bossed around. It was part of the reason he fled Earth and came to Mars in search of a new life. Only that new life hadn't turned out so well. Constantly near broke and growing more bitter daily, he presented the front of being a tough guy from the streets while in all secrecy he sold insurance to new arrivals. Not the daring lifestyle he dreamed of, but it was his. Thankfully there was no way Charlotte or, by extension, Gerald could have known that.

Her finger pointing did nothing to conceal her glare. Charlotte tried to compose herself as she searched nearby faces. She didn't see either man. The longer they stayed on the street, the more she began to feel like she was being caged in, guided in a certain direction without hope of escape. Once again, the urge to abandon the quest surged and it took every ounce of resolve to fight it. She was close. She felt it. Close enough to envision the glory that would be laid at her feet.

"To the train," she uttered. "We can still board and escape."

"The more you say it, the less I believe it."

She didn't argue. There was no point when she felt the same way.

Charlotte stepped onto the boarding ramp and felt an instant of relief for the first time since leaving the Waldorf-Astoria, that is until the shorter of the two men chasing her emerged on the stairwell to block her way. Curiously, he was cleaning his glasses with a bored look. Charlotte tried to push Creeps back—

It was too late.

The tall man, the killer, was directly behind them. One hand was tucked deep in his jacket pocket, suggesting he had a weapon. He used the other to idly scratch his jaw.

"If you please, my associate and I have had enough running for one day," the short man said.

"You've got the wrong people," Charlotte protested.

"Do we?" he asked in reply. "Interesting. I don't recall either of us mentioning who or what we were looking for."

"Making you exactly who we want," the tall man ground out.

Creeps swallowed hard. "Look guys, this is all a mistake. Let's talk about this."

"Shut your lips before I slice them off," the tall man threatened.

"You're a real tough guy with that piece in your pocket," Creeps challenged.

The tall man snorted.

"We are wasting valuable time here, my friends," the short man said, replacing his glasses and blinking. "Where is Mr. LaPlant? We very much with to speak with him."

"Who?" Creeps asked and was gut punched for the effort.

"That's enough, Edgemeyer. They won't serve any purpose if they're incapacitated."

Edgemeyer shrugged but backed away a step. Lines were forming now, trying to move around them to board. He didn't like crowds. He wasn't comfortable being around so many people without the ability to defend himself properly.

"We must leave, Gholson," he said in monotone.

"Indeed. I do hope we aren't going to get any trouble out of the two of you," Gholson said as he gestured for them to leave the ramp.

Reluctant but unwilling to get shot, Charlotte and Creeps did as they were told. Until a better solution presented itself. She hoped Gerald was having an easier time.

SIXTEEN

2273 A.D.
Enroute to Creighton Colony

Night had fallen with remarkable speed, painting the landscape in smooth tones of red and purple. The atmosphere of Mars wasn't anywhere close to being established to support human life, despite the decades of colonization. Faint wisps of clouds decorated the horizon, but nowhere near enough to produce the necessary levels of oxygen. In many ways Mars was the equivalent of the Wild West. Lawless, the outback of Mars presented challenges and difficulties seldom found on many colonized worlds. It was the perfect place for those with less than honorable intentions to search out an easy mark or find a place to hide.

Carter Gaetis sat in the dining car of the bullet train casually sipping a harsh local coffee. The race from his last mission to get to Mars wore him out. Mr. Shine was the most demanding man he'd ever worked for, expecting perfection in everything at all times. Carter was often hard pressed to maintain operational standards. The lives of the Lazarus Men were harsh on the best days. Shine's disappointment resulted in untimely demise. Carter had no intention of marring his spotless record or invoking Shine's ire.

All the more reason he found the urgency in his latest assignment disturbing. Clearly Shine had stumbled upon a plot of great significance, but what? What could be so important to make Carter terminate his previous assignment abruptly and fly halfway across the galaxy just to wait? He wasn't sure he wanted to know. He liked to think he was a simple man with simple needs.

Pulling the trigger came naturally for Carter once he accepted his position, after all it was what sent him to prison in the first place. Or so he told himself. In truth it had all been a mistake, thus causing all of his life's problems. What began as a drunken brawl ended with him taking a life. The violence was always there he decided, lurking deep within. His wife and daughter paid for that sin. Now their bones were rotting deep underground as he made his way across the galaxy with a blaster in one hand and a knife in the other.

Carter winced at the revolting taste echoing in his mouth as he swallowed his coffee. Unrefined. Uncivilized. It burned all the way down his throat. He found it amusing the coffee nearly brought a tear to his eye. Taking another sip, Carter fell into his role and began searching the thin sea of faces in the half empty car. Businessmen, blue collar workers, the occasional student. He glanced down at the small video screen attached to his left wrist to identify the face of his target.

Carter knew Shine would be furious should he report back with negative contact.

"Would you care for anything else, sir?"

Disturbed from his ruminations, Carter flashed annoyance. "No. Thank you."

If the server took offense, he had the good sense not to show it, choosing instead to scurry away to the furthest table in the car. Carter didn't bother watching him go. People like that were little more than necessary disturbances, but disturbances nonetheless.

He resumed searching. All of his previous reconnaissance pointed to his target being aboard this particular train. But where? Precious minutes ticked by without progress. Minutes dragging him closer to his report time with Shine.

Then fortune smiled down upon him. He watched as his primary target sauntered into the dining car, but with a different individual at his side. Carter pursed his lips, fearing matters had somehow already spiraled beyond his control. He rechecked the image. The man was correct, but the woman was all wrong. Wrong hair color, wrong build. Wrong everything. Carter was forced to sit back and take this new information into account. His one saving grave was he had positive identification to send back to Shine.

The unlikely pair was escorted to their table and seated with typical flourish. Carter absorbed every detail, every nuance. There was nothing significant about his target. He'd seen the type countless times before and found absolutely nothing interesting. Men like that were content with watching life speed by, never jumping in to make great things happen. Carter snorted.

It was the woman who drew his complete attention. Her classic looks were captivating, but only on the surface. To Carter's eyes she screamed danger in an all too familiar way. Taking another sip of coffee, Carter leaned back in his chair and tried to put the puzzle pieces together. There was no obvious reason for the pair to be together. None. For his part, the man seemed oblivious of his companion's thinly veiled skills. A shame really. Carter imagined stepping up to that woman would be an exercise in survival.

"What have you gotten yourself into, Gerald LaPlant?"

"I need to lay down," Gerald said, covering a small burp with his hand.

The train, travelling at a high rate of speed that did not normally induce motion sickness, felt like it was cast upon the ocean. Gerald swayed as they left the dining car. His knees bounced unnaturally with each step, giving him a rubbery look. He couldn't focus. Gerald saw three of everything. If it hadn't been for Tianna guiding him down the corridor, he doubted he would have been able to make it.

"We're almost there, Gerald," Tianna said with grace and smoothness that stirred the fires deep within him.

He nodded, already having forgot what he'd said mere moments earlier. His head swam, far worse than any drunken night he'd experienced. As much as he wanted to collapse and let the night play out in the corridor he couldn't. Raw determination propelled him. Tianna said they were almost there, but where were they going? He frowned, only to lose the thought as fresh waves of dizziness hammered into him. He fumbled for the key, relaxing only when his fingertips brushed against the alien hardware.

Tianna showed no concern. She was surprisingly strong for her slender build. Gerald allowed her to continue dragging him down the hall. Stomach in revolt, pursing the angle of seduction was out of the question. He struggled to get free briefly. She gripped tighter to keep him from falling.

"Almost there," she soothed after he calmed.

His head dropped. "Where?"

"Don't worry about that. You won't be disappointed."

The side of his head clipped the doorframe as the thin metallic door hissed open. Tianna giggled as she guided him in. The room was dark, almost unnaturally so, yet she managed to effortlessly work their way over to the pull-out bed. He landed hard; breath driven from his lungs. The cling-cling of the train barreling on accompanied the pounding in his head.

"Wha … what happened to me?" he asked.

A faint glow lit the side of the cabin suddenly, illuminating her silhouette. He blinked rapidly, hoping to clear the liquid from his vision. Gerald tried to rise and failed. Strength fled his muscles. He didn't want to get up anymore. The soft sound of a zipper being undone drew his attention. He stared, disbelieving what was happening on the other side of the cabin.

Tianna appeared as little more than a dark shape, enhancing the mood as she slowly undid the zipper on the back of her dress. The thin fabric slid down her body and pooled on the carpet. She made a show of ruffling her hair, knowing he was already captivated. Placing a hand on her hip, she sauntered over and straddled him. Her fingers touched his lips when he tried to speak.

"Shh," she whispered. "No more words."

Mouth still open, Gerald tried to reply but her lips covered his. He managed little more than a groan as her tongue darted into his mouth. Temptation won and he caressed her back, tracing down over her hips as she pressed down on him.

Tianna finished buttoning her dark leather jacket. Tying her hair back in a tail, she glanced down at Gerald's unconscious form. Their act of intimacy was pleasurable, but little more than a minor distraction. He was capable enough, just not what she needed or was looking for. His snores now filled the cabin.

Gerald was the likeable sort, but she hadn't come all the way to Mars for amusement. She'd been given specific instructions with no leeway for deviation. Tianna worked better under pressure, and even better with strict guidance. The human mind was almost as complex as the most advanced computers, leaving plenty of room for error or worse. Her training honed her speed, strength, and skills while focusing on her mind. Such conditioning kept her operating at peak performance. A fact her employer enjoyed.

She crossed the small space in two strides before snaking her hands into Gerald's pockets. Assured her prize was close, Tianna moved quickly. Her face remained impassive as she deftly searched each pocket. Her expression remained the same even after her long fingers curled around the slender object.

The light was still dim. Thieves' work demanded obscurity and, truth be told, Tianna much preferred to work in the dark. She held up the small cylinder for inspection. Nothing in her training suggested any significance in it. She failed to understand the urgency for its recovery.

Tianna returned to the other side of the cabin, where she activated the small communications terminal attached to the desk. Roland McMasters' face appeared in waves of blue and grey.

"Report," was all he said.

Tianna held the object up. "I have it. Just as you said."

"Good. Good. I've arranged for transport to bring you home. It will be awaiting your arrival in Creighton Colony."

She dropped the object into her pocketbook. “Yes, sir. What are your instructions for Gerald?”

McMasters scowled. “He is no longer of consequence. Kill him or leave him. The decision is yours.”

“Sir, the Lazarus Men will be searching for him as well. Perhaps it would be best if I brought him with me,” she ventured.

“I told you he is of no consequence. Let Shine’s agents take him. There is nothing that insipid upstart can do without the key,” McMasters paused. “Still, it might be best if you eliminated LaPlant. He knows much more than he should.”

“Yes, sir,” Tianna said. Again, she betrayed no emotion.

The transmission faded, leaving her alone with her decision. Tianna calmly pulled the small plastic handgun from her hip pocket and pressed the barrel against his temple. The silenced round was small, only .22 caliber but more than enough to do the job while being quiet enough to go unheard. She clicked the safety off and cocked the hammer.

Gerald stirred, smacking his lips twice before flopping over with the ghost of a smile. Tianna frowned. He was no threat. How this man became entangled in McMaster’s scheme wasn’t her concern. Whatever his perceived slight against her boss was, Gerald didn’t deserve to die. She waivered, knowing that pulling the trigger was her best bet. Still, there was a quality of innocence to Gerald giving her pause.

Just this once, Tianna was willing to give the benefit of the doubt. Her thumb slipped the hammer forward, releasing pressure as she placed the weapon on safe and tucked it away. McMasters would be furious when he discovered her blatant act of humanity, but he was easy enough to deal with.

She reached down to caress Gerald's cheek before gathering her belonging. Once the drugs she slipped into his drink wore off, Gerald would awaken to a horrendous hangover and much confusion. At least he would awaken. She doubted he'd find the mercy in it, but her conscience rested easier knowing an innocent man would live.

Tianna slipped out the cabin and locked the door behind her.

SEVENTEEN

2273 A.D.
Io Operation Facility, moon of Jupiter

The gas giant was resplendent in the fading sunlight. Warm, earthy tones of brown, yellow, and red swirled as ferocious storms scoured Jupiter's surface. There'd been a time when scientists and leadership from Old Earth tried to pierce the storms and land on the planet's surface. After numerous failed attempts, the deaths of more than a few brave volunteers, and billions of dollars in equipment lost, the program was scrapped. Governments continued sending satellites and fresh crew to the seven monitoring stations in Jupiter's orbit but talk of penetrating the thick veil of storms was over.

Shine watched the planet turn far beneath the cold steel decks of his space station. Hands ceremoniously clasped behind his back; he took time each morning to reflect on the good circumstances that had placed him in his current position. Decades of plotting and toil propelled him to create the Lazarus Men, a position he had no plans of relinquishing. Genetic enhancement technology was capable of extending the human lifespan by half and was expected to increase as new, less regulated techniques and procedures were developed on outlying worlds far from Earth's antiquated belief systems. But he had something much better.

Few alive knew the true depth of Shine's involvement in the Jupiter program. He'd overseen some of it personally. Virtually every mention or record of his past had been systematically removed from databases. Officially he didn't exist. His real history swept away. It was all thanks to Jupiter. He found the pull of the gas giant irresistible. A symbol of might. Of power. Shine's one arrogance was in his secret proclamation of being the Lord of Jupiter. An excess of ego, he admitted to himself only.

Shine reveled in his affiliation with the planet. While mankind sped across the stars in search of new worlds to carve out new empires, he kept to his quiet isolation. After all, he was a man who had everything he needed. Why waste time and resources in search of unsettled worlds when his carefully laid plans were about to net him the entire Terran system? Shine was a puppet master, orchestrating feats of such audacity his crimes would surely result in immediate execution if he were ever caught.

The facility in orbit to Io was his pride. State of the art and unparalleled in any of the settled systems, it was capable of running without resupply for five years. Fruits and vegetables filled massive gardens running along the interior decks. Water was always an issue, but he managed to compensate by installing artificial aquafers. Regenerator systems kept his skeleton crew fully hydrated almost as well as being planetside. Shine even boasted a large swimming pool for his personal use.

All of these accomplishments paled in comparison to the hustle of activity occurring just below the station. Shine funneled trillions of dollars into a clandestine project capable of shifting the balance of power in the universe permanently. Construction crews worked around the clock to build a fleet of dreadnaughts beholden solely to Shine. Private militaries were illegal; a unified accord agreed upon by every major ruling body prohibited them.

Shine aimed to change that. Once his fleet of dreadnaughts was combat ready and deployable, he would become a major player on the board.

Soon, but not yet. There was still much to be done before he was ready to announce his bid for dominance. Shine ground his teeth in frustration, it had been over a day since he reassigned Carter Gaetis, one of the best he'd ever hired, to the Mars mission. A day with limited communication. There was no worse feeling for a man like Shine than being kept from the information flow.

There was also little he could do but wait. Carter was highly capable and if anything negative had happened Shine would have already been alerted. Each agent was fitted with biometric readers surgically implanted that reported a continuous flow of vitals. If an agent were terminated, Shine would know. He also had, without their knowledge, the ability to end their lives should they become compromised. He'd done so three times. It was a failsafe system allowing total control and anonymity—puppet master, indeed.

Shine knew his frustrations weren't directed at Carter as much as McMasters. The Fat Man was becoming an increasing problem that would soon require solving. His fingers dug into government pockets on a dozen world. Whereas Shine remained behind the scenes, McMasters preferred the limelight. He made no pretenses about his deeds, nor offered excuses. Bribes and political manipulations were no obstacles for Roland McMasters.

Fat Man. Shine snorted at the ridiculousness of the moniker. McMasters' weight aside, Shine found the title a joke. Little enough differentiated the Fat Man from a circus performer. Business acumen and childish nicknames did little to diminish the threat, however. McMasters was a deadly predator lurking just out of reach.

On a personal level, Shine abhorred dealing with the Fat Man. There was no such thing as a casual encounter. Every conversation came with an ask. A demand so slight many failed to notice. To be fair, Shine made a small fortune off the Fat Man. Normal business thrived off competition. McMasters insisted on eliminating his to advance his agendas. More the fool he. Shine reaped the rewards while building his own quiet empire.

Suddenly frustrated, Shine abandoned his view and stalked back to his desk where a hot cup of tea awaited. It was his one luxury. Sliding into the soft cushion of his chair, he sighed. Reflected was always a dangerous time and he found himself slipping deeper into it. Thoughts of Jupiter and the Fat Man incited his melancholy.

His skeleton-like fingers drummed a hollow song on the desktop. Eyes narrowed, focusing on an obscure point on the far wall. Why now? After decades of going without mention or thought, why did the Fat Man show renewed interest in the Eye and Karakzaheim? Shine came to one, the only one, inescapable conclusion. McMasters knew where the Eye was.

Shine's palm slapped the desk. A thin smile creased his lips, giving him a cadaverous appearance. "Very wise, Roland. Very wise indeed."

He never expected McMasters to succeed. Decades of failure turned to disheartenment, forcing Shine to conclude the quest was over. While he gathered McMasters was hiding something during their last conversation, he had no idea what. Until now.

Leaning forward, Shine activated his intercom. "Get me in touch with Mr. Gaetis immediately."

Carter Gaetis was already on Mars and, unless Shine missed his guess, so was the Eye to the treasure of Karakzaheim. He tried to recall the legends. Karakzaheim was a general in an obscure civilization. A ruthless warlord by all accounts. One who'd amassed the wealth of a thousand dreams. But the difference between truth and legend often proved disappointing.

Yet now he found himself behind in a race with the potential to redefine human history. The Fat Man insinuated at having stumbled upon something big but had not even hinted at the particulars. He should have known better. He and Shine were now competitors for the same great prize. The future of the Lazarus Men now rested in the hands of Carter Gaetis.

***

Absolution, Cestus III

Roland McMasters knew what people said behind his back. Knew and ignored it. Let those smaller individuals worry over petty names or whispers of what might have happened. He wasn't accustomed to pandering to lesser people. Empires were created on the backs of strong workers through the domination of stronger minds. Visionaries. McMasters view himself as one. The events of today merely shaped the profits of tomorrow.

Nestled in his chair aboard his private shuttle, he glanced out the viewport as the city of Absolution raced past. The city was nice enough, cosmetically pleasing, but he wasn't interested. Hailed as one of the jewels of the outer worlds, Absolution was created as a place to let go of the past while embracing new futures. McMasters found it fitting to establish the heart of his new empire here.

Most planetary officials were deep in his back pocket. They did what he wanted, and when he wanted for the rewards he offered. In return he was given access to rights and land grants unparalleled by any rivals. It still wasn't enough. Greed was McMasters' greatest attribute. He wielded it like a sword on an ancient battlefield.

It was greed that saw him leave the comforts of his private hillside residence this morning. Overnight he'd received the best news he could have hoped for. The key was finally in his grasp. The debacle on Earth could now be forgotten. He despised incompetence and planned a thorough reprimand of Gholson and Edgemeyer upon their return to Cestus. But for now, he was content knowing Tianna had the key and had removed the troublesome Gerald LaPlant. Now he could begin his quest for the Eye in earnest.

"Why am I going to this meeting?" he demanded of his assistant who sat a row behind.

"Sir, the city council seeks reassurances that renovation projects previously approved under last quarter's budget are going to proceed on schedule. They believe …" He cut off abruptly, unwilling to risk McMaster's ire.

Roland thumbed the control switch and swiveled his chair around. His tiny eyes were almost lost within the excess folds of flesh on his face. "Believe what?"

The assistant swallowed. Others had come and gone, their bodies found in untidy places or not at all. By his count, he was the seventh this year. Painfully thin and quite pale, his hands trembled as he clutched the datapad. "Sir, they believe you won't fulfill your promises. There is talk of pulling out of your programs if this proves untrue."

"Is there now?"

The assistant nodded, too vigorously. He tensed, waiting for his employer's snap. Heartbeats felt like thunder. Beads of sweat formed on his upper lip.

Roland spun the chair around …

Thinking himself safe, the assistant sank back into his chair to exhale quietly. Then he heard it. The snap. That was it. The simple click of two fingers. He looked up in time to see one of McMasters black clad paramilitary guards approach him.

EIGHTEEN

2273 A.D.
Enroute to Creighton Colony

Darkness. Raw pounding echoing deep in the trapped cages of his soul. The world spun, out of control on a collision course that could only end in eventual demise. Each pinprick of light was a dying star exploding across the sun. Heartbeats raced like comets fleeing black holes. The universe conspired against him in a game of cosmic jest. How much can one man take when life is stacked against him?

Gerald LaPlant awakened with a groan. His hand shot to his forehead in a futile attempt at quelling the nightmare raging within. He struggled to recall the events leading up to his current condition. He failed to remember. The last few hours were blank. He couldn't remember a thing after telling Tianna he felt bad in the dining car.

The car. Dinner. Excessively strong drinks.

Gerald frowned. There was no conceivable way three drinks intoxicated him to the point of unconsciousness. He opened his mouth to call out to Tianna, but his throat was so dry naught but a pained squawk emerged. Jets of fire lanced down his throat and he nearly vomited. Sheer will prevented the act, for he knew doing so was to invite more torment.

Unable to move or speak, he let unconsciousness reclaim him.

Without any chronometer, there was no telling how long he'd been out before he awoke a second time. His immediate condition rushed back to him.

This time the pain was less. It was a minor gift he was immeasurably thankful for.

The intensity from the faint light illuminating the far side of the cabin was so disturbing, allowing him to look around and see where he was. Quieter rumbles in his stomach suggested the worst was past and he dared to rise. The bed was a mess, but the rest of the cabin was pristine. His bags should have been strewn about in a careless manner, but this room showed no signs of being inhabited aside from the bed. Whose cabin was it?

Tianna.

"Shit."

Three drinks normally had little effect on him, prompting Gerald to suspect he'd been drugged. Why would she drug him when she didn't even know him? He didn't have much money or any valuable possessions …

Except for the key.

Frantic, Gerald dug into his pocket.

He found nothing.

He'd been robbed.

Just like that all of his hopes and dreams vanished. With murderers on his tail, he'd been taken by one of the oldest cons. He cursed himself for being such a fool. There was no way a pretty face should have derailed all the wards he'd worked so hard establishing since fleeing his apartment what felt like months ago.

The whirlwind ride of the last few days was nauseating, making it all he could do to keep up as events continued spiraling out of his grasp. Gerald regretted slipping up with Charlotte and Creeps. There was strength in numbers and none of this might have happened if they'd all boarded the same train. He let fear dictate his actions. Now he was without his friends and potential allies in what he assumed was an ultimate confrontation with McMasters' henchmen … and the key was gone.

"How am I going to explain this?" he muttered, finally finding the strength to get out of bed.

There was no good way to explain what had happened. The trip was a debacle so far and Gerald was on the verge of giving up. Then there was Tianna, who either worked for a separate group looking for the treasure or, much worse in his opinion, was one of McMasters' assets.

He snorted. *Add her to the list. This trip is going to be the death of me*.

A little strength began flowing back into his limbs, giving rebirth to his desire to get moving. He needed to return to his cabin and collect himself. Once he was fully recovered, he'd set out to find Tianna and get the key back. The train was only so big and their time on it had to be coming to an end. She couldn't escape into the Martian landscape with the key. Not now.

Gerald dressed as fast as his weary body could manage and snatched what few of his belongings he could find: his wallet and wrist chrono were carelessly placed on the floor. One of his shoes was by the window, the other under the bed.

Getting dressed took longer than anticipated. Minor effects from his drugging continued hampering him. He nearly abandoned tying his shoes twice as his head swam and darkness crawled into his vision. Stuffing his wallet in his jacket pocket, Gerald stumbled toward the door. Clammy fingers hit the access pad and the door slid open with a pneumatic hiss. He was about to take a step into the darkened hallway when the scene playing out before him froze him in place.

"Stay where you are and raise your hands. Now," the black clad man growled as he rose over the pair of bodies bleeding out in the hall.

Gerald felt the last of his strength give way. His knees buckled and he would have fallen if the killer hadn't reach out, snatching him by the collar and slammed him back into the wall.

His day continued getting worse.

***

Night had fallen across the western half of Mars, casting an eerie scene on the bullet train as it sped across the red dunes. Carter Gaetis slunk down the largely empty hall through the sleeping cabins in search of his prey. The last communique he'd received from Shine spun up his operational pace. Shine claimed his actions were urgent with no room for error but left it up to Carter on how best to deal with the situation. Murder was his first option upon securing the item Shine desired. The train moved fast enough he would have little trouble disposing of the bodies before they reached the Colony.

Working his way down the hall, he was forced to flatten against the inner wall as a very drunk couple stumbled and bumped their way past. He couldn't help but notice the way their hands found their way inside clothing to feel and grope—to him it was disgusting. People should show more restraint when in public, but societal standards continued to drop as new excesses were discovered on different worlds. Mankind had lost its moral compass.

"S'rry," the man mumbled in passing.

His female counterpart giggled and dragged her hand across Carter's groin as she passed. Neither saw his glower.

Carter kept moving.

Doors hissed open and closed, allowing him easy passage as he finally reached the first car where the woman LaPlant had been seen with had a cabin. He'd taken a guess, based on the footage he had seen of them hanging on each other earlier, that they would likely go to her cabin instead of LaPlant's.

Lightning fast reflexes kicked in the moment he stepped into the car as a pair of poorly dressed men with weapons in hand were preparing to break into the cabin. Carter covered the distance between them in two heartbeats. His right hand slapped out, catching the first man's wrist. An audible snap preceded the sharp cry. The second man used the distraction to spin and draw a bead on Carter, but the Lazarus Man was too quick.

Dipping low, Carter brought the now crippled first man between him and the shooter—the muffled round punched into his friend's chest. Blood misted in a light cloud. Carter shoved the body at the shooter and both fell to the floor. He lashed out, kicking the weapon away before the shooter could recover. Dropping to a knee, Carter punched the man's throat, crushing the windpipe and snapping his spinal column. The shooter died with an addled look and drool spilling from the corner of his mouth.

The stench of fresh urine filled his nostrils as Carter rose. These two presented a new set of difficulties he wasn't prepared for. Shine wouldn't have contracted local hit men for a priority assignment, though he'd been known to do so for lesser objectives. No, these two were rank amateurs, more liability than asset. Whispers of the Fat Man being involved returned to him. Shine had hinted at such without confirming. Still, Carter had a hard time believing these two were caliber the Fat Man hired.

The cabin door opened suddenly …

He attacked. "Stay where you are and raise your hands. Now."

Carter slammed the bewildered man against the wall and began patting him down for weapons. Only when the target was clear did he bother looking at his face—Gerald LaPlant. The man he'd been sent across half the galaxy to find. Only the pair of bodies at his feet prevented Carter from feeling elation at successfully completing his mission. He snatched Gerald's collar tightly and half shoved, half dragged the man back into the cabin.

"Where's the woman?" he demanded after clearing the empty room.

Gerald struggled to talk past his already bruising throat.

Carter pushed harder. "The woman! Where?"

Gerald shook against his hold.

Suddenly concerned, Carter backed off slightly. He studied the man before him, noticing for the first time the dazed look in his eyes. Carter had seen this many times before; Gerald was drugged. The woman had most likely taken the artifact Shine desperately wanted.

"Move and I'll kill you before you can swallow. Understand?" he threatened.

Gerald offered the barest hint of a nod. He kept his hands up as Carter returned to the hall and dragged both bodies in.

Under any other circumstance Gerald might have been upset at the scene, but he was growing accustomed to being around death. First the man on Earth, then his neighbor, and now this. who knew how many others were unceremoniously dumped in trash bins or dark alleys in the process?

He couldn't take his eyes off the blank looks in the dead men's eyes. Seeing them made his stomach churn. More than anything he wanted to throw his hands up and beg for it all to stop.

Gerald thought of Tianna then. Of her lies, the artful deception. How had he been so blind? Knowing he held the key to the most valuable treasure in the galaxy, or so Charlotte assured him, should have forced him to act smarter. Instead, he fell prey to a pretty face. And now here he was, held at gunpoint by a man he'd never seen before.

The desire to find Tianna and get the key back drove his decision. Gerald only had one move if he didn't want to end up alongside the two being unceremoniously folded and shoved under the bed.

"I don't have it," he croaked.

The man rose and turned in such a fluid movement Gerald wondered if he had rehearsed it.

"Have what?"

The man's tone told Gerald all he needed to know. Any lies or deception would be met with the brutal application of force. Gerald needed to play this right in order to survive. "What you're looking for. Tianna took it."

Seeing the man tense at the name, Gerald frowned. *Interesting. They must know each other.* "She drugged me and took it when I was out."

"Why should I believe you?"

"Because its true. Search me if you want, but you won't find it in here," Gerald replied, purposefully making his tone sound weak to appear non-threatening.

Finished concealing the last body, Carter wiped his hands on the bed sheet. "Where is she?"

Tianna Everson. One of the Fat Man's favorite tools. A weapon of unparalleled beauty, genetically enhanced to seduce the weak-minded while simultaneously having the quickness of mind to get what she wanted. She was formidable. He had hoped he was mistaken after seeing them together in the dining car. Hoped that it was anyone but her. Very few things in the galaxy troubled him. She was on that list. If Tianna had possession of the artifact he needed to move fast if there was any chance of saving his career. Mr. Shine would not be pleased with this new information.

He pointed a finger at Gerald. "If I discover you're lying …"

"Why would I? Look, this is all one big mistake. I shouldn't be here," Gerald said.

Carter gave another look around the cabin. "Explain, and you'd better make it believable, or you don't walk away."

"It all started a few days ago back on Earth," Gerald began.

NINETEEN

2273 A.D.
Enroute to Creighton Colony

Carter Gaetis paced like a caged tiger. He felt betrayed. Years of service to Mr. Shine and he was being treated like a common hood. The betrayal was … insufferable. All emotion aside, he was trapped into continuing with his forward momentum. The only escape from this sudden revelation was to carry on. Perhaps there'd come a time of reckoning. Perhaps not. Until that moment chose to reveal itself, he was a Lazarus Man. Bound to perform his duties.

He looked Gerald in the eyes, searching for any trace of deception. He wanted to disbelieve Gerald's tale but, in his heart, he knew there was far too much truth involved to feel comfortable with the parameters of his assignment. Far too many power players were introduced to the game, changing the rules and making this more than a simple recovery operation. Like Gerald, he too was beginning to understand he was caught in a web much too large for his liking.

"If," Carter began, "If I choose to believe you, give me one good reason why I shouldn't kill you now and move on."

Gerald looked stunned. "Do you have a family?"

Carter paused. That singular question reopened wounds he'd long thought permanently closed. Visions popped up. Random. Meaningful. They lasted a split second before fading back into obscurity. His wife. His daughter. Flames. Tears. The strength of these visions threatened to drive him to his knees. He hadn't thought of his family since the days immediately following his transformation.

Yet Gerald's seemingly innocent question rocked the foundations of his life without a moment's hesitation. They'd been dead for so long now; his past life little more than illusion. They held no position in his current life. Performance demanded strict adherence. In order to become the fully trained assassin he was, Carter purged the past from his mind. Or so he thought.

"Where's your cabin?" he asked abruptly, not wanting to consider his past a moment longer. Not when Tianna Everson was getting away with the key.

Treasure didn't interest him much. The organization provided everything he'd ever desired. Money, a home, women. Everything. There was no such thing as excess for successful operatives. The only way to refocus his attention was by pursuing his rivals. Getting the key back was the priority, but should he manage to disable or even kill Tianna …

"A few cars down, I think. I'm not even sure where I am," Gerald admitted.

Carter could tell the effects of the drugs were wearing off and Gerald's initial fear of him was starting to fade. Perhaps he had been through several traumas.

"Three cars down from the dining car," Carter supplied. "Take me to your cabin now."

"Sure. Just don't do anything brash," Gerald agreed, taking an uneasy first step.

Carter eyed him curiously. He almost admired Gerald's ability to at least partially function after all that had happened to him. Gerald bumbled his way through his order thus far without suffering substantial harm. Carter found that fact encouraging for reasons he failed to understand. Dumb luck wasn't much luck at all but seemed enough to keep Gerald alive.

"Walk in front of me. No sudden movements. No stopping unless clearing it with me first. Do you understand?"

"I understand," Gerald affirmed and led them out of the cabin. "What do I call you anyway?"

Carter nudged him. Conversations with targets was discouraged. But banded together until he found Tianna and recovered the key, Carter saw little choice than to quell Gerald's nerves.

"Carter," he replied.

Gerald nodded. "Fair enough, Carter. I don't suppose you mind telling me what this is all about? Why all of you are so damned determined to find this Eye?"

"Keep moving and keep quiet," Carter warned. "No more talking unless I say."

He didn't want to kill Gerald but would if it came down to it. Carter, like most people in the galaxy, didn't believe in the legend of General Karakzaheim. Such notions of vast lost treasures were foolish. Yet here he was, locked in the middle of a treasure hunt with Mr. Shine on one side and Roland McMasters on the other. He wasn't happy about this at all.

They made it to Gerald's cabin without incident. It wouldn't be long before stewards discovered the bodies Carter had stuffed under the bed. By his estimate they still had several hours before pulling into the station. Hours in which Tianna would either fortify her current position or find a way to depart the train in motion. Moving at speeds topping 200 miles per hour, trying to depart the train was tantamount to suicide.

But no. The Fat Man wouldn't allow his best agent to be cast to the wolves without adequate resources to get out of trouble as fast as found it. Options were limited in Carter's opinion. She would have to have a way off. Then again, he determined, there was no reason for McMasters to suspect any of Shine's agents were on Mars.

A quick search of the cabin told Carter all he needed to know. Tianna hadn't been here and, more than likely, had no intentions of doing so. She'd already gotten what she wanted. It was his turn to play catch up. Carter decided his next approach.

Gerald was a hindrance. He could tie the man up and go about his business or he could kill the hapless Earthman. Both prospects provided drawbacks he needed to consider before making his final decision. For now, he was in no position to delay.

***

One of the marvels of Martian travel was the seeming ease with which the trains could travel without the feeling of motion. Tianna stared out the small, round window but failed to notice the dunes and dry streambeds. None of the red landscape interested her much. She'd completed her mission yet felt oddly empty. As if a small wound opened with the potential to grow and fester.

The half empty glass of water in her right hand offered minor solace. What she needed most was to deboard the train and get back to Cestus. McMasters would be pleased with her success. She was pleased with besting the insufferable Gholson and Edgemeyer. She'd never cared for them. One was highly useless in the field, though he managed to perform certain technical services she lacked the skillset for. Edgemeyer, however, was the closest thing to an outright psychopath she'd ever seen. He frightened her.

Under other circumstances she would have prepared transportation for an immediate retrieval. Instead, she took it upon herself to have a shuttle waiting at Creighton Colony. The trip across the planet was comfortable enough and she'd ensured Gerald wouldn't be able to find him again once he awoke. She'd taken care of everything. When did she feel like the walls were closing in?

Roland McMasters had always been a fair man when it came to commissions and quality of employ. She'd been taken in by McMasters at an early age when an unexpected pox on the continent of where she'd been raised wiped out her family and nearly three-fourths of the entire population. Tianna owed him her life and would do anything to repay him. She'd killed, seduced, and betrayed in order to further McMasters' agenda and would continue to do so as long as she remained by his side.

Her conscience was clear for all save one thing: Gerald LaPlant. Seduction was no small part of her skillset. She'd used it often enough to be more than convincing but, as she sat and reflected, there'd never been a reason to sleep with her targets. None whatsoever. So why had she done it? The answer was one she wasn't sure she wanted to know. There was no affection between them. He was just another mark. An unaware target.

Drugging him was almost too easy and her concoction was potent enough to rob him of time and memory. A little trick that took years to perfect. She thought about the trail of bodies left in her wake during the experimentation days. McMasters demanded total loyalty without emotion or regard. She gave it. Those bodies honed her skills. She knew their names by heart. Recalled their face with utter surety. Clarity of the past sent her strength for the future.

Only now that future was slightly obscure. Hidden from view as she tried to work past her deeds.

Gerald LaPlant. There was nothing suave or memorable about him. What he lacked in stature and charisma he more than made up for with honesty. Gerald had a good heart and, in her estimation, didn't deserve to be in the situation he found himself. She knew that all it took was a spark to ignite and set him on a course of self-discovery. That frightened her.

A brief conversation with Gholson told her enough. Gerald had stumbled upon Zilke's murder. An act of being in the wrong place at the wrong time. Fate seldom treated the innocent kindly. She harbored every expectation that unless he abandoned his foolhardy quest here and now, Gerald would be chewed up and spit out without any regard.

Tianna sincerely hoped that wasn't so. Plagued by visions of his face, she angrily shook her head in the hopes of clearing her mind and tried focusing on the key. Water sloshed from her glass. Oh yes, the key. McMasters had told her as much as he could about the key and the treasure waiting on the other side of the destination. Legend said the key, when paired with a map of the western continent of Cestus III, a map McMasters purportedly had in his possession, would point the way to the location of the Eye. From there it was a small matter of locating the treasure and claiming it before any government or rival agency could interdict.

Treasure beyond counting. She thrilled at the notion but saw little relevance to her position. McMasters would continue sending her on assignments until his dying breath. He kept his plans for the treasure hidden from her and the others outside of his inner circle. She didn't mind. Some things needed to be kept secret.

What she found most interesting was word of the capture of two individuals known to be associates with Gerald. Gholson was secretive about their significance. Tianna was halfway around the planet and unable to ascertain who they were or what they represented. She wanted to know their connection with Gerald and the key. The only way of finding out was to head back to Oberon City and intercept Gholson before he got off planet.

Having made up her mind, Tianna finished her water and was about to return to her cabin when a squad of security guards rushed past. Her nerves jumped despite years of training. One of the conductors noticed her sudden apprehension and approached. His sidearm looked awkward on his hip.

"Ma'am, there is nothing to worry about," he tried to console.

She nodded slowly, playing the part. "What's going on? Is there something wrong?"

He shifted his gaze from her to his departing guards. Each had a rifle and wore riot gear. The conductor leaned conspiratorially close and said in a hushed voice. "We've discovered a pair of bodies in one of the cabins."

"Bodies?" she said too quickly.

He nodded. "Murdered, or so we believe. Stay here and wait until the aft of the train is clear. It shouldn't be long."

Tianna flashed a nervous smile. "How can I relax when there's a murderer onboard? This is most dangerous."

"Our security teams will have the train secure before you know it. Please remain here."

Tianna reached out to touch his arm in a smooth caress. "Can you tell me which cabin this happened in, please?"

Against policy and his better judgement, he did then hurried off, trying to catch up to the rest of his squad.

Tianna leaned back and frowned. Two bodies; murdered no less. She wasn't alone in trying to recover the key. She wondered how many contingencies McMasters sent in the event she failed. She didn't have the answer.

She'd already guessed the bodies were in the cabin where she'd left Gerald. The conductor confirmed that. She went from being the alpha predator on the train to a target. Whoever else was onboard would already be hunting her and the key. Tianna could handle herself well enough. That part didn't concern her. What did bother her was that someone else was after the treasure. McMasters had competition he apparently didn't know about.

Tianna decided it was time to change her appearance and move to a more secure fallback position until the train arrived at station. Looking around to ensure she was alone and unwatched; she pinched the tiny node surgically implanted at the base of her right ear. In the blink of any eye her hair changed from blonde to deep, almost crimson red. Her eyes transformed to a rich emerald.

Her change of appearance wouldn't protect her for long though, especially if the conductors started going cabin by cabin with the passenger manifest. One thing became certain. She needed to get off the train before the killer decided to make his move on her.

TWENTY

2273 A.D.
Oberon City, Mars

Creeps couldn't stop fidgeting. It was driving Charlotte crazy. Yet as much as she wanted to lash out, to bark at him to stop, she knew it wouldn't do any good. They were trapped with men lacking the natural hesitancy of committing violence most people had. Her kidnappers sat in the front of the service car ensuring she and Creeps were kept in the dark and quiet. Neither seemed especially concerned with their prisoners escaping. But was it an advantage? She reckoned Gholson could be dealt with easy enough. His broken glasses and swollen nose suggested as much. It was the lanky killer at his side that scared her.

"This isn't happening," Creeps said.

Charlotte shot him an annoyed glance. What little she knew of the man suggested he was the sort to cut and run when trouble arose. Not that she blamed him. Given the opportunity, she planned on disappearing and never being found again. His nervous attitude was already setting her on edge.

"Yes, you've said that a hundred times. You'd think once would be enough."

He waved her off. "I haven't heard you come up with an idea to get us out of her."

"What am I supposed to say, Creeps?" she paused, suddenly unable to keep her anger from boiling over. "This isn't what Gerald had in mind when he told me the story about the treasure."

"What treasure?" Creeps perked up.

It dawned on her that Gerald wasn't a fool after all. Blissfully ignorant perhaps, but not a fool. "I don't think its my place to say."

"Bullshit!" Creeps grew indignant. "I knew you two were keeping something from me. Gerald hasn't spoken to me in years, and I get a call out of the blue? You two are up to something aren't you?"

Charlotte looked toward the front of the truck, only slightly relieve neither man showed signs of overhearing the conversation. "Keep quiet, you idiot. What are you trying to do to us?"

"Me? What am I trying to do? You're the one keeping secrets," Creeps hissed. "Give me one reason why I shouldn't go up there and tell them about the treasure."

"Because you don't know anything about it, stupid," Charlotte replied.

She kept her voice under control, if barely, but grew worried of Creeps doing something foolish to put them both in jeopardy. His potential for betrayal threatened her life directly. After all, he'd already told her that he was only looking out for himself. Betraying her wouldn't take much effort.

Creeps opened then close his mouth before muttering, "Tell me something now."

She breathed a little easier. Maybe she could keep Creeps on their side. "Where would you like me to begin?"

"The treasure," he told her. "Gerald already told me enough about the rest. What treasure and how much?"

She paused to clear her throat, carefully choosing her words. "The largest in the galaxy. Gerald and I were about to begin hunting for it."

"Go on, I'm listening."

Oh I know you are. Falling for each little bit I choose to give you. Aloud, Charlotte replied, "The treasure of Karakzaheim."

Creeps rolled his eyes. "Nonsense. There's no such thing."

"Isn't there?"

Her words gave him pause. Head cocked, he edged closer. "You expect me to believe in those foolish children's tales? Do you have any idea how many people have died in search of that myth?"

She didn't. In fact, it hadn't occurred to her until now. Death was a regrettable part of her studies. She worked with it. In it. Around it. Death held the key to all of humanity's future endeavors. No matter how great or small one's deeds in life were, death swallowed them all. Charlotte tried to think differently. Now more than ever she had to believe it was all worth it. That her life had meaning and purpose and that purpose was to find the infamous treasure of Karakzaheim. Only then would she find true satisfaction.

"Gerald and I are on the trail to the real treasure," she affirmed.

"Where is it?" he asked. Creeps wasn't a fool. To become a willing accomplice to this mad scheme he'd need more convincing this wasn't just a farfetched dream.

Charlotte hesitated. "Well, we don't know."

"Bullshit. I knew it."

"Wait, listen!"

"Last chance," Creeps warned.

Charlotte blew out a deep breath. "He has the first part to finding all of the clues. It's called the key.

There is a map that goes with the key. I was hoping to find the map in Creighton Colony."

"And this map will lead us to the impossible treasure?" Creeps rubbed his jaw.

"In theory," she hedged. "And it is much more than treasure. It will be the archaeological find of the century!"

Creeps grinned before pointing at the two men in the front of the truck. "Too bad they don't seem interested in your theory." He shrugged. "Got any plans for getting us out of this mess?"

She didn't and that troubled her more than she was willing to admit. Making matters worse, she had no idea where Gerald was or even if he was still enroute to the museum annex. Frustrated and tired, Charlotte wanted to ball her fists and scream. She didn't. If for no other reason than the preservation of her life from the two killers in front of her.

What she guessed was hours later, the truck pulled into a quiet, abandoned warehouse in the labor district. Edgemeyer jumped out and opened the back doors. Artificial light flooded in, blinding both Charlotte and Creeps. Firm, incredibly strong hands reached in and snatched Creeps by the collar.

"Hey! Let go of me!" he shouted, but he was helpless to stop Edgemeyer.

Charlotte climbed out unmolested, daring an equally hard glare to the hard-faced killer. Gholson slipped behind her.

"He's a rough man, but he won't lay a hand on a lady," Gholson told her.

Edgemeyer shoved Creeps back, turning to give Gholson a warning glare.

"Killing you, on the other hand, won't be an issue," the shorted man continued.

Charlotte stepped away from him. His presence disgusted her. "What do you want with us? We've done nothing?"

"That may be true, but our employer has taken interest in you, Ms. Bailey."

"Me? Why me?" she protested.

"She talks too much," Edgemeyer growled. She spied his sidearm in his left hand.

"Patience, Mr. Edgemeyer," Gholson chided. "She must not be harmed."

Glowering, Edgemeyer turned back to his prisoner, leaving Gholson to continue: "It has come to our attention that you are an archaeologist."

'What of it?" she asked.

Gholson removed his glasses and started cleaning them. "Mr. McMasters has need of your services in order to find the treasure. And before you embarrass yourself by proclaiming ignorance, we already know what you know about the treasure. You were in the company of one Gerald LaPlant who has an artifact necessary for us to find the Eye. Your expertise is precisely what we need to succeed."

She fired a smirk at Creeps, who shrugged. "If I don't agree?"

"We should kill them both now, especially her," Edgemeyer muttered.

Gholson ignored him. Many years of working together left him armored against Edgemeyer's perpetual gruffness. "You have no other choice. You will either assist us or, well you really don't want to know the alternative."

It was that moment Charlotte realized she had more control than she thought. Being invaluable gave her wiggle room. "What's in it for me?"

Gholson replaced his glasses, blinking rapidly to clear his eyes. The frame was bent, giving them a crooked appearance. "A sensible woman after all. We are prepared to compensate you handsomely for your services, provided we are successful of course."

"Of course," she said with a false smile.

Edgemeyer had lost all patience, snapping, "Gholson, we must leave now."

"In due time, my friend. Now, Ms. Bailey, do we have an accord?"

Charlotte extended her hand without second thought. "Deal. But one question."

"Go on."

"What happens to Gerald? He didn't ask for any of this to happen."

Edgemeyer growled, "He should have died on Earth."

"Indeed, he should have," Gholson seconded. "Gerald LaPlant had a most unfortunate experience. He witnessed our … actions. Regrettable, but he must die. It would also be a shame if you … disappoint us before fulfilling your part. I do so frown on unnecessary bloodshed, but then again, it is not my decision to make."

She froze. "There must be some other way. He … he," she fumbled, at a loss for words. "He has the key, and you don't have him."

Gholson shrugged. "Does he? We are not the only ones in Mr. McMasters' employ. Another agent has already secured the key and incapacitated LaPlant. You see, you really don't have a choice."

Her knees gave out and she slumped to the floor. Gerald. Dead. What started at a frantic pace continued to barrel on, devouring lives at will. Was she next? Was Creeps? The only way of deterring her own death was to agree to work with McMasters. Her stomach roiled.

"You bastards," Creeps growled and struggled harder to get away.

The thin man kept him pinned in place with little effort. Gholson walked up to them and jabbed a finger in Creeps' chest. "The only reason you continue to draw breath is because my employer wishes it so. Do not presume you are important enough to keep your tongue."

"You wouldn't dare," Creeps seethed.

"Wouldn't I? Mr. McMasters said to bring you in alive as insurance to make Ms. Bailey cooperate. He didn't specify you had to be intact. Remember that."

Edgemeyer grinned, the visage of a hungry wolf.

"What are you?" Creeps asked in a whisper.

Edgemeyer brought his face an inch away from Creeps' ear and said, "Death."

"Get them loaded on the shuttle. We must return to Cestus immediately," Gholson ordered.

Edgemeyer forced a dazed Creeps toward the boarding ramp. The local managed a final, defeated look at Charlotte as she struggled to get off the ground. It was all she could do to remain on unsteady feet. So much had changed over the last two days.

"Move," was all Edgemeyer said.

Charlotte obeyed. She and Creeps were now in the willing employ of Roland McMasters. Yet as she was being hurried toward the waiting shuttle carefully camouflaged in the rear of the warehouse, she couldn't help but think of the way Gerald looked at her. That awkward smile and those soft yet suspicious eyes.

Gerald was a mystery. She knew next to nothing about him other than he was a hard worker, or so he claimed, and was on the run from the men who had abducted her. There wasn't anything overly special about him, yet she couldn't get him out of her head. Was it his laugh? The twinkle in his eyes he tried desperately to hide when he looked at her? She hadn't known until now, but a man like Gerald was exactly what she was missing in her life.

And now he was gone.

TWENTY-ONE

2273 A.D.
Creighton Colony, Mars

Carter Gaetis secured Gerald in the corner of a small cabin then busied himself cleaning his weapon. The largest part of the mission was still incomplete. He had Gerald in custody, but not the artifact. Cleaning his weapon calmed his nerves and allowed him to think more clearly.

The train was getting close to Creighton Colony. He figured they had another thirty minutes before pulling into the station where Tianna Everson would leave the train and disappear. He couldn't allow that to happen. Everything hinged on finding her.

Unbidden memories returned. Three years ago he'd been on assignment, monitoring a purported corrupt government official from the Earth Alliance. Termination was the order, but he needed to collect as much data to send back to Shine as possible. When the moment arrived for Carter to complete the assignment, he was too late. He discovered Tianna standing over the body, hands covered in blood.

Carter made the mistake of going after her and failed, badly. Tianna proved more than a match in hand-to-hand combat, leaving him lying on the floor with a broken arm. That was where the authorities found him. He spent nearly a week in prison before Mr. Shine was able to secure his release. During that week he thought what went wrong and the possible repercussions he would face upon release.

The next three years were spent pining for retribution. Carter became obsessed with hunting

Tianna down. It was his intention to kill her and close a chapter of his career.

"You do that a lot," Gerald remarked, gesturing with his head to Carter's weapon.

"What's your point?" he growled.

Gerald shrugged. "A thing can only get so clean before you're wasting your time."

"I can always get the barrel dirty again," Carter replied, casually swinging the weapon to point at Gerald's chest.

"I'd rather like to keep on living."

"Wouldn't we all. I told you to keep quiet."

Gerald decided to press. "We're almost at the station. The train is slowing down."

Carter didn't need the reminder. He was no closer to a plan for finding Tianna or getting the key. Making matters worse, he hadn't produced any useful intelligence from Gerald. Carter could not figure out if Gerald was obstinate out of fear or simply didn't know anything.

"Once the train stops and she gets off, you won't have any need for me, right?"

Carter sat straight up, letting the cabin's light define his muscular build. "Nothing in my orders mentions you being dead … or alive. Keep running your lips and putting you in a body bag starts sounding good."

Taking the water for what it was, Gerald nodded. "So what are we going to do?"

"Shut up and let me think or I will put a round between your eyes."

Any pretense of putting up with Gerald's childish questioning washed away, leaving a chill in the cabin. A quick glance at his wrist chrono confirmed Carter was due to check in. Failing to get the artifact was already a colossal failure. He didn't need Shine doubting his ability to follow standard procedures.

Carter kept his blaster trained on Gerald. "Not a word out of you, or they'll be scraping your brains off that wall. Understand?"

Gerald nodded. He sat on the high-backed chair, taking a moment to smooth out the tiny ripple in his pants.

Carter turned away with a grunt and activated the call.

"Mr. Gaetis, I was beginning to grow worried." Shine's rasping voice was heard before his image appeared on the holoprojector attached to the faux wood table on the far side of the cabin.

"Sir, there have been complications," Carter said.

Shine's image stiffened. His cadaverous face creased with fresh lines of disappointment. "Would you care to elaborate?"

"The Fat Man's agents have infiltrated the situation. Everson got to the target before I could. I am in the pro—"

"Where is the artifact?" Shine's voice turned cold.

"She has it," Carter replied in defeat.

Shine pursed his lips. "That is … unfortunate. I had every expectation you would already be enroute with my prize secure, Mr. Gaetis. Perhaps my instructions were unclear?"

"No, sir."

"Then please explain why a rival got the best of one of my best field agents."

"Sir, she was an unexpected variable," Carter admitted. "I am in the process of tracking her and retrieving the item before she can get it into the Fat Man's hands. I anticipate this matter being resolved within the next twenty-four standard Earth hours."

"It had better be, or …" Shine fell silent. His threat successfully conveyed. "I want the artifact in my possession at once. Do not fail me again, Mr. Gaetis."

"On my honor," Carter said.

The transmission ended.

Gerald looked at Carter, daring to ask, "Who was that?"

Carter finally looked up, mixed feelings crossing his face. "A man you'd best pray never crosses your path."

"It doesn't seem like I have much choice in who crosses my path these days," Gerald replied.

Carter tucked his blaster away in the concealed holster built into his synthetic jacket. "The mission always comes first. Always."

"Fair enough, but I'm not part of this mission," Gerald countered.

Carter paused, hand lingering on his jacket. "Like it or not, your world has changed. You're part of this hunt now. Whether you come out of this dead or alive makes no difference to me."

"Does my opinion matter?"

Carter gave him a hard look. "I tell you what. You help me run this bitch down and I'll conveniently forget I ever saw you. The artifact goes with me, and you can fade away back into an obscure life."

Left with little real choice, Gerald unsurprisingly said, "Deal. What's our first move?"

"Our first move," Carter started, "is to figure out how Tianna plans to get back to Cestus III and then stop her before she can do it."

Nothing more to say, he ushered Gerald into the main hallway and they headed aft. There was no possible way to cover all exits, forcing Carter to hedge his bets. He had no real plan, other than hurrying through the train in the hopes of running into her.

Passengers were beginning to leave their cabins, cluttering the hall. Carter frowned and lowered his shoulder to force his way through. He moved fast, trusting that Gerald's need to find Tianna would keep him in tow for a while at least. He also judged Gerald to be at the end of his rope, and willing to latch onto any offered help.

They passed through a dozen cars without any luck. Carter was beginning to think they'd missed her, and she was already preparing to deboard. He needed to remain focused. Of course, thoughts of what he was going to do to her made his heart race. There was nothing like the screams of competitors knowing they'd failed.

Carter prided himself on carrying out his assignments cleanly, not with the intention of causing pain. For Tianna Everson he was willing to make an exception. She was an embarrassment he'd suffered too long. The only blemish on his otherwise perfect record in the Lazarus Men. This one time, Carter found the mission personal.

They stepped over the entrance to the second to last passenger car. Hope dwindled. The train slowed to a crawl. They were pulling into the Creighton Colony station. Time was up. Doors hissed open. Passengers lined the walkway in an unmannerly procession.

Carter turned back in frustration and bumped into a tall, stunning redhead. He was about to apologize when recognition dawned. Tianna offered a womanly smile before gut punching him. Carter doubled over, his breath fleeing with a pronounced whuff. Pain rippled through his stomach and up into his ribcage. The solar plexus. *Fucking bitch.* Carter groaned.

Tianna shouldered past and slipped into the growing crowd.

TWENTY-TWO

2273 A.D.
Creighton Colony, Mars

Gerald hears the rising shouts and curses as Tianna forced her way through the growing crowd. Seconds slipped away. He watched everything without knowing what to do next. Instinct screamed at him to hurry after Tianna; to do anything to stop her long enough to retrieve the key. After watching how efficiently and ruthlessly she disabled Carter, Gerald had no doubt she would dispatch him with no difficulty.

A muffled voice announcing the destination came over the intercom. The main doors opened and the crowds started pushing into the terminal. Tianna slipped out and was gone. options terminated. Gerald turned back to Carter, grabbing his arm and dragging him out of the stampede before he was trampled.

"Are you all right?" he asked.

Carter tried to wave him off. "After … her. That was … Tianna."

"I know. She just got off the train."

Carter finally managed a deep breath and straightened. Fire surged through his lungs. "Move, before she's gone."

Unsure if following Tianna was a good idea, Gerald offered Carter support while the man continued to regain his breath—they headed in the direction he saw Tianna head.

The station was remarkably plain. Faded and dirty tile covered the floor, walls, and arched ceiling. Chipped and scarred columns of now brown plaster had been added for decoration by the original builders but had long since fallen into disrepair. Hundreds of passengers filled the rounded main hall. Hundreds of people making it all but impossible to find a single woman with the ability to transform her looks. Then it hit Gerald.

"I can't see her," he said, exasperated. "Why doesn't she look the same?"

Carter pushed away, able to stand on his own at last. "She's a *splicer*. Genetically enhanced to be able to blend in, like a largdros bug."

"Like a what?"

Carter paused; his face twisted with thought. "Ah … like an Earth chameleon. The point is, she can change her looks at random."

That explains the hair. "Can you track her?"

"If you stop asking me idiotic questions. Come on."

Gerald struggled to keep up with the assassin. How many people were going to get involved in this hunt before someone else died?"

Then there was the Fat Man mystery. He could only assume the unfortunate moniker referred to Roland McMasters.

Carter gripped Gerald's upper arm and hauled him sharply left. "There."

Gerald stumbled along; his senses overwhelmed. Face blended together. Trying to look for familiar features was futile with Tianna. The obvious came to him and he felt foolish for not thinking of it before.

"Hey, Carter!" he shouted.

Carter kept moving, picking up speed.

"Carter, her clothes!" Gerald raised his voice over the din of the crowd.

The Lazarus Man jerked to a stop. "What did you say?"

"She can change her looks, but her clothes stay the same," Gerald explained.

The quickest flash of a smile crossed Carter's face. "Come on."

Gerald's heart began racing. Another ten meters of progress and the man beside him pitched backwards, arms flailing up in surprise. Gerald skidded to a halt and looked down into the man's blank eyes. Blood pooled from under his head. He was frozen in place, staring deep into the eyes of a murdered man.

"Down!" Carter yelled, shoving Gerald out of the way before firing three quick shots.

Gerald slipped in the blood and he crashed down beside the body. He scrambled to get away, even as he wondered who the man was. Why he was here. Gerald tried feeling empathy but couldn't. The dead were dead. A few inches to the left and it would have been him bleeding out. Self-preservation dominated his thoughts. He needed to find a way out of this mess before he wound up on the ground as well.

Hands wet and sticky, Gerald struggled back to his feet.

The crowds were scattering in panic.

Through the jumble of legs and bags, Gerald was able to spot the blue-green dress Tianna was wearing. People screamed as gunfire continued to trade between the killers. A woman five meters in front of Gerald fell. Her shoulder blossomed with blood. The flow pattern of her dress turned obscene. Gerald felt the bile rising in his throat. The acidic sting made his stomach convulse.

"Gerald! Move right and find cover," Carter barked.

Two rounds struck the ground in front of him, kicking tile chips into his face and hands. Gerald pushed off and dashed behind the nearest column. Tianna's rounds ricocheted off the column. A few struck innocent bystanders unlucky enough to be near him.

Gerald decided Carter and Tianna were crazy. No treasure in the galaxy was worth this. He slammed into the column, heart thundering in his chest. He dared a quick look to where he'd last spied Tianna—

She wasn't there. *Shit. Where'd she go*?

Frantic, he scanned the crowds. Men and women pushed and shoved their way toward perceived safety. A handful of bodies littered the dirty floor. Gerald heard a piercing wail. A small boy who couldn't have been more than ten crouched in the middle of it all. Hands pressed to his ears; his face was filled with tears. Without thinking, Gerald dashed to the child. Snatching the boy around the waist, Gerald stumbled back to the relative safety of the column.

He slid to the floor and grabbed the boy by the shoulders, trying to catch his gaze. His hands left bloody prints on the boy's shirt. "Look at me. Where are your parents?"

The boy cried harder upon seeing the blood. A snap-hiss from a round narrowly missing Gerald's head made him duck.

"Your parents, boy. Where are they? We can't stay here."

Seeing he wasn't about to get an answer, Gerald cursed and pinned the boy between himself and the column.

The shooting stopped. Hands snatched him to his feet. Weaponless, Gerald clenched his fists to strike.

"She's gone, but we need to move," Carter told him once Gerald relaxed enough to recognize him. "Local security is already on the way. Lose the kid. We need to go now."

Gerald offered a last, sad look at the boy, praying one or both of his parents were somewhere in this madness, and hurried after Carter.

Neither man said a thing as they did their best to blend in with the fleeing civilians.

"Where can she go from here?" Gerald asked as they hurried into a stolen vehicle and down Creighton Colony's main avenue in search of their elusive target.

"There's a small airfield that's off the grid just outside of the colony. My guess is she's headed there and booking out on unregistered transport."

"Is that legal?" Gerald regretted asking it the moment the words left his mouth. Of course it wasn't. Nothing about this entire venture had been legal thus far.

Carter shook his head. "The Fat Man has greased the palms of many officials on the outer worlds and in the Earth Alliance. No one will bother looking if she does head there and I have every reason to believe she will."

"Fat Man?" Gerald asked.

"Roland McMasters."

Gerald nodded; his suspicions confirmed.

Carter caught the movement out of the corner of an eye and asked, "What is this object everyone is willing to kill for? And what, precisely, is your role in all of this?"

Ah, so you haven't been told everything either. Guess that puts us on even footing. He hesitated before replying. "I'm still trying to figure that out. All I know is a lot of people have been killed and I'm no closer to getting out of danger than I was before. I'm trapped, Carter."

"Finding the artifact is the only way out for either of us." Carter paused. "Why Creighton Colony?"

Gerald didn't see much reason in keeping secrets, especially considering there was almost no chance of following through. "I met an archaeologist who knew what the artifact was; she was certain the museum annex here had the data she was looking for."

"Are you certain you can trust her?"

Gerald's own pause was just long enough to be unnatural. "I … I don't know."

He was trying to protect Charlotte, but with her being halfway around the planet, he had no idea is she was still safe or not. Then a thought struck, "What do you know about a pair of goons named Edgemeyer and Gholberg?"

"Gholson. Avoid them at all costs," Carter answered. "Tell me they're not involved."

Gerald nodded more quickly this time. "They chased me off Earth and found me in the main terminal at Oberon City."

Carter winced.

Gerald reached for the closest piece of the bar-style cage fortifying the vehicle's cabin and clenched his teeth. Each bump and rattle seemed a prelude to the roller being slammed into a rock formation in the Martian emptiness.

Gerald saw death a dozen times before finding the courage to cast a sharp glare at Carter. "Slow down, you're going to get us killed."

We're both dead if she gets away," Carter snapped. "You didn't tell me Edgemeyer and Gholson were involved. What else are you hiding?"

Faint lights could be seen breaking the horizon. Gerald hadn't noticed they were already free from the constraints of the city. He assumed the landing strip was straight ahead. It was the conduit to a new life. A means of getting off Mars. A trio of orangish-red lights bounced through the darkness several hundred meters ahead of them. Could it be?

Tianna and the artifact.

"I don't suppose I can get one of those guns?" he asked, focused again on settling the score so he could be free of this nightmare.

Carter ignored him.

TWENTY-THREE

2273 A.D.

Clandestine landing strip outside of Creighton Colony.

The landing strip was situated in the center of a small basin created after a meteor strike sometime in the distant past. Though it was not under Martian authority, the landing strip was concealed beneath a shimmering dome of bioelectrical static. Stimulated atmosphere made the air within the dome breathable, if slightly uncomfortable. It was like walking atop the Himalayan Mountains. Doable, but difficult.

Gerald stayed a few feet behind Carter as instructed. He mimicked Carter's movements, ducking and sprinting like a drunken sailor in port for the first time in years.

So far, they'd seen no one and, aside from the empty roller parked on the edge of the landing strip, there wasn't any sign of occupation. As far as Gerald could tell, the dome was deserted. He was about to mention that to Carter when the top of a small cluster of red tinged boulders evaporated in dust. Tianna's voice sang over the echo of gunfire.

"Stay where you are."

Gerald dropped as fast as he could as self-preservation took control. In his clumsiness, he bumped into Carter. He was rewarded with a sharp elbow to his stomach. A second and then a third round hit where his head had been.

***

"Show yourself, Tianna. Let's do this like civilized people."

Her laughter echoed over the rocks, light and oddly carefree. "Ah Carter, how long has it been?"

"Not long enough."

His right hand slid up his torso to touch the spot where she'd shot him in their previous encounter.

"You're not still upset about that little bullet, are you?" she taunted.

Tianna held all the advantages in the situation. She had the artifact. She was concealed and had the perfect line of sight on them. It was a desperate scenario Carter struggled with. He needed to end this now.

"You should have killed me then," he scanned the rocks. She was cleverly hidden, taking up an impossible firing position that kept them pinned down.

And yet … She could have killed him outright back then if she wanted, but she continued letting him live. Why? Carter frowned. That was three years ago. There'd be no second chance this time.

Only one of them was going to walk away.

"I won't make that mistake again. Tell me, is Gerald still with you?"

Carter gave Gerald a stern look, keeping him silent.

"That's not your concern. Be a good girl and give me the artifact. We can forget this nasty business ever happened and go our separate ways."

Her laugh took on a sharp edge. "You don't know McMasters very well if you think I won't be severely punished for failing him."

"It's no more than you deserve!" Gerald shouted.

Carter glared.

"Hello, Gerald. Did you miss me?" Tianna called out.

"Not as much as you missed me back in the train station."

Carter snorted.

"Simple fool. I wasn't trying to kill you. If I wanted to do that you never would have left my cabin. Carter, on the other hand …"

To his credit, Carter didn't rise to the challenge.

"Tianna, give me the key back," Gerald said.

"I wish you wouldn't have said that," she said. "Now I have to kill you. Don't be mad, Gerald. Business is business. There can be no loose ends, and your knowledge of the key makes you a loose end."

Carter tensed at the sound of a faint whistle.

"What was th—" Gerald tried asking.

Carter waved him off, ears trained to the slightest sound. Six armed men in black flight suits burst from cover, surrounding the pair. Their faces were concealed behind the reflective faceplates of their helmets.

***

The biggest attacker brandished a wicked looking curved blade. Contact happened in the blink of an eye. Carter struck faster than Gerald could believe. He ducked under a vicious lethal swing meant to decapitate and jammed the barrel of his blaster up under the helmet before pulling the trigger three times. Plexi-steel and brain matter blossomed from the top of the man's head.

Gerald cried out as the man fell to the ground, a mountain of lifeless flesh. Carter continued the movement and rolled forward. He came up on one knee and took aim. The round struck true, piercing his victim's heart as the man raised his own weapon.

The third man took advantage of the scenario and maneuvered behind Carter unseen. He raised his blaster and readied to fire. Gerald shouted and leaped on the man's back.

The shot went wild.

The shooter threw an elbow back into Gerald's ribs. Instead of pitching back, Gerald drove three quick blows to the back of the assailant's head and neck with a fist sized rock he snatched up in the confusion. Stunned, the shooter tilted his head back, giving Gerald the opportunity to slip his forearm around the shooter's throat. Squeezing, Gerald dropped the rock and slipped his right arm in front of the left, locking the grip the shooter could not break. The helmet worked in Gerald's favor, driving the chinstrap deeper into the folds of soft flesh and cutting air flow. Gerald heard a gurgle before the shooter's knees gave out and they both toppled to the red dirt.

Gerald rolled to his side and was rewarded with the loose blaster only inches away. He snatched up the weapon and fired two rounds into the shooter's unprotected chest. Blood spread across the front of the flight suit faster than Gerald thought possible. Breathing heavily and his heart racing, Gerald slumped down. It felt good turning the tables after being hunted for the last week.

Then realization of what he had done struck and his stomach tightened with sickness. He looked at the corpse—a man dead by his hand. Now *he* was a killer. Gerald struggled with the urge to cry and the desire to stand with one foot atop the body and bellow a triumphant roar.

The adrenalin rush subsided, and shame infiltrated his raw nerves. He stared down on the body and wondered who he was. Did he have a family? A home? Continued torment pointless, Gerald took the man for what he was, a paid killer in the employ of Roland McMasters. As such, he got what he deserved.

Gerald stirred himself out of his rumination and watched Carter dispatch the last of their attackers. It was in that moment he realized he held an unexpected advantage. Gerald tucked his new blaster into a pocket and waited for Carter to return.

The Lazarus Man looked haggard. Blood ran freely down his left arm. His face was battered. Despite having saved each other's lives, Gerald felt no compassion for his companion. Carter was as much of the problem to him as Tianna.

Shit! Tianna.

In the confusion of their fight, they'd lost her … again.

"Carter," he began.

Carter bent down to place his good hand on a knee for stability while waving Gerald's question off. "Where is the other man?"

"I killed him."

"You what?"

"He was going to shoot you in the back. He's right there," Gerald gestured toward the body.

Carter looked at him differently, as if understanding Gerald was no longer helpless.

"Thank you," was all he managed before dashing toward the nearby flight line.

Gerald gave the bodies a final glance before hurrying after. His sole concern lay in stopping Tianna from leaving Mars. Recovering the key was secondary, yet vital to his survival.

They rounded a bend on the trail and skidded to a halt as the long flight line came into view. Flanked by the skeletal remains of buildings once meant to house administrations and remote star liner headquarters, a single craft sat in the center. Grey shelled and ovoid, it was designed for one pilot and built for speed. Gerald spied Tianna climbing the small ladder built into the side and then the cockpit.

They were too late.

Carter emptied his magazine at the craft but only a few rounds struck. He was too far away to cause any real damage. He sprinted forward without waiting for Gerald.

They were halfway there when the engines cranked to life. Their bright blue lights flared, and the craft slowly inched off the ground. Carter was blown from his feet by the force of propulsion. Gerald stopped, crouched down, and shielded his face with a forearm as a cloud of debris blasted him.

The sleek vehicle entered the upper atmosphere and disappeared from sight.

TWENTY-FOUR

2273 A.D.
Absolution, Cestus III

He swirled the amber bourbon in the crystal glass in his right hand. The subtle clink-clink of ice striking the glass was soothing, comforting to his ears. Smoke from the finest cigar money could buy wafted in thinning clouds overhead, transforming the formal parlor into a pleasant environment ripe for relaxation. Old Earth classical music, timeless in its presentation, played softly in the background. Roland had a fondness for Mahler. The music had a way of reducing his stress, almost enchanting him through its simple brilliance.

Roland was a man with one desire. He wanted everything. To think his search for the treasure of Karakzaheim was hampered by the most unlikely person, a nobody, set him on edge. He was used to getting what he wanted. A man who dined with presidents, dictators, ambassadors, and the most influential people in the galaxy, yet insignificant Gerald LaPlant managed to stymy his every more. Were it not for the importance of the prize, Roland might have taken amusement in the game. Fate seemed to enjoy toying with him.

Yet he was prepared and had already taken measure to neutralize LaPlant's interference. Roland's agents falsified employment termination orders with Trans Stellar and Earth law enforcement agencies were already waiting for Gerald's return to New York

City. If Roland had his way, and he usually did, Gerald would be found, caught, and cut into quarters before being disposed of among the stars. No one got the upper hand against Roland McMasters without paying for it.

A puff of smoke later and his thoughts shifted to the enigmatic leader of the Lazarus Men. His strained relationship with Mr. Shine compounded his dilemma. It infuriated him that the weasel of a man had no first name, or if he did, managed to bury it deep enough not even Roland's expansive capabilities could discover. The mystery of the Lazarus Men stretched back much further than Roland had been able to penetrate. He remained at a disadvantage until he learned Shine's secrets.

Roland knew it was a calculated risk involving Shine in his business, but felt it was necessary after the debacle on Earth. Shine's agents were highly trained and more focused on outcome than the usual mercenaries Roland typically used. That did not less his concern about betrayal, however. Shadow organizations like Shine's had many enemies and, since they insisted on working outside of the law, Roland knew they were prone to attack with impunity by the right people.

"A decidedly tangled web," he muttered aloud, letting the last sip of smooth bourbon roll across his tongue. "Well, Shine, it's your move. I wonder which direction you will go."

Roland was fairly certain Shine was going to make a play for the treasure if he hadn't done so already. Since Roland had his three top agents on Mars, it only made sense to his business mind that Shine would send an equally experienced agent. Or more than one. Fair enough. This was business after all.

Pouring another drink, Roland enjoyed seeing the golden liquor slide down the side of his glass. A thousand other bottles just like this filled his cellars, along with fine wines and other liquors from across the galaxy. A walk-in humidor curated five thousand cigars. Naturally there was no way he'd consume everything before his demise. Nor did he feel the need to. He just desired to own them and keep others from having them.

"Your pardon, sir, but they have arrived," his new assistant announced after clearing his throat to make Roland aware of his presence.

Roland felt no urgency. He already knew what his agents had to report. Waving the assistant away without looking, he continued the pour. The scuffle of feet, that heavy sound of rubber dragging across tile—a sound he despised—soon filled his parlor. Roland was certain they did so on purpose, just to irritate him.

"Mr. McMasters," Gholson said upon entering the room.

"What were my instructions?"

Gholson pulled back, confused. "Sir?"

Roland spun, his face the twisted vision of wrath. "Answer my question, Gholson."

"We were supposed to bring you the key," Edgemeyer said, stepping in for his stammering partner. He betrayed no emotion.

"Exactly." Roland paused to take a sip. "Yet you return without it. Oh, there's a line of bodies stretching all the way back to New York City, but I still have no key. Without this I cannot find the Eye. Perhaps there was misunderstanding on your parts?"

"No sir, just complications," Gholson offered.

Roland slammed his glass onto a beautiful mahogany table; the glass shattered. "I don't give a damn about complications! Your idiocy is hampering my efforts, and now the wolves have smelled blood. I should have you both vented into space."

He shook his hand, frowning at the waste of bourbon as it poured down his fingertips and onto the crimson carpet. "Still, you have delivered an item of some value. Bring them in."

Edgemeyer folded his arms across his chest and stiffened as Gholson hurried to do as ordered.

Once they were alone, Roland said, "You should have taken control of this matter sooner. Gholson lacks the ability to think ahead."

"He has his uses," Edgemeyer replied. "It was my fault. Zilke had already passed the key off to LaPlant. Matters became … complicated after that."

"If you weren't such a valuable asset I would relegate you to the kitchens," Roland grunted. "Or I could always have you reprogrammed."

"You could, but it would serve no good purpose," Edgemeyer countered.

Roland idly scratched at his chin. His bourbon was gone. His cigar was out. He'd had Edgemeyer commissioned as a personal favor from the Dromn Artificial Development Corps some years ago. The android was state of the art and designed to be a ruthless, efficient killer. It was the muscle a man like Roland needed in order to further certain nefarious aspects of his business. Androids were still relatively rare in the galaxy. This gave both Roland and Edgemeyer a distinct edge over the competition, at least until Dromn secured defense contracts for synthesized soldiers. Only a handful alive knew Edgemeyer's secret.

Gholson returned with Charlotte and Creeps at gunpoint. Roland studied the odd pair with minor amusement. The archaeologist stood indignant as she was being herded into his presence. The other glared daggers at Edgemeyer and then back over his shoulder at the squat man holding the gun. Neither of them was in a position to do more than listen.

"What is the meaning of this? I de—" Charlotte was cut off by the muzzle pressing into her back.

"There is no need to be rude to our guests, Gholson," Roland said, more for Charlotte's benefit than any disciplinary measure.

Gholson shrugged and stepped back. His mind raced, knowing he was in trouble and desperate to find a way to improve his standing with McMasters.

"I've got a score to settle with you, little man," Creeps snarled at him.

Roland laughed. "I dare say the time for deception is quickly coming to an end, Creeps. Come, stand over there with the rest of my employees."

Charlotte spun to face Creeps. "What does he mean by that?"

Creeps held up both hands. "Hey, a man's got to eat. Don't take it personally, sweet stuff."

The slap echoed sharply and Edgemeyer bolted forward to stop Charlotte from driving her fist into Creeps' face. She continued struggling, using her legs to kick and thrash.

"Come now, Ms. Bailey, it's most certainly not his fault," Roland supplied, amused. "My men got to him before you landed on Mars. You see, it's a simple matter of economics. We had tapped LaPlant's communication devices, leading us to Creeps here."

"And you turned him for what? Pennies?" she asked.

Roland gestured with empty hands. "Every man has a monetary breaking point. Fortunately for my coffers his was exceedingly low."

"It'll pay the bills," Creeps defended.

"Indeed."

Charlotte stopped struggling. "Why did you have to kill Gerald?"

Roland snorted. "He is still alive according to the last report I received. Fortunate for you, though I admit he has raised my ire and for that I will see him punished. He won't be alive long."

Roland dashed any hope she might have had. "Rest assured, the key is in my possession. It will be here soon. Then we can move forward."

Charlotte stiffened. "What's next? You have the key. What do you need me for?"

"Need? Oh no, my dear. I don't *need* you at all. I have the key and the map. You are merely a pleasant diversion. Although, I may have use of your services before the end."

"Meaning what?" she demanded.

Roland moved back to his deck and sat with an audible huff. His hands rested on the expanse of his stomach, fingers drumming in thought on the light grey fabric of his waistcoat. His eyes narrowed.

All of the tools he needed to find the treasure were in place. With what he had learned lately, and his knowledge of Cestus, he had a good idea where to begin searching. Once he got the key in his hands he would discover if he was correct. What he lacked however, was a credible source who understood and could recognize any traps and pitfalls around ancient ruins.

"Meaning, young lady, there is room in my employ for a woman of your particular talent," he supplied. "Tell me, what is your specialty in the field of archaeology?"

"Predynastic Old Earth at the moment," she replied slowly.

"Good. Would this include other empires?" he asked. It was common knowledge that many of the now colonized worlds once held other civilizations. A few worlds yet maintained remnants of those peoples. Cestus III included.

"It can. That all depends on what you're specifically looking for." She paused. "Look, Mr. McMasters, I understand you're a very powerful man, but you could speed this process up by coming out and telling me exactly what you want. I've never had much tolerance for dithering."

Roland leaned forward, planting his elbows on the desk. "No, I can see that. Very well, come sit and I will explain to you the legend of the treasure of General Karakzaheim and what I intend to do with it."

Edgemeyer released her and she took the nearest chair opposite McMasters.

"We all have a price," Creeps chided as she passed him.

Roland smiled.

***

"Unidentified craft, this is the civil defense authority. State your business on Cestus III
and transmit credentials now or prepare to be fired on."

The pilot exhaled his frustrations at being spotted so quickly after entering the atmosphere. Government technicians had assured him this shuttle was equipped with the most up to date stealth technology available, supposedly making it next to impossible for any planetary governments in the Outer Worlds to detect. Clearly, they suffered from gross miscalculation or perhaps just hubris.

Spies were abundant on every political side, making any effort of secrecy largely impossible. It was the same game states and governments had been playing since the dawn of the first empire. Years spent as an Earth Defense Force pilot made him confident in his abilities, but when he couldn't trust the men who made his aircraft, he had little choice but to acquiesce.

"Civil defense authority, this is shuttle A-377 out of Mars. I am transmitting my clearance codes now," the pilot said.

His tension rose as several flights of fighters lifted through the clouds to flank his inbound shuttle. They'd shoot him down without compunction if the order was given. Sensors indicated an even half dozen surrounded him in a loose semi-circle—it was overkill. He was unarmed. Why the display of force then?

He reduced his speed to appear less of a threat. Following instructions meant a longer life expectancy. Getting on the ground was supposed to be the easy part. The trick began with what followed. The pilot, known to one man as Fake Earl, was a seasoned professional. Right now, he needed to get on the ground and link up with the local Earth embassy.

After that was a matter of locating Gerald LaPlant and getting him safely back to the Earth Alliance before Roland McMasters succeeded in stealing the treasure of Karakzaheim. Already ridiculously rich, McMasters had secret holdings in most major weapons manufacturing companies on a dozen world. Everything from bullets to tanks. Million would die while his wallet continued fattening from the proceeds of his quest.

Fake Earl was sent to stop it before it got started. He smirked at the name Gerald was so intent on forcing upon him. His real name was Agent O'Hara, a loyal agent to the Earth government for nearly two decades. He'd been assigned to watch over the New York City spaceport as soon as the government caught wind of McMasters' move. Several agents were scattered across every major transportation hub. It was O'Hara's good fortune that Gerald stumbled upon the untimely murder of Zilke, tripping the entire scheme.

"Shuttle A-377, you are cleared to land. Proceed to docking pad 32 without deviation."

O'Hara sighed. Without deviation meant officials would be there to meet him. Well enough, so long as they were deep in McMasters' pockets. Setting the autopilot controls, O'Hara leaned back in the webbing of his pilot chair and headed into what he assumed was a web of deception, violence, and danger. All in a day's pay.

TWENTY-FIVE

2273 A.D.
Enroute to Cestus III

"You lied."

It was more accusation than statement. Carter used every ounce of restraint he had not to throttle Gerald before leaving Mars.

"I had to. Tell me you would have done anything different?" Gerald challenged. "This may be just a game for you people, but this is my life. Dying for some mythological treasure isn't what I had in mind for the week."

"Gerald, this is not a game. Powerful people want that artifact."

"If I had told you I knew what the key was while we were on the train you'd have killed me. I'd be dead and stuffed under the bed with those other two bodies. I've paid attention. I've seen what you can do and, frankly, it scares the living shit out of me."

Carter continued staring into the vast emptiness of space. Being among the stars like this was momentarily peaceful, despite the situation.

"You should be afraid. Death isn't the worst that can happen to you. And yes, I would have killed you."

Gerald blanched at the admission.

Several moments of awkward silence raised the tension in the cabin. "How did you get involved in this mess? You seem like a good guy. Definitely not the sort to be mixed up with bad people."

What could he say? "I was in the wrong place at the wrong time."

"Yeah, that's how most bad things begin," Carter agreed for the sake of avoiding further conversation.

"What about you?"

Carter refused to take his eyes off the stars. "What about me?"

"Why do you do this?" Gerald asked with a wave of his hand.

Carter stiffened. "Desperation."

"What could be so bat to turn a man into a contract killer?"

"Is that what you think I am?" Carter asked. "A random murderer without morals? You don't know the half of it." He drew a deep breath. "I got into some trouble when I was younger. Kids doing stupid shit, you know. Anyway, my old man turned me in, sent me to a youth adjustment camp. I hated him for it then and I still do."

The words flowed. He hadn't told the story to anyone except his wife. Once begun, he found he couldn't stop. It was a confession a long time coming. "My old man made me finish school. Turns out he did me a favor. I met a girl there and fell in love. We got married a few years after school. Things were good for a time, but the credits are hard to come by when you're living poor. It was difficult, but we managed until I got her pregnant. Neither of us realized how expensive having a child was. It broke us. I started stealing to make ends meet. Petty theft, nothing serious."

"Doesn't sound that much different from my life," Gerald said. Old regrets resurfaced. He wondered if any of this would have happened if he'd remained married.

"It gets worse. I wound up getting in with the wrong crowd. We started jacking vehicles for a local chop shop. That lasted a few months before the Earth government came down and sent the lot of us to a maximum planetary penitentiary after a deal went wrong. A lot of people were killed. I got pinched in a bar after I accidentally killed a man. Spent five years in that hell before being paroled. Can you imagine how difficult it is to find honest work being a convicted felon?"

"I—"

Carter continued, ignoring the interruption. "Things got harder and harder for all three of us. My wife turned to drugs. My child went unattended. It was a downward spiral without an escape. I don't remember how long it went on before I was approached by Mr. Shine. He found me when I was at my lowest. His words were golden, inspiring, and enticing. He made me want to listen, to sign on to what he was selling. He promised me I could restart my life without repercussions. How … how could I say no?"

"Makes sense," Gerald said. "That's how you got involved?"

Memories of that final, fateful night played out in the dark corners of Carter's mind. He remembered the peaceful look on his daughter's face as she slept. The muzzle flashes temporarily blinding him. The smell of gunpowder. Worst was the smug, almost satisfied look on Shine's face as he casually strolled out of the apartment hab.

"More or less."

That's it. No further explanation.

If Gerald picked up on the hesitation it didn't stop him from asking, "Do you get pleasure from your work?"

"I only kill when necessary." Which was true. Carter took no enjoyment in robbing others of their lives. It was a job. One he was good at performing but the heap of sins resting around his head like an obscene laurel weighed him down.

"Which is why I'm still alive."

"More or less. What are you getting at?" Carter asked, unsure and slightly annoyed.

"I just want to know how much longer I have to live."

"Don't we all."

Gerald paused, then sighed. "Who do you work for?"

"You really don't want to know. There are people in the galaxy you should never meet. Mr. Shine is one of them. One minute of straying off the normal path and you collide with shadows, my friend. Don't push into nightmares unless you have no choice."

***

They landed without fanfare. Gerald watched with rapt fascination as he got his first glimpses of a planet comparable to what Earth used to be. Lush jungles and forests covered the sprawling land masses of the four continents. Oceans of purple tinged waters dominated Cestus. Comparable oxygen levels made the planet perfect for colonization.

Cestus was the largest inhabited planet in the galaxy, roughly one-third larger than Earth. Yet it harbored a population of only a few hundred million. Most were crowded into the major population centers located in strategic areas on the two largest continents. As Gerald took it all in, he could envision building a new life here. Starting over with a fresh slate.

There was the small matter of finding Charlotte and Creeps, both of whom they confirmed were taken by McMasters' people on Mars and locating Tianna and the key again. Then came clearing his name with Roland McMasters.

Soon they were through customs and moving in search of their quarry. Gerald followed Carter's lead. Their differences settled by a fractious bond. The gun tucked neatly inside his trousers bolstered his confidence as they made their way through busy marketplace.

Throngs of people flocked to the open-air market stretching between many streets. Absolution was precisely what the name inspired. A fresh start and a bright future. In Absolution there was only tomorrow. If you could successfully navigate the darker underbelly the government refused to acknowledge.

Gerald found the city itself unremarkable in appearance yet decidedly more livable than old New York. Absolution lacked the tens of millions of destitute and fragile people crowding together for undelivered mutual assurance. Only a few hundred thousand called this city home, with others flying in and out on transports and supply runs. Officially, reported crime was low, the police force small and military presence light.

The architecture left something to be desire, at least in his opinion. Gerald was used to the efficient box shaped buildings of home dominating the skyline. The homes here had a cottage-like feel. Wood and stone decorated most of them, including the local shops. It all felt … alien.

A light pall of blue-grey smoke danced between rooftops. Night fires were slowly dying as the new day awakened and roused the world back to life.

"Is the whole planet like this?" Gerald asked, with only the casual frown from stepping in the soft mud of the dirt streets. He tried, and failed, to think of the last time he stepped in honest to God mud.

Carter nodded. "It has its charms."

"What I don't get is why the city isn't as advance as Earth or Mars."

"The further away from the central planets you get the harder it is to get supplies and equipment. Don't misjudge these people. They are some of the most honest, genuine people you'll ever meet. Life can be hard at times, but most everyone here came to make a better life for themselves. More people should have that opportunity."

"How can they when men like McMasters control the galaxy?" Gerald asked.

Carter stopped abruptly, laying the back of his hand on Gerald's chest. "Don't speak his name out loud. You never know who works for him, or who is looking for a few extra credits. Absolution may seem quaint, but it has some of the finest obscure technology available where it counts. You never know what *he* has put in place."

"Right. So don't trust anything," Gerald said.

"Keep that up and you might just make it out of this alive."

Mention of McMasters' reach within every faction of civilization made him nervous all over again. Whatever confidence he was building evaporated. Gerald was slowly starting to understand the rules of the game.

He looked into the faces of the early birds seeking deals before the main population ventured out their front doors. How many worked for McMasters? Was he being monitored? Was McMasters aware of enemies already in his backyard and moving in on him? Gerald frowned at the thought of being anyone's enemy. He'd never been one before. That Roland McMasters, arguably the most powerful figure in the galaxy, wanted him, of all people, dead was still unfathomable.

"What's our next move?" Gerald asked, the charm of Absolution evaporating.

"I need to figure out a way to get into his private stronghold. It's a good guess that your friends are already here. Along with Tianna and the key."

"You make it sound like he's some mad scientist living in a castle."

Carter gave Gerald a blank look before turning away.

Io Operations Facility, moons of Jupiter

Shine studied the holographic three-dimensional maps of Cestus III's main continent. His relationship with McMasters continued to degrade, forcing him to consider extreme conclusions. He already had one agent in position to deliver the killing blow. His best agent by all accounts, but recent failures on Carter Gaetis' part awakened fresh doubt.

Yet all was not going wrong. He finally deciphered what McMasters was going after. Shine initially dismissed the notion as another foolish waste of time and precious resources. All after, there wasn't a shred of evidence that General Karakzaheim existed other than remnants of dubious legends. Thousands had gone out in search of the treasure. All returned emptyhanded. Many others failed to return.

Shine had no tolerance for tall tales, at least not until Carter confirmed that the object Tianna Everson absconded was in fact the key to unraveling the entire mystery. Maybe, just maybe, the treasure did exist. And the Fat Man now had the one item necessary to break the ages old code. Shine couldn't allow that to happen.

There were millions of places on Cestus to hide a treasure. Much of the planet remained undocumented. Shine felt the impulse to fly immediately to the giant planet, but that was unwise without concrete evidence of the treasure's location. He needed Carter to infiltrate McMasters' inner sanctum. With events on Cestus beyond his control for the moment, Shine decided to refocus on his own projects.

His fleet of private dreadnaughts was well under construction. Three were already complete, but the other twenty-two remained skeletons of metal and potential in the dark of Io's rotation. Project Daedalus was his greatest aspiration, outpacing that of the organization he'd built in the shadows. Daedalus promised to make Shine unstoppable. The Lazarus Men were powerful in the dark but lacked the capability to enforce policy through strength of arms. With his own private fleet of warships, Shine would become a premier power among the planetary governments.

Whistling an old song from his childhood, Shine clasped his hands behind his back and strolled down the viewing corridor to admire and inspect his ships.

TWENTY-SIX

2273 A.D.

Absolution, Cestus III

"We're being followed."

Gerald avoided turning and giving them away. Instead, he followed Carter's lead, walking casually through the open market as if nothing was wrong. He saw Carter slip a hand inside one of his pockets. That didn't make him feel any safer.

"By whom?" he asked after they'd gone another few meters.

"One identified and five other possibles," Carter answered. His eyes continued roaming over the throngs of pedestrians.

"Shouldn't we do something?"

"Such as? We're in the middle of one of the busiest crowds on the planet. No one is going to make a move here, not unless they have a death wish. I most certainly do not. Stay calm and follow my lead. If I had stopped back there we'd either be dead or on the way to the nearest detention facility."

Gerald's cheeks felt hot after being rebuked. "What are we supposed to do then? We just can't let six people hunt us down and strike when they're ready."

Carter muttered through gritted teeth, "Gerald, keep your voice down and take a deep breath. This is nothing. Trust me. We're in no immediate danger."

"Whatever you say." Gerald decided not to bother arguing. With a gun in his own pocket, he dreaded the moment when he'd be forced to use it again.

He pretended to be calm despite having nerves so jittery it was all he could to put one foot in front of the other. To distract himself, Gerald studied Carter. The way the agent moved reminded him of holovids he'd seen of Old Earth jungle cats. His gait was measured, calculated. His eyes never stopped roving.

They ducked behind a carpet vendor and followed a narrow alleyway between stone-faced buildings Gerald was certain were going to topple over onto each other. Carter picked up the pace. The path became so narrow Gerald was forced to turn sideways to make it through. Stone and dust from the wall trickled down his back between flesh and shirt.

Instead of waiting to check on their pursuers, Carter surprised him by pushing ahead. Every impulse screamed for Gerald to turn, to look back over his shoulder. His heartbeat quickened at the thought of unknown enemies just a step behind, ready to reach out and snatch him by the collar. The subtropical heat of Cestus III added to his misery, leaving him suddenly nauseous.

"Carter, I don't feel good" he managed before stopping to bend over and place his hands on his knees. His mouth flooded with saliva. He watched Carter move to peer around the corner through tear filled eyes.

Carter doubled back. "I think we lost them. What's wrong with you?"

"I-I don't know."

"Stay still. You're probably suffering from exposure. It's common the first time someone comes to Cestus. It'll pass, but you'll feel sick for a few hours." He paused. "Can you keep going?"

Gerald opened his mouth to reply then quickly turned away. He vomited against the wall and would have collapsed if Carter hadn't eased him down to the ground. His vision swam, blotches of darkness coming and going. His breathing quickened before slowing. He felt better after a few minutes but was drained.

"I don't think I care for this place," he said, wiping the spittle from the corner of his mouth. "This is normal?"

Carter nodded. "Yes, but we can't stay here. Can you walk?"

"I'll crawl if I have to."

Carter poked his head around the corner again before hefting Gerald to his feet. They headed down a nearby winding street with no clear angles. Gerald found it disturbing that Carter seemed to know every road no matter what planet they were on. The possibility of escape on his own dwindled with each passing step.

They made it a few blocks before Carter jerked them to a halt. Gerald looked up and saw three *beings* blocking the street. Each stood close to seven feet tall and were a confusing combination of thin and muscled, with long, ropey arms and bony knees. What startled Gerald the most was the almost crimson color of their skin. Looking closer, he saw thin blue stripes running across their arms and legs.

"What are they?" he whispered.

"Not now," Carter snapped. Letting Gerald's arm slip from his shoulder, he stepped forward with his hands open and out to his sides.

Gerald watched. He wanted to help. Wanted to draw his weapon, giving away his one advantage, and face them down at Carter's side. But killing them didn't feel right. The fact they were aliens, creatures he hadn't believed in until just, reinforced his opinion.

"We aren't here to harm you," Carter said, his voice surprisingly submissive.

Gerald struggled to understand why the assassin hadn't already acted.

The tallest of the trio took a step forward and gestured with his head. "He sickens?"

Carter nodded. "It will pass. A common illness for visitors to your world."

"Worlds not same. Pain. Suffering."

"There is, but we are not here to harm you," Carter reiterated.

The native leader bared his teeth, long fangs that curled down into his lower jaw. They were a race of predators. "Harm? No. Not that one. You …"

Gerald saw Carter tense and started, slowly, to reach for his gun. The aliens' awkwardness, initially disarming, was likely a ruse.

"Me, yes. I am dangerous, but I am no enemy to your people." Lacking fangs, Carter straightened and flexed to present the proper show of force.

"Prove."

The singular word was both demand and challenge. All three bounced on their heels, ready to leap on the humans without further provocation. Their actions depended on how Carter responded. Wincing, Gerald looked to see what Carter had in mind. At least it appeared the Lazarus Man understood the challenge for what it was. One false move, a moment of hesitation, and both he and Gerald would be eviscerated.

Carter raised his right hand up over his head and slowly reached into his outer jacked pocket with his left. A collective snarl escaped the three aliens in warning to Gerald, who was spied snaking his hand closer to the handle of his concealed blaster. Carter ignored them as he produced a small pendant, letting it dangle on a pewter chain for them to see. Round with a cross in the center, the pendant was a blood red jewel.

The aliens attacked.

Each moved in a crimson blur. Carter managed to raise a blocking forearm before the alien leader clubbed him across the forehead, dropping him unconscious in the span of a breath.

Gerald tried shouting for help, but darkness fell a split second after pain lanced across the back of his head.

Gerald woke to a pounding headache. When he tried to reach up to check for blood, he discovered he couldn't move. He was shackled. He was a prisoner … again.

"Carter?"

He heard a slight shuffling from the darkness in the room.

"Yeah," came the hoarse reply.

A wave of relief washed over him. At least they were both still alive.

Twin lights blinked on, banishing the darkness. Gerald blinked rapidly, trying to get the burn from his eyes. A light was positioned directly over him and the other on Carter, leaving the rest of the room in shadow.

"Sorry if the light is a bit bright for you."

"Who are you? Show yourself?" Carter demanded.

Crimson legs with thin blue stripes appeared at the very edge of the circle of light.

"I apologize for the harsh mannerisms of the Naem. They are a proud people who have seen better times. I trust your injuries are relatively minor?"

Gerald stopped blinking and frowned. "Wait. Why do I know your voice?"

The Naem parted, allowing a well dressed man in official clothes to step forward.

"You!"

Fake Earl smiled. "Hello Gerald. Allow me to introduce myself. My name is Agent O'Hara of the Earth Alliance Intelligence Corps. Welcome to Cestus III."

TWENTY-SEVEN

2273 A.D.
Earth Alliance Safe House, Absolution, Cestus III

For the thousandth time since fleeing his apartment, Gerald felt thoroughly outmatched. He recognized Fake Earl but refused to accept the man once posing as his friend and colleague was a planted government agent. He lifted his head to look at Carter, who appeared to accept it all with remarkable calm. Even so, there was no denying the animosity smoldering in the assassin's eyes. Gerald hated to think what might happen if Carter managed to break his bonds.

The shuffle of clawed feet reminded Gerald that the crimson skinned natives of Cestus were still there. Naem, Fake Earl called them. Funny that he had not noticed until now the Naem had clawed feet. Their presence was enough to deter further confrontation, at least for the moment.

"I realize this may be too much for you to swallow, Gerald, but I can assure you this is no game," O'Hara said.

"That explains why I was beaten unconscious and tied up, right?" Gerald fired back. "Why am I talking to you? I don't even know you."

One of the Naem shuffled and O'Hara flashed a sympathetic smile. "A necessity given your choice of travelling companion. There's nothing permanent in a few bruises. You'll be fine and I am precisely who I told you I am. I've never lied to you."

"Except about who you are."

"He'd be better if you let us go now," Carter said. "Let us go, and I'll forget I ran across you, *spook.*"

"That's a term I haven't heard thrown around in a long time, *assassin.*"

Gerald shifted his gaze between them. Hundreds of millions of miles from home and he was trapped in an old fashioned pissing contest.

"Since you know what I am, you should accept the offer. I won't give it again."

O'Hara crossed his arms. "Perhaps, but I won't accept. Not yet. We have to talk."

"I'm listening," Carter relaxed, leaning back into his chair.

"Good. Most of the Lazarus Men we've encountered over the years have proven unreasonable in the best of situations," O'Hara said. "I should thank you for your cooperation."

"As long as you have me in chains and under guard there's not too much I can do. Is there?"

"Fair enough."

"How do you two know each other?" Gerald interrupted.

"Ask him," Carter said with a gesture of his head.

"Earth Alliance keeps tabs on all of the known subversive agents operating in the galaxy. We know about the Lazarus Men," O'Hara admitted.

Carter shrugged, prompting Gerald to ask, "Who are the Lazarus Men?"

O'Hara's eyebrow rose. "You really do like keeping secrets, don't you, Carter?"

"A man in my line of work doesn't live long otherwise."

"No, I suppose not. Gerald, the Lazarus Men is a clandestine mercenary outfit. They procure contracts on people's lives, influence elections, that sort of thing. The nasty of the nasty."

Feeling Carter's gaze on him, Gerald closed his eyes. "I am sick of all this bullshit. For the last week I've watched people die, been hunted for an ancient piece of rock, been kidnapped, and been on the run like an escaped convict. I'm done. No more. Earl, Fake Earl, O'Hara—whatever you want to call yourself. Let me go and send me back to Earth. You two can have all of this."

"I would if I could, but your knowledge makes you dangerous, Gerald. You are much safer among us."

Gerald laughed. "To whom? I'm a nobody trapped between spies and killers."

"To the Fat Man, Gerald," Carter answered. "You know too much to be allowed to go free. I've told you this."

"I need you to focus, Gerald. Events are starting to pick up. McMasters is in possession of the key and your friends," O'Hara said.

"They're not even my friends. I've only known Charlotte for a few days and Creeps is, well, I don't really know what he is." Still, that didn't change the outrage he felt at their being held prisoner in McMasters' compound. If anything, he felt responsible.

"We're here to stop the Fat Man," Carter cut in.

"Then we're after the same thing," O'Hara said. "I propose an accord."

"I'm listening."

O'Hara carefully considered his next words. "First, a truce. I'm not here for you, Carter. Nor am I here for you, Gerald. Though I have an interest in seeing you get home again."

"Comforting," Gerald muttered with a snort.

The Naem edged closer, anxious at the angry undertone in his voice.

"Truthful," O'Hara corrected. "We team up. Join forces to prevent McMasters from finding the treasure."

"I can't return emptyhanded," Carter said.

"You're not going anywhere at the moment," O'Hara replied.

"Who gets the treasure?" Gerald asked.

"The Naem. Karakzaheim is their legacy. The general was their greatest champion. Any treasure we find goes back to them"

Gerald found it difficult to accept a relatively primitive species like the Naem, which reminded him of big cats on steroids, were capable of producing great leaders or globe spanning empires. The convenience of giving the treasure to a neutral party was disturbing and entirely unconvincing.

"Deal," Carter said, interrupting Gerald's next thought.

O'Hara paused, then gestured to the Naem. "Release them. We have work to do."

"Why all of the deception? Why me?" Gerald asked, rubbing his aching wrists where the bonds had dug into his flesh.

O'Hara held out his hands as if to apologize. "I wish it hadn't been you, but we don't often get to choose what happens to us. You just have bad luck."

Bad luck. A handy excuse for anyone who ever felt things were not going their way. The deeper Gerald got involved in this tangled mess the less he believed in luck.

"How long were you watching me?"

"I wasn't watching you. You were just one of the guys. The government knew that McMasters was going to try and pass something important through illegal channels out of the spaceport. You just happened to stumble into the situation and got caught up. I wish it were otherwise. I came to like you during our time together."

Gerald still wasn't ready to trust O'Hara. The man spent the better part of a year lying to him. "This is pure nonsense."

He was getting tired of saying the same thing without anyone listening.

"As far as you're concerned, I agree. I don't expect you to accept everything that is going on. I wouldn't," O'Hara leaned conspiratorially close and whispered, "What has he told you?"

Gerald paused to consider the sleeping Carter. Even in the midst of dreams, the man looked ready to spring into an attack.

"Nothing. He's close lipped," Gerald answered. "All I know is he's after this Fat Man. His boss wants the key to the treasure."

"Why are you with him?"

Gerald told him the story, watching O'Hara's reaction as the tale developed. Much to his surprise and relief, he found the Earth Alliance agent listening intently. The lie he told about not being close to Charlotte bothered him, but it was necessary. He couldn't risk either Carter or O'Hara using his feelings against him.

When he finished, he placed his hands behind his head and propped his legs up on the small stool the Naem provided him. Three of the creatures were still there, now crouched in the far corner conversing in a guttural tongue reminding Gerald of clicking noises. They appeared largely unconcerned with the human affairs. Gerald found them strange and frightening in equal measure.

"Can we trust him?" O'Hara asked, gesturing toward Carter.

"Can I trust you?" Gerald countered.

"Fair enough."

"If we recover the key, will the treasure really go to the Naem?"

The look on O'Hara's face told him everything. The Earth Alliance wanted the treasure for itself, leaving the Naem exactly where they were. A once proud species forced to beg for scraps. Gerald was repulsed but not surprised. No one with an iota of common sense trusted the government.

***

Carter listened to every word. Feigning sleep, he allowed his body to recover from the beatings on Mars and the Naem while catching every word O'Hara and Gerald said. It was no surprise the Earth Alliance agent intended treachery. Were he in the same position, he knew his orders would be the same. So long as O'Hara had the Naem with him there was little Carter could do.

Eyes closed, he tensed at the question of trust. Gerald's answer was telling. Enough for Carter to be relived. He didn't view Gerald as a threat, despite the hidden gun he assumed Carter didn't know he had.

Deciding to play along with O'Hara until he could thwart McMasters' plans, Carter formulated his future. Focus was placed on stealing the key. He needed it if there was to be any hope of prolonging his future among the Lazarus Men.

TWENTY-EIGHT

2273 A.D.
McMasters Compound, Cestus III

Heavy winds blasted the southern approach to what was a castle in all but name. Roland McMasters had modeled his mountaintop home after the Eagles Nest, an Alps retreat for one of the most powerful and homicidal men in the mid-20th century. The original was eternally stained from the horrid nature of the men who once thought to rule the world from there, but the idea of what it was meant to be was what sparked Roland's inspiration to build his own empire.

While Cestus wasn't known for high mountain ranges, McMasters claimed the closest area suitable for dominating the central continent. White walls rose up from the foundations of the world. Windows, covering entire walls, provided expansive views of the central plain. Soaring trees of a thousand different species and nearly as many colors stretched beyond human sight. Clouds gliding over the canopy assured a peaceful scene complete with birds of many species dotting the sky.

This house was the heart of the McMasters empire. Not as large, both house and empire, as he desired, but it was growing daily as his wealth and status improved among the different planets. In the distance, so far away as to appear little more than a bright stain on the horizon, sat Absolution. The city of hope. Of the promise that tomorrow would not be as dark as yesterday.

It was a lie.

Absolution may have been intended with grand promise, but the reality of the situation left much to be desired. Poverty and crime were rampant among the under population. The planetary government spent billions of credits attempting to reclaim the city image in the hopes of drawing a better class of immigrant. Still, whole neighborhoods went untended by planetary law enforcement without ever being reported. A continual influx of newcomers kept the population growth sustained with tax paying citizens. Taxes needed to be paid for the government machine to grind on—McMasters had a profitable hand in that machine.

He mused over the strange companions filing along behind him as he led them to his private study on the second floor. They were an odd collection; not one belonged with another. He found Charlotte the most enigmatic. Her inherent drive to learn and discover ancient secrets prompted her to make dangerous decisions. It was a trait he specialized in exploiting. McMasters would focus on converting her to his cause by dangling a steady stream of ancient lore.

Creeps, her former companion, was a mere petty thug with limited ambition. He was scarcely better than an informant like Zilke. Still, he served his purposes in betraying Charlotte and Gerald. Indirectly, his actions were responsible for allowing Tianna to retrieve the key.

McMasters chuckled as the more devious part of his mind entertained wicked way in which to dispose of Creeps. Every man had his use, be it important or insignificant. More so, men like Creeps had a solitary purpose before becoming expendable.

Then there was Gholson and Edgemeyer, both his willing servants for years. Ruthless and intelligent, they made the perfect pair. It was a rare occasion when they failed in any assigned task. But their failure in delivering the key and removing all loose ends demanded retribution. Reprimand at the least, but that could wait.

It was the promise of yet more power spurring McMasters on. He wasn't always this way. Once, so long ago he barely remembered, he'd been poor. His family lived in an old garage with curtains for walls. Food was scarce on a world with dwindling resources, so he was often hungry. His father died when Roland was still a child.

His father's death not only changed the course of his future, but his family life as well. His mother wasn't strong. She sent him to live with distant relations in New Africa. Earth wasn't home any longer. It couldn't be. Boarding that offworld shuttle was the last time he heard from her. Roland tried making a new life with his aunt and uncle, but nothing he did worked. By the time he was old enough to make his own road through life, he'd grown bitter and resentful. Dissatisfaction became the cornerstone of his very being.

He always wanted more.

So he did the only thing he could do he joined the fledgling military of the Outer Worlds. They provided a bed and three hot meals a day, at least when his main unit wasn't out in the field conducting training. Army life suited him, and he soon thrived. By the time he made squad leader, he was ready for more. And a Naem rebellion on the far continent provided that opportunity.

His regiment deployed in support of peacekeeping operations. There, in the jungles of Cestus III, Roland McMasters took his first life and became aware of the legend of General Karakzaheim. Awareness turned to obsession. Years passed and his enlistment contract expired. He went into business with a swindler, losing almost all of his money before realizing what was happening and … correcting the problem. Once he gained control, he uncovered the full treachery of his former partner. A small fortune appeared under his name.

McMasters turned next to developing his fledgling enterprises, expanding his range of influence wherever and however he could. He quickly discovered how it easy it was to bribe the right person needed to accomplish a task. A decade later, he was one of the most influential men on several planets. Life was good for Roland McMasters, but he still wasn't content. The name Karakzaheim bounced around in the corners of his mind.

And now, after nearly six decades, he was close to achieving the one goal that had come to dominate so much of his life. He was about to uncover the treasure of Karakzaheim, giving him immense financial resources leading to more power. The treasure held the promise of an unprecedented future, ripe with the spoils of a new age. McMasters' concern would finally be reduced to having enough time to enjoy it. He was still too young for life extension treatments. He wanted, needed, more time.

McMasters stepped aside and gestured for the others to enter the study ahead of him, maintaining the semblance of being a gentleman. He found that the pretense helped resolve situations favorably. Besides, he was in a good mood. The message he received shortly before confronting Charlotte pleased him. Tianna was enroute with the key.

"Please, be seated. All of you. Refreshments are on that back table along the wall. Do help yourselves. Ah, Charlotte, if you wouldn't mind. I have a map on my desk I would like for you to see."

"May I?" she asked, reaching out to touch the map. Her eyes were wide, excited.

McMasters gestured with an open palm. "Be my guest. Without you I am assured my quest would be much more difficult."

"What about the rest of us?" Creeps demanded.

McMasters' eyes narrowed dangerously, but he kept his anger in check. "As I said, refreshments are available. Help yourself. I don't imagine this will take long."

Roland McMasters was many things, patient not among them. He wrung his hands in helplessness, turning from the others to collect himself. Truthfully, there was nothing he could do until Tianna landed and delivered his prize. Charlotte was a potential asset as well, but even her trained eye was all but worthless without the key.

"Where did you get this?" Charlotte asked, curiosity in her voice.

"Don't concern yourself with that," McMasters answered. "All that matters is the map is in my possession. Can you decipher it?"

Charlotte peered closer.

McMasters adjusted with her. He studied her as she studied the map. It was quite an ordinary topographic map with traced lines across ridges and circled depressions. The jungle dominated the center. A line of hills ran for over a hundred kilometers along the northern edge. Swamps and the ocean lay far to the south. Yellow marks showing theorized locations for the ruins were joined by red marks showing locations already undergoing excavation. Treasure seekers and pillagers of tombs had combed those areas long before his archaeological teams started digging.

"Nothing to indicate the location of the treasure. It's a very generic map," she concluded.

McMasters gave a gruff node then moved to a handcrafted cherry display cabinet with glass doors. Inside sat three ornate crystal decanters, each with an exotic liquor, an antique firearm, a helmet of alien origin, and a folio of what appeared to be journals. Each was a war trophy from his earlier years. He cherished them; they gave him focus. He picked up the folio and turned back to Charlotte.

"I suspected as much. We should be able to learn more when the key arrives," he said. "These journals might be useful. They were collected from abandoned Naem villages after the rebellion."

"Is that where you got your experience?" she asked.

He jerked back in surprise.

"From some of these artifacts I'd guess you spent time in the military and come from a humble background," she continued. Charlotte waved her hands toward his trophies. "Otherwise you wouldn't have these on display in such pristine order."

McMasters sneered. He'd gone so long without anyone discovering his origins, he was caught off guard by her observation. "What makes you say that?"

Charlotte smiled.

Gholson cleared his throat and McMasters glanced at him. His anxious face bore a faint crimson flush, and he hadn't stopped fidgeting since they entered the room. The bruising on his face was mostly gone and he'd gotten an alternate pair of glasses. His nose was still swollen.

"Mr. McMasters, the shuttle has landed. She's on her way to the compound now," he said, touching the earpiece in his left ear.

Edgemeyer lowered his near empty glass, the stain of whiskey sliding down to the bottom, and scowled at McMasters.

"Ah, very good. Soon our names will make history." McMasters felt almost gleeful, choosing to ignore Edgemeyer's apparent jealousy. "Have her brought here immediately. We've delayed enough already."

Creeps threw back the rest of his drink and slammed the glass down on the end table. "It's about time. All I want is the payment promised so I can get back to Mars."

"Creeps, you'll get everything coming to you. On my word," McMasters assured with a predatory smile.

TWENTY-NINE

2273 A.D.
McMasters Compound, Cestus III

Tianna Everson entered the study with a confident stride. Her formfitting black flight suit, while specifically designed for survivability in harsh conditions, was suggestive enough to elicit a low whistle from Creeps. She ignored him and halted before her employer.

"Welcome, Tianna, my dear!" McMasters said.

"Roland," she replied with a gracious nod.

McMasters noticed the others confused by her familiarity. Jealousy rearing when least needed. One mouth dropped open in casual shock. None of those assembled had ever heard him called by his first name or in such a brazen manner. It went without saying doing so was automatically fatal.

"Did you experience any difficulty in extracting from Mars?" he asked.

Her pause was slight. "Nothing significant. We lost eight men in the process however."

A snicker from across the room—Edgemeyer most likely.

"Eight?" McMasters' eyebrow rose in question.

She nodded. "Unfortunately. I wasn't anticipating the arrival of a Lazarus Man. He was … most efficient, but I managed to escape with the item."

McMasters balled a fist and slammed it into his palm, inwardly cursing Shine. The weasel meant to backstab him from the beginning. Shine knew what Roland was after. Now he was in a race with one of the most powerful organizations in the galaxy. The Lazarus Men would be coming after the treasure, and McMasters by extension.

Fine, let them. He had an ace Shine wasn't counting on. McMasters knew about the fleet of private dreadnaughts being constructed in the shadow of Io. No doubt Shine needed the treasure to finish building his fleet. Advantage to Roland.

"Some losses are to be expected in the midst of matters such as this. Besides which, they were hired guns. We have all the pieces we need and a considerable jump on Mr. Shine."

"Of course, Roland," she agreed, almost placating him.

Knowing Shine, arguably one of the most homicidal people in the galaxy, was after the same prize changed everything. McMasters secretly enjoyed the thrill of competition, though he would never admit it.

"Good. Good. Now, please give Ms. Bailey the key," he ordered.

Tianna reached into her pocket but hesitated. "Her?"

"Yes. It's all right. She has come to see the light, if you will," McMasters explained. "Until she proves me wrong, she has my trust."

Clearly still wary but accepting his explanation and confidence, Tianna produced the key that had caused so much havoc on three worlds, much to McMasters' displeasure, and handed it to Charlotte.

"Thank you, but what am I supposed to do with this?" Charlotte asked.

Tianna scowled.

"Use it of course," McMasters said.

***

His intensity made Charlotte nervous. She'd never thought the key would arrive and, now that she held it in her hands, she had no idea how to use it. All accounts suggested the key was an ancient technology. She didn't see how he expected her to know what to do without a lengthy research period.

A closer inspection confirmed the key was altogether unremarkable. Cylindrical with one pointed end and void of markings, it held an almost hypnotic allure. None of that changed the face Charlotte didn't know what to do with it.

With a sigh, she laid the key on the map and turned to face the others. "I've never seen anything like this before. The simplicity of …"

Her words died in her throat as she watched their faces transform from idle boredom to amazement. Charlotte looked down and her breath caught in her throat. The key rose off the table to stand upright with the point hovering a fraction of an inch above the ancient parchment. It began glowing pale blue.

"Wha …"

McMasters smiled for the first time. His eyes blazed with greed and pleasure. "See, I told you. Never doubt your own abilities, Charlotte. Never."

She smiled despite herself and reached a tentative hand out, wary of being shocked. The key was cold to the touch. Whatever powered it was beyond her knowledge and understanding. The way she saw it, she had two options; either pretend she knew what she was doing and wind up looking like a fool when it collapsed around her, or stumble through the experience until something worked. Charlotte went with option two.

Fingers curling around the key, she closed her eyes and whispered a quick prayer. *Where would I hide the treasure if I were a fanatic warlord knowing my time was coming to an end?*

The key moved.

Did it? She wasn't sure. At this stage it was easy to imagine what might have been.

Charlotte closed her eyes again, redoubling her concentration. The key moved again, sliding across the map. She felt the press of bodies, figuring the others were now crowding closer for a better look.

Charlotte's eyes opened as she struggled to hold the key as minor sonic vibrations from its core tickled up her hand and numbed her fingertips.

The key never touched the map, instead it connected the user and map by an odd blue light emanating from the lower point. This bridge was well beyond her scope of understanding. Her initial rection was to control the key, but that faded as she began to understand. Horrified at the prospect of the key being sentient, Charlotte knew stopping was in her best interests. Some secrets needed to remain so. Why then did she continue?

Mankind had already made great strides into the realm of synthetic flesh, so why not an alien species? An entire universe of possibility rested in her hands, ridiculously simple in design and next to impossible to understand. The one word circling through her mind was a thing that did not exist; magic.

Forcing distractions out, she concentrated on the gentle hum, the effortless movement as the key traced a light burned line across the map. The starting point was McMasters' compound. It led across the capital city of Absolution, over a small forested plain and through the depths of the jungle where it stopped.

Charlotte squinted, trying to make out the prominent land features even as the light bored a pinprick hole in the map.

The blue light suddenly winked out and the key stopped humming. It felt cold in her hand. She let it fall and stepped back. The key disintegrated before their eyes, leaving behind a small pile of ash. Charlotte stepped back as McMasters gently pushed her aside.

***

"Gholson, bring up the schematics of the jungle," he ordered, studying the burned center on the map. "I want precise grid coordinates."

"Yes, sir." Gholson's hurried to the computer terminal. His fingers flew over the keyboard. Each click added tension as the rest of the group peered down on the map.

A sharp bleep announced the activation of a three-dimensional image of the jungle above the table. The key had stopped in the center of a small plateau roughly fifty kilometers from the compound. Rising to an elevation of one hundred thirty-seven meters, the plateau was heavily vegetated and unpopulated. Natural clearings dominated the middle of a four-kilometer square area.

McMasters traced the image, ignoring the clearings, as he focused on the honeycomb of tunnels burrowing deep underground. If the treasure was here, it would be in the tunnels.

He had a starting point.

"My friends, we leave at dawn. Edgemeyer, I want a security detail assembled and ready to depart immediately. There are to sweep that plateau clear of immediate threats. I don't want to risk my personal safety due to haste."

While the others were expendable to his mind, he refused to leave unprotected.

"Outstanding," Creeps announced. "You all have fun on your little jungle adventure. I'll try to forget you while I'm on my liner back to Mars."

"Perhaps you misunderstand," McMasters corrected. "You are coming with us."

"I don't think so. You said I could leave."

"Of course, but only after this quest is complete. You know far too much to be allowed to go free until then," McMasters said.

"That's bullshit!" Creeps fumed, his face darkening. "I don't want any part of this. I did what you wanted me to do. Our contract has ended."

A look from McMasters sent Edgemeyer behind Creeps. The thief cried out as the android grabbed his right and arm and twisted before bringing his wrist up between his shoulder blades.

"You may not have noticed, but I am not a man one says no to," McMasters threatened. "Of course, if you prefer, I can find a way to dispose of you now. I doubt you would be missed. Men like you come and go without lasting impression."

In pain, sweat beading on his forehead, Creeps hung his head. "N…no, I'll cooperate."

"Good! Mr. Edgemeyer, release our guest."

McMasters turned his attention back to the map and dismissed the others. The jungle called to him in ways he'd only dreamed of. At last, after decades, it was nearly time.

THIRTY

2273 A.D.
Absolution, Cestus III

The unlikely trio finished a quick meal of local fruits and meat O'Hara assured them was akin to chicken, though Gerald found that claim dubious with each new bite. Hunger made him finish his plate, but the unpleasant aftertaste lingered on his tongue. He didn't know whether to spit or vomit. Local cuisine didn't agree with his Earthly tastes.

He looked down at his plate and swore something wiggled in the few scraps remaining. Gerald pushed the plate away and leaned back. At least the local brew, while bitter and pungent, was drinkable after the first few swallows.

"Not hungry?" O'Hara grinned.

Gerald frowned.

"It takes some getting used to, but the gnosta bugs aren't half bad."

"Those are the ones crawling out from beneath your bergu steak," Carter eagerly supplied, making a show of crunching down on one of the squirming red and black insects.

"I'll pass," Gerald said as bile rushed up from his stomach.

Both Carter and O'Hara shared a laugh. It was the first real sign of cooperation they'd shown, but it was not enough to inspire Gerald's confidence. Or calm his restless stomach. It was only a matter of time before the opposing agents were at each other's throats. Or so he assumed. Gerald hoped to be long gone before that happened. His mission was to find

Charlotte and Creeps and get the hell out of here. Nothing else mattered.

He listened as the discussion slowly turned toward the coming task. Gerald thought of it as an impossible heist. They meant to break in, abscond with two human beings, an ancient artifact, and get away without being noticed. Even his untrained mind was wise enough to know there'd be violence. Surprisingly, he found the prospect both exhilarating and terrifying.

When he closed his eyes, Gerald saw life as it once was, even while knowing it could never return to normal. The daily grind of working on the flight line had been satisfying without reward. Now his name and reputation were irreparably shattered. His promotion gone. The body of Mrs. Moorhead no doubt already found in his apartment. Gerald had nothing to return to. O'Hara had explained the warrants for his arrest to him. He'd be taken into custody the instant his foot touched Earth soil.

Friendless, alone, and locked in an alien environment, Gerald decided not to waste his time with dreams of what might be. Judging from past events, he doubted he was going to make it out this nightmare alive. Despair crept closer, wanting to invade and subsume his mind.

He clenched his hands and focused all of his thoughts on Charlotte. He couldn't foresee a future with her, though the idea was pleasing and left him with a faint smile. He was determined to rescue her from McMasters, even if it meant his own demise.

"Hey, you listening?"

Gerald blinked rapidly to clear the tears threatening to form. "Huh?"

O'Hara stared at him with bemusement. "Don't start daydreaming now. We need you focused for this part."

"Sorry," he mumbled.

Carter popped the last bite of bergu steak in his mouth and watched. He did that a lot, Gerald noticed. Always watching, listening, assessing the situation. Gerald already knew the man was calculating, but this singular facet showed him on a deeper level. Carter was a man with the presence of mind to always think ahead to gain advantage over any situation he found himself in.

"We can go in through the access tunnels under the main compound. Security will be lightest there."

"Assuming the Fat Man isn't paranoid," Carter said. "As most powerful people tend to be. I suggest dropping in through the roof. Infiltrated through the ventilation conduits."

"Too risky. His surveillance capabilities will detect any aircraft long before we get within drop range," O'Hara countered.

Gerald placed his face in his palms. "So we're screwed either way."

"That's the spirit!" O'Hara said with a grin.

Carter wiped his mouth. "Gerald, you're not exactly wrong, but there are mitigating factors involved. The Fat Man has his hands deep in the local government, but he's not all powerful. There are plenty of money hungry politicians who resent his influence. We have allies among them. He also can't risk getting into a running gunfight on the outskirts of the planetary capital. Law enforcement would have no choice but to intervene and he won't want the attention."

"Time he can't afford to lose if, what you both said is remotely accurate, the key to finding the treasure is already in his grasp. He'll want to act immediately," O'Hara added.

"Precisely. Giving us the advantage," Carter said.

"How is his ability to spot us long before we get there our advantage?" Gerald asked. "I thought the idea was stealth?"

"It is, but when a man is expecting something he tends to overlook the obvious," O'Hara said.

Gerald shook his head. "You two are nuts. We're going to get killed."

"An occupational hazard, Gerald. No one is asking you to become a hero overnight, or even a hero at all. No one. We both understand that you're a victim of circumstance in all this, but that doesn't mean you get to sit idle by while the rest of us risk our lives. Like it or not, you are part of this. As long as McMasters remains in power, he will hunt you for what you've witnessed."

"In what way?" Gerald demanded, glaring at Carter. "I can turn around now and leave, and nothing will change. I'm not necessary."

"No, you're really not," Carter agreed. "But you still have a role to play in all of this. The Fat Man doesn't know what you know, and that will worry him. Once he discovers you're still in the picture he'll go out of his way to deal with you."

"So I'm a distraction A puppet dangling for him to snatch at while the two of you sneak in and disable his plans?"

Gerald was incensed. How far would Carter and O'Hara let him dangle to suit their motives? Would they let him die if it meant stopping McMasters and claiming the treasure? As much as he wished it weren't the case, Gerald knew neither would hesitate to sacrifice him if the needs justified the deed. Neither would be friends, but now he felt the desire to classify them as closer to being enemies. Ones he couldn't afford if he had any hopes of detracting himself from this debacle. The prospect of finding Charlotte and Creeps significantly lowered with each passing revelation.

"No, that's not—" O'Hara began.

"Yes," Carter interrupted. "Gerald, this is not your old life. You're involved in something you have no control over now. We're all going into a dangerous situation. Anyone one of us could be killed and we must be willing to accept it. You're not in your pleasant little world with no implications to the greater galaxy any longer. This is real life. People die. Obviously, we don't wish you harm, but I believe both of us are willing to accept that if or when it happens."

"The same goes if either of us is killed or captured," O'Hara added.

Silence settled over them. Each lost in conflicting thought.

"I don't pretend to understand the world you operate in," Gerald said after a while. His words were deliberate, slow. "I won't let you use me. I'm not a carrot on a stick. I have a mind, a life of my own. It may have been reduced to ashes because of all this, but it's still *mine*. What gives you the right to decide whether I live or die? Because you have guns? Or is because you think you work for a righteous cause?"

He paused, letting his words sink in. "I am going to make it clear to you. I am here because I *want* to be here. Not for your little power games."

"Fair enough," O'Hara agreed. "Now that the issue is settled, we can move on to finalizing our plans. Time is against us."

***

"Mr. Gaetis, I am most disappointed with your performance to date," Shine's image admonished as it materialized above the access terminal.

Carter braced for the worst, knowing he was due for a reprimand for his actions on Mars. Shine's piercing glare, even through the technological distortion of the viewing screen, left him hollow. "Sir, I …"

"I am not interested in your excuses, Carter," Shine snapped. "The key is already in McMasters' compound. I suspect he is even now preparing a party to begin searching. He must be stopped. I'm not sure you are up to the task. My … faith in you has greatly diminished."

"Sir, McMasters will be stopped," Carter said.

"Of course he will. I've ensured it. A team is enroute to Cestus as we speak."

Carter felt gut punched. "You're replacing me?"

"Reinforcing. Operational control remains in your purview. I am simply giving you the assets required to ensure mission completion. Is this a problem?"

Defeated, Carter said, "No, sir. I understand."

Shine broke into a rare smile. "Good. Stop McMasters and get me my treasure." His image wavered. "Oh, and Carter, do not fail to tie all of this up. I don't need to remind you of our clandestine nature and what happens to those who fail me."

The transmission faded even as Carter swore under his breath. It didn't take much to imagine Shine ordering his execution once the mission was complete. He needed to take precautions to ensure he didn't fall into a trap—one that was no doubt already in development.

***

Gerald stared at the setting sun as it transformed the atmosphere into shades of purple and red over Absolution. The sunsets of Cestus III were spectacular. It was unlike anything he had ever seen on Old Earth. The drab buildings blocking out the sky back home left him feeling akin to a prisoner at times. This, this was simply amazing.

Watching the fire in the sky made him think about those things in life he wished he'd done differently. He could have been a better husband, lover. He could have spent more time developing his character. Regrets were a heavy part of his life. He resolved to start making amends the moment he returned to Earth. He owed it to himself, if no one else.

There was still time, though not much. His redemption rested solely in his hands as he sped toward a conflict he still didn't profess to understand fully. There had to be more than just this rumored treasure at stake. Money was powerful, but not enough to drive numerous men to the brink of insanity. Or was it?

Kidnapping. Murder. What else would McMasters or the strange, pale man Carter worked for consider doing to find the treasure? Gerald didn't want to know. He also knew there was no way these organizations could continue keeping to their hidden agendas as the quest drew closer to an inevitable conclusion.

"Gerald, it's time," O'Hara called.

Gerald closed his eyes, exhaled his pent-up frustrations, and nodded. There was no point in delaying. Not even for the grandeur among the clouds.

THIRTY-ONE

2273 A.D.
McMasters Compound, Cestus III

Three figures dressed in black camouflage slipped across the small field leading up to the half-slope on the eastern approach to the McMasters compound. The moon had yet to rise, making them all but invisible to the naked eye. Thermal distortion circuitry built into their suits rendered night vision ineffective. McMasters' impressive security systems were blind. Mr. Shine had spent a small fortune on research and development of stealth technology and bioengineering. Carter hoped the suit worked well enough to let him infiltrate the compound and take down the outer defense grid.

He and O'Hara agreed that McMasters wouldn't rely on human intelligence to keep his compound secure. Not with Dromn Corporation steadily producing androids. Loyal and fierce, they would soon provide the backbone of any internal defense. For the right price.

Carter would deal with that situation if he needed to. His initial priority was getting past the outer defense grid. Using schematics provided by O'Hara, he knew there was an impressive array of automated small arms rifles and light caliber machine guns linked through a central computer. These weapons were highly sensitive to movement, light, and sound. Each was capable of firing several hundred rounds per minute in a web covering virtually every square inch of surface space encircling the compound. It was, in all regards, an airtight perimeter any infantry commander would have been proud to defend. It also made Carter's approach much more dangerous than dealing with a few poorly trained men on roving patrol in the middle of the night.

He reached the edge of rifle range and crouched behind a low stone wall marking the limits to McMasters' property. From here the ground continued to incline over a hundred meters before hitting an iron frame fence surrounding the buildings. Guards with dogs moved in two man teams, circling the compound in opposite directions and crossing paths twice every thirty minutes. The longer they were on duty, the less observant they'd become. Carter planned on taking advantage of this by making his assault in the predawn hours.

Their earlier plan of infiltrating through the subterranean tunnel network was abandoned after a hasty reconnaissance showed steel bars blocking every approach. They didn't have the time or equipment to cut the bars to get McMasters.

Making a direct approach was unwise under the best of circumstances, but there wasn't any other choice. McMasters had an air defense grid concealed in the roof of his expansive complex. Heat seeking rockets would launch the instant hostile aircraft were identified by the sentry computer in the main house. They could not get in through the tunnel network and they couldn't get in by air. That left the small chance of the direct approach.

The trio place their faith in the enhanced suits Shine provided and waited.

***

Gerald was convinced his companions shared

a death wish. His knees lost strength at visions of being riddled with bullets. He really didn't want to die. Saving Charlotte and Creeps was the one thing holding him together.

"When I give the signal, we sprint all the way to the fence. Don't stop for anything," Carter instructed in a hushed voice.

"Is this going to work?" Gerald asked.

"Have a little faith," Carter replied. "We don't want to die any more than you."

"The EMP burst should be powerful enough to disarm and reset the defense grid. It's only a hundred meters. Run fast and do not stop. Understood?" O'Hara added.

Gerald didn't, but that didn't matter.

"Three."

He hoped he didn't trip.

"Two."

Dying the middle of an open area because he tripped over his own feet would be embarrassing but at least he wouldn't have to live with the ridicule.

"Go!"

They scaled the stone wall simultaneously and ran for the fence. Each second terrified Gerald. Each footstep was one closer to a round in the chest. His brains splattered in pink mist. Thunder pounded in his head. *I'm not going to die. I'm not going to die*. He repeated the mantra until he slammed into the iron bars. A dog barked in the night.

He watched O'Hara produce a small handheld torch and begin cutting through the nearest bar. Gerald jerked around, looking for any signs they'd been discovered. The sun was beginning to lighten the sky to grey and deep blue. It wouldn't be long before dawn broke. An electronic hum whirred nearby. He jumped.

Twin gatling guns spun to life, tracking a line across the sky before levelling on the immediate terrain. Gerald's stomach clenched.

"Relax. The system is just rebooting. That's all," Carter whispered.

O'Hara was already through the second bar and cutting the third.

"Are you sure?" Gerald asked.

Carter's nod was meant to be reassuring but left him with a growing sense of unease.

"I'm through," O'Hara announced before slipping through the hole he'd created.

Carter shoved Gerald in and brought up the rear. Once through, he unslung the short-barrel tactical assault rifle strapped to his back. Gerald noticed the man had already slipped into combat mode. O'Hara let the Lazarus Man take point. Gerald decided the safest place on Cestus III was directly behind Carter Gaetis. Of course if Carter managed to get killed …

They crossed the driveway, sliding between the main house and secondary quarters built for visiting CEOs and dignitaries. Carter moved with well-rehearsed efficiency. As if he knew the compound like the back of his hand. He unerringly led them down the winding path and across a small garden with a fountain in the middle. Gerald nearly tripped when he noticed the statue in the center of the fountain was of two naked women locked in tender embrace. *Who does that*?

"Keep up. We're almost there," Carter hissed, forcing Gerald to focus and keep running.

Interior light flooded from wall height windows lining the entire wall at four-foot intervals. Gerald suspected they were about to be caught. How could anyone move through so much light without being discovered? He wanted to voice his opinion even while knowing he'd be shut down without pause. The other two men were cold, efficient and already slipped back into their professional demeanors. For him to speak now would result in another reprimand and delay their mission. It was time they didn't have to waste.

They were a heartbeat away from the rectangular blocks of light stretching across the lawn when darkness fell. Gerald resisted the urge to halt. His immediate reaction was they had fallen into a trap. McMasters and his goon were no doubt watching from a hidden location, waiting for the right moment to swoop in from all sides and take them into custody, or worse.

"Move, move, move," Carter ordered.

The trio sprinted to the far end of the building.

Barking dogs from the opposite side of the compound jolted them into action. Carter led the way, going down a short flight of stairs before they stopped. Panting, they huddled in the lee of a recessed door with a three-foot overhang.

"What was that?" Gerald demanded. His nerves were at their breaking point.

"Quiet," O'Hara cautioned.

Gerald ignored him. "What did you do, Carter? We should have been caught."

"We should have, but we weren't. My organization has many infiltration tools at our disposal. I enacted a low frequency level electromagnetic pulse."

Lights flickered.

"Come on, the power grid is already resetting. We need to get inside before the security sensors are back up,' Carter said.

He pulled a small tool from his belt. He aimed it at the locking mechanism and turned away a split-second before the lock melted under high pressure heat.

"Go."

O'Hara took point, weapon drawn. Gerald followed close behind. Their cushioned boots made no sound as they stole down the semi-darkened hall. Gerald's heart hammered. Fear rose, threatening to undo everything.

O'Hara pulled up at the first corner and waited for Carter to catch up.

"Which way from here?" Carter asked.

O'Hara checked the three-dimensional map built into the back of his glove. A red dot represented where the Fat Man was suspected to be. Two floors up and in what appeared to be an expansive study. Smaller dots showed the location of security guards and house staff going about their business. O'Hara laid out a route to avoid contact until they gained the study.

"We need to go up."

Gerald marveled at the way the two enemies were working together. Carter's knowledge of infiltration tactics played perfectly with O'Hara's internal navigation skills. Gerald almost allowed himself to feel hope that they might find Charlotte yet. The Lazarus Man was content with allowing the Earth Alliance agent to assume the lead, opposite of their way in. Once again, Gerald was stuck in the middle. He didn't mind.

They wormed deeper through the impressive building without being discovered. O'Hara stopped only after climbing a second flight of stairs. The main doors to the study were wide open. Full power was restored, robbing them of all cover. He gave a silent three count—just enough time to ready their weapons. Gerald reached for his stolen pistol, stopping only when he remembered that no one knew he was armed. It was the one advantage he had in this sorry affair. It also never occurred to him why the Naem hadn't searched him when he was captured.

O'Hara and Carter burst forward with weapons trained at chest level. They split. Each took a flank and moved into the study. The first corners were cleared as they pushed deeper. Without any resistance, they were able to reach the second single door marking the entrance to the private room without incident. Gerald played it safe and stayed behind O'Hara. He viewed Fake Earl as the lesser of two evils.

Carter didn't wait. Heavy boots slammed into the door. The locking mechanism snapped, and the door broke open in a tiny shower of splinters. Both he and O'Hara charged in shouting orders and threatening violence.

It was Gerald who broke the tension. "Shit."

"Check the back. We need to ensure there's no trapdoors," O'Hara ordered.

Carter swept the room while Gerald remained frozen in place.

"Nothing," Carter announced. "How could they have escaped? We moved in time."

O'Hara placed his hands on his hips. A dark expression crawled across his face. He sniffed the hint of spilled alcohol. "I don't know. We must have missed something."

Gerald didn't care why things went wrong, only that they did. Instead of focusing on the problem, he looked for a solution. They knew McMasters was still planetside with Charlotte and Creeps. All intelligence pointed to the mythical treasure being on

Cestus. But where? He stumbled through the study, taking in the various artifacts and trophies collected over a lifetime of excess. Only when his eyes fell on the partially scorched map half curled on the desk did he stop.

"Guys, look at this," he called.

Together the others rushed to the desk and peeled open the map. O'Hara slapped Gerald on the back. "Good job, Gerald. You just showed us where he went. We have them."

Gerald didn't share the enthusiasm but was confident enough they weren't too far behind McMasters. With a little luck they'd be able to catch up to him and end this nightmare.

He was tired of running.

THIRTY-TWO

2273 A.D.
Outskirts of Absolution, Cestus III

"Sir, we have a problem," Gholson said shortly after they'd left the compound.

The three vehicle convoy was crawling through Absolution just as the sun broke the horizon. McMasters placed a hand on the leather cushion console and waited.

Gholson swallowed the lump in his throat. "It appears the compound has been infiltrated. Three men were detected moving through the main floors … including your private study."

Jowls trembling, McMasters demanded, "Who are these men and where are they now?"

His harsh tone slashed through the cabin, bleeding vehemence with each syllable.

Gholson flinched. "Security is unclear, but their objective was definitely the study …"

"They were coming for me," McMasters concluded.

He admired boldness in an adversary, but this went beyond blatant disrespect. It didn't take much imagination to know Shine had a hand in the raid. No one else would be so bold or foolish—this action demanded retribution.

"Mr. Gholson, I want those men found and eliminated," McMasters said. His tone shifted to one of deceptive mildness. "No one breaks into my inner sanctum without suffering consequences."

"I can return and ensure the matter is properly handled," Edgemeyer offered.

McMasters almost agreed, however, he couldn't spare one of his most valuable assets right when he had the most need. "No, Edgemeyer. I have suspicion that your special brand of justice will be needed where we are going."

The android sank back into his seat and shrugged.

"It appears as if your expedition is beginning on uncertain footing, Mr. McMasters," Charlotte said from across the vehicle.

His eyes narrowed, but he offered a disarming smile. "Nonsense. All adventures have bumps. I have many enemies, my dear. Any one of whom would be more than pleased with my failure. Fortunately, none of them know what I am attempting to achieve. You need not worry. We will find the treasure and your name will live eternal."

The convoy rolled past a group of robed Naem lingering on a street corner. Their cold eyes followed the vehicles until they were lost to dust and distance. No one in the convoy paid them any heed.

***

Charlotte took quiet enjoyment from McMasters' obvious discomfort with the news Gholson delivered. His foundations had been rocked, even if but slightly. Overconfidence was ever the downfall for many powerful men over the course of human history and she had no doubt that Roland McMasters was going to get his before the end.

"You should keep your teeth together," Tianna warned. "Little flowers like you often get crushed underfoot."

"Leave our guest alone, Tianna. She's quite harmless and, as it turns out, a most willing accomplice to my quest. I admit that we would not be where we are now if not for her calculations and brilliance in her field."

Brilliance? Inwardly, Charlotte scoffed. All she had done was stumble through learning the map with a piece of alien tech on the whims of becoming famous. How did that make her brilliant? Then again, compared to the rest of the menagerie he'd collected she was a genius.

"Your words are most kind and accepted," Charlotte lied. "But if you don't mind, I do have a question."

"Ask. I'll decide whether you get an answer," he said.

Tianna cast a cold look at her. The message was clear. Don't overstep your bounds.

Charlotte did her best to ignore her. "What makes this treasure so important you are willing to risk everything?"

"What determines the importance of a single life? Governments continually seek to consolidate power through the manipulation of the masses. No one at that level cares about the plight of the lesser man. Pick a planet, they are all the same. My corporation has been accused of similar attitudes, but I treat my employees well. Without them I am nothing but a shell."

"With an exceptional bank account," she muttered.

"The treasure of General Karakzaheim is regarded as legend by most, but I know better. You see, I was stationed here when I was very young. The local indigenous population rebelled against the central government, and military operations were executed. It was during that campaign I first stumbled upon the clues and rumors. The Naem believed the stories had been handed down over the centuries from father to son, mother to daughter."

"How would outsiders learn of this? There was no human presence here until eighty years ago," she asked. What little she knew of the Naem suggested a primitive, reclusive culture.

His smile darkened. "My company was ordered to surround and secure a Naem village, not far from our target coordinates in fact. Matters spiraled out of control once our infantry entered the village. The Naem were incensed by our presence. They resisted. Mayhem ensued after the first shot was fired." He paused, face twisting. "Their leader was the first to die. Many others on both sides soon followed."

"What happened next?" Creeps asked. He was drawn into the tale along with the rest of them. The cigarette drooping from the corner of his mouth trembled.

"What would happen anywhere in that type of situation? Slaughter. We killed the Naem to the last infant. Once their leader died, they fought fiercely to defend their homes. It wasn't enough."

"That's horrible," Charlotte gasped.

"That's war."

***

The screams of women and children unceremoniously murdered while forced to their knees had troubled McMasters deeply at the time. He still saw the muzzle flashes. Smelled the cordite and superheated laser burns. When it was over, he walked through what remained of the village. Bodies littered the ground. The Naem had been defenseless against the superior firepower that brought them down.

Perhaps the most vivid memory came from when he halted before the body of a young Naem boy.

McMasters judged he couldn't have been more than ten standard years. The boy's stomach was shredded, and he was bleeding out. McMasters didn't know what made him stop, but he did. Kneeling, he looked at the pain the boy's eyes. Defiance remained. The boy was dying in absolute agony yet continued showing the strength of his people. It was admirable.

McMasters did the only thing he could. He drew his sidearm and placed the barrel to the young Naem's heart. He could still hear the sound of that shot. It haunted his waking moments.

"You have no idea," McMasters replied. A look of sorrow flit through the lines of his face. "At any rate, part of our task was to clear the huts and treehouses. I was fortunate enough to be assigned the village leader's. It was there I found my first clue. A stone the size of my fist. It was crimson with shimmering blue flecks. I was immediately enthralled by the beauty of it. The Naem were little better than savages to our eyes. What use would they have of immense jewels? I took it and spent the new few decades looking for more."

"Leading us to this point," Charlotte concluded.

"Quite so," McMasters said.

"And it never bothered you? Killing these women and children?" Creeps asked.

McMasters was genuinely surprised at the question. His eyes widened. "It was a lesson on power that I have never forgotten. I did what had to be done."

Charlotte, wiping the corner of her right eye with the edge of her sleeve, asked, "How can you live with yourself?"

Folding his hands on his lap, McMasters said, "It isn't very hard. Besides, the moment of reckoning is approaching."

"In what way?" Creeps asked.

"After all these years I am returning to the scene. The coordinated pointed out by the key are exactly where that Naem village was."

Creeps snorted. "I hope you don't believe in ghosts."

They rode on in silence through the last outskirts of Absolution and onto the broad plain leading to the waiting jungle. Thirty kilometers later they arrived at the massive green wall swallowing the road. Tropical trees in every shade of green rose high into the sky. Though Cestus was largely uninhabited, McMasters ensured a road was kept open across the continent. It connected Absolution with the port city of Mariner Bay, running the entire length of the jungle. The local government thought it was out of a sense of patriotism, but McMasters had an entirely different purpose in mind. He knew that at some point he would be returning to the jungle in search of the treasure. He just didn't expect it to be at the scene of a great crime.

***

Charlotte pretended to sleep as she listened to McMasters and Tianna converse in quiet tones. The others had all fallen asleep a while ago. All but Edgemeyer.

"This is dangerous. We shouldn't have brought them."

McMasters sighed. "Tianna, you are going to have to learn to trust at some point. These two are harmless."

"Not from my point of view."

"Creeps is a petty thug at heart. He may have some use before this is over. I've had trouble with the Martian government blocking my intelligence network. He might prove useful."

"He's already sold out a friend. What makes you think his loyalty to you will be any stronger?" she countered.

"I think Creeps—what a foolish name—knows that to double cross me will result in his immediate disappearance. It's the woman who bothers me more."

Charlotte almost opened her eyes at the admission.

"How so? She is mousey. Not the type built for our world," Tianna said.

"No, she's not built for our world, but she is far more cunning than she would have us believe," he said. "People like that have great potential, but they are harder to turn. Between you and me, I believe there is more to her relationship with Mr. LaPlant than she would have us think. We must watch her."

Charlotte held her breath. How did they know? She'd done everything to downplay her plans with Gerald. How much more do they suspect and, perhaps more importantly, what steps are they willing to implement to prevent a reunion?

"I wish you have removed LaPlant from the equation on Mars," he said, then paused. "Or Earth when Edgemeyer had the opportunity."

Risking a glance, Charlotte noticed the android glowering, but he said nothing. Tianna, however, wasn't so courteous.

"That opportunity was thwarted the moment one of the Lazarus Men found him," Tianna said.

"The very same one who I presume managed to break into my home," McMasters conclude. *And the one who you ran into three years ago, no doubt. We all keep secrets, don't we, my dear?* "I fear we may be in a hunt."

"For your life?" she asked.

"No. The treasure. Mr. Shine is a shrewd man. I have yet to come against a man of his … talents. This should prove interesting."

"We should have brought additional security. The Lazarus Men are trained killers and, if what you say about this Shine is accurate, he will not stop until he has defeated you."

"Exactly. Shine has never been bested as far as I know," he said.

"Then how do you plan on defeating him?"

"All men have secrets, Tianna. It's a matter of finding his."

Their silence left Charlotte burdened by yet more mysteries and questions. She didn't know what was going to happen once they reached the plateau. Part of her was suddenly afraid to find out.

THIRTY-THREE

2273 A.D.

Absolution, Cestus III

"They have already left the city," O'Hara told the small group in an abandoned warehouse shortly after dawn.

The Earth Alliance agent had secretly bought and established the facility for clandestine use under the auspice of interstellar shipping. Flights carrying supplies would occasionally arrive and distribute food, supplies, and weapons to the local population. Dissidents were always helpful in the event an armed uprising became necessary. Earth had supplied dissident cells on every one of the outer worlds in anticipation of an insurrection.

Gerald looked up from the rectangular table covered with an impressive array of weapons and tech they had already selected for the mission.

"How do you know that? How could you possibly know where McMasters is?"

"Orbital telemetry picked up a convoy of three vehicles breeching the jungle wall two hours ago. They are moving at speed and laden with excavation equipment," O'Hara supplied. "Contractual agreements between the Naem and the local government prevent any use of machinery or human interference on traditional Naem land unless sanctioned by the archeological authority. There haven't been any digs authorized in almost a decade."

At some point, and he wasn't sure when, Gerald's mind started to wander. The mention of digs brought Charlotte to mind. As much as he wanted her to be alive, to be unharmed, he couldn't trust to fate.

Everything he knew and had been told about McMasters suggested a ruthless man capable of producing great harm on those allied against him. Was Charlotte wise enough to play along? Or had she turned at the promise of finally getting her name out there for the universe to adore? He wasn't a gambling man for a reason.

"Can we stop them before they reach the site?" Carter asked.

O'Hara finished reassembling a short barrel rifle. The clank of the charging handle jerking back and releasing echoed throughout the warehouse. "Unlikely, but that doesn't matter. We already know his destination."

"That doesn't help," Gerald said, returning to the conversation.

"It does if McMasters is distracted. His security will be dealt with by the Naem. Something about an old score to settle. I don't know. Regardless, this will give us the opportunity to sneak in and do what is necessary."

Kill. You mean kill anyone not wise enough to surrender so you can claim the treasure. What will happen to me then? When you both get what you want? Gerald didn't want to ask, content to stew in private conspiracy theories. Both men offered false assurances that he'd be set free while telling him he was a loose end that couldn't be left alone. He knew they both lied.

"Are you going to show me how to use that?" he asked Carter to break the silence. It was a stretch, but one he needed to take. He'd already proven a measure of worth back on Mars and was hoping Carter would entrust him further.

Much to his surprise, Carter said, “Sure. We can use all the firepower we can get. Just as long as you don’t shoot me first.”

“I wouldn’t dream of it,” Gerald lied.

Gerald added the jungle wall of Cestus III to the list of impressive sights he never expected to witness. No expert, he guessed the trees in this dense jungle stretched up at least a hundred feet, making a nearly impassable wall to deter all but the strongest willed. He sensed an ominous appeal lurking within the triple canopy. It unsettled his nerves. Again.

But whatever affected him seemed to have missed his companions. He didn’t see how the three of them were going to stop an entire work party—no doubt laden with armed guards in addition to Tianna and Edgemeyer. Gerald was wise enough to the game now to figure McMasters wouldn’t be separated from his two favorite killers at this point.

O’Hara assured him that all would be taken care of. It didn’t dawn on him to ask about the Naem. They’d disappeared sometime before leaving the warehouse. A shame, considering how savage and intimidating they proved earlier. Gerald tried to relax as they entered the shadow of the jungle. Somewhere in the dense mass of vegetation was the culmination of everything he hated and adored.

“You doing all right?” O’Hara asked. He saw the apprehension clouding Gerald’s face.

Gerald didn’t know how he was doing. “I suppose. What’s the plan for when we catch up? You know we’re outnumbered and outgunned.”

Carter grinned. It was a look ill suited to his personality.

"If you say so," O'Hara replied. "The primary objective is to capture McMasters and secure the treasure."

"Without killing anyone," Gerald ventured.

O'Hara took a moment to answer. "I don't think any of us want more bloodshed."

"Speak for yourself," Carter scoffed.

"Earth Alliance doesn't advocate the use of violence to solve potentially political issues," O'Hara added.

"I don't fall under your jurisdiction."

Gerald winced at the rebuke, getting an instant headache from their back and forth display of machismo. They were worse than the Baker brothers he'd been forced to sit next to during his middle school years. One always trying to outdo the other. The combination of constant posturing left him considering backing out when they weren't looking. After all, he wasn't necessary to the mission. Letting the at odds pair continue to bicker only served to degrade everything and could quite potentially lead to an altercation from which only one would walk away.

No matter what I do, I can't avoid being stuck in the middle. He listened with little interest as their vehicle entered the jungle. Gerald didn't know what to expect, though his mind was already racing with impossible theories. His eyes couldn't remain fixed in one place. Every sight, sound, and smell was alien to him. It didn't take long before the towering height of the trees blocked out the sun entirely. Gerald clutched at the handrail. He wasn't sure why, but it felt like going underwater.

Where he thought the temperature would drop in the shadows, he was surprised to find the heat and humidity increased to a miserable level. Gerald raised the window, realizing O'Hara and Carter were still sniping at each other. Pointless, really. Chances were McMasters would be more than prepared enough to deal with the three of them.

Then there was O'Hara. Gerald found it difficult to believe that the man who had played himself off as being Earl was covertly inserted by the planetary government. Life was making a habit of throwing so many twists at him he couldn't keep up. He stared at the back of O'Hara's head, wondering if there was even a hint of truth between them. He had genuinely liked Earl, after a fashion. Learning Earl was no more than a character made him angry. If he were a different man, a stronger one, he would shoot O'Hara in the back of the head and pray Carter let him escape.

Gerald let out a frustrated sigh and returned to looking out the window. The jungle road was compacted dirt wide enough for one vehicle. He marveled at how the majority of vehicles on Cestus still had wheels. It was hard to find such an archaic vehicle in an Earth museum, much less on the road. The jarring of each hole or bump was mildly disturbing.

The trees were packed so tightly it was hard to see what was ahead. Branches arched and intertwined over the road. Gerald imagined all sorts of creatures and insects crawling through the canopy. Or the Naem. Where were their villages? How many were there? The long-legged natives of Cestus had once ruled their world and were now regulated to skulking in a jungle. He could only imagine how the Naem felt about humans taking over their planet.

"Why are they helping you?" Gerald asked suddenly.

"Come again?" Carter asked.

Gerald gestured with his head. "Not you. O'Hara. Why do the Naem bother with you? Humans took their world. I'd be looking at sticking a spear in your back the moment you let your guard down."

"The Naem want what is theirs."

Gerald didn't buy it. "No, can't be. You and I both know the treasure won't stay here."

"It's not for me to decide, Gerald," he replied. "The Naem are useful allies and will remain so for as long as we need them. It's the same throughout history. Man has moved from one area to the next. Expansionism has been the cornerstone of our success as a species. The Naem were displaced, yes, but the local government is making efforts to amend earlier actions."

"That doesn't change the fact that they no longer own their world," Gerald countered. His suspicions that both O'Hara and Carter were going to backdoor them the instant McMasters was removed from the equation grew.

"No one can own a world," Carter said. "We're fortunate enough to be born and live on any world capable of sustaining life. The Naem are closer to their world than any of us, but even their relatively primitive minds understand the concept of advancement."

"Neither of you answered my question," Gerald reinforced.

O'Hara craned his neck around to look him in the eye. "Gerald, the galaxy isn't a nice place. The Naem help us because they want the glory of Karakzaheim restored. They are proud, but not foolish. Helping us helps them."

"Why would they believe that? You know Earth won't allow them to keep the treasure, even if it does belong to them. Neither will your Mr. Shine, Carter."

"Watch your tongue, Gerald. My employer doesn't take kindly to those who don't fall into his vision of the future," Carter warned.

His tone lacked malice, which Gerald took as a good sign. It showed him Carter wasn't the coldhearted assassin he portrayed. At least not always. Partially satisfied he could negotiate with the man, Gerald decided that O'Hara was going to prove his most difficult obstacle. There was an underhandedness about the man he refused to trust.

"We're going to have to stop for the night soon," O'Hara changed the conversation.

"Its still early afternoon," Gerald said.

The Earth Alliance agent nodded. "And we don't have an accurate recon of the area. The Naem are supposed to link up with us not far from here. They'll lead us to the dig site, ensuring we won't run into any of McMasters' security in the process."

"We can't risk running into an enemy patrol. Not this close to the end," Carter seconded. "No one is saying we shouldn't keep pressing ahead. We need to do so in a logical sense. This is a combat operation, Gerald."

So, we're going to war now? Gerald leaned his head back and did his best to forget everything he'd just heard. Sometimes ignorance was the best policy. Walls of green continued to blur past.

THIRTY-FOUR

2273 A.D.
Northeast of Absolution

Day or night, he couldn't really tell. Carter assured him it was closer to dusk than night, but Gerald found it difficult to care. The discomfort of the moment continued rising the deeper into the jungle they delved. Gerald felt entombed. Green walls closed in on him with each step. He felt, without seeing, thousands of eyes watching him. It was only a matter of time before some jungle creature threw caution aside and attacked. Would either of his companions bother saving him?

Bastards. Probably not. I might as well just storm off into the trees and get it over with. Trapped among his current set of associates was akin to being locked in an asylum cell—only the lunatics were running the show. *And I'm one of them. A glorious fool skipping to my doom. Why did this have to happen to me?*

Carter pulled off the main road three hours into the jungle. A service road led them a hundred meters deeper to a small, manmade clearing. He killed the engine and the trio got out. Carter and O'Hara secured the immediate area; Gerald felt awkward walking around in a perimeter circle by himself, fighting feelings that the jungle was encroaching. Millions of insects groaned, chirped, and creaked unseen. The engine cutting off was the loudest sound he'd ever heard.

"Here, eat. You'll need your strength for what's ahead," Carter handed him a military issue ration packet and canteen.

Gerald glanced down at them. His disappointment was obvious. "Are you sure this is edible?"

He'd never eaten food in a bag before, especially not army food, but he'd heard stories from men and women in passing back in New York. None of them ended with positivity.

Carter grinned and slapped him on the shoulder. "Food's food. What did you expect?"

Flipping the package over, Gerald said, "Something hot would be nice."

"They have heater packets inside. Just like being in a nice restaurant," Carter chuckled. "I heard once they found traces of rat and other vermin in the processed meats, but that was a few years back. There's even flavor packets now."

Gerald's stomach lurched.

"Don't be proud now," O'Hara added. He set his assault rifle down on the vehicle hood and opened his own meal. "Give it a few more days and you'll be willing to eat just about anything. Besides, rat doesn't taste so bad."

There was no joke in his face. Gerald swallowed back bile.

"Look at it this way, you've already eaten live bugs," Carter threw in.

"Wonderful. How much longer do we have to wait for the Naem to arrive?" Gerald asked. The ration pack found a place beside his rifle and remained there.

"They're already here," Carter pointed to the trees on the far side of the clearing.

There, standing under the branches of a giant boayan tree, were a pair of Naem. To Gerald's untrained eye all Naem looked alike, but as he peered closer, he saw noticeable differences. Length and thickness of the blue stripes. The varying shades of crimson skin.

At O'Hara's gestures, the Naem emerged from their cover and walked over to the vehicle. The Earth Alliance agent greeted them with what sound to Gerald like a manufactured growl and then presented a clawed fist. The movement was reciprocated. Gerald watched with fascination as these animalistic and seemingly brutal jungle dwellers displayed unquestionable civilized behaviors.

"Is everything set?" O'Hara asked them.

The shorter Naem hissed. "Yes, Earth Man. Our enemy almost at ruins."

"Wait, what?" Gerald blurted out.

Carter elbowed him softly in the ribs to silence him.

"Very good. How fast can you take us there?" O'Hara inquired.

"Few hours. We arrive before midnight."

Gerald listened intently. There were bits about a plateau. A long march through the jungle. More hours pounding away through the jungle did not seem fast to him. The thought of marching uphill in the middle of the night was ridiculous and, more than likely, deadly. No one in their right mind would attempt such. Not only would the going be slow, but it would give McMasters an even bigger lead. That McMasters might find the treasure while they were still deep on their jungle excursion mired him in unease.

"Get everything from the trunk and drink water now. We still have miles to go," O'Hara said to his companions.

Gerald wanted to yell, shout, anything to get O'Hara's attention. "We can't waste time walking through the jungle! Not when we have a vehicle. We'll never make it."

O'Hara winced, watching the Naem for any sign of a potentially violent reaction before squaring on Gerald. "McMasters will have surveillance on the road. Armed men with superior firepower and tech support. We'd be spotted and gunned down without ever getting close. This isn't a game, Gerald. The treasure is not the only thing at stake."

"What do you mean by that?" Gerald's eyes narrowed. It took great willpower to keep from drawing his pistol.

"One way or another, there will be blood spilled tonight. You need to get it through that wall in your mind that we're playing for life or death," Carter supplied.

Frustrated, Gerald waved them both off and went to the back of the truck to get his gear. "Let's just get this over with. If we're going to die, it might as well be in the jungle."

Night had fallen, turning the jungle into an extremely dangerous place. Gerald listened as both Carter and O'Hara took turns quietly explaining everything that could kill him. Cats almost as large as the truck that brought him. Lizards longer than a man with rows of razor-sharp teeth. A species of bear-like creatures known only to Cestus. He stopped keeping track between the myriad species of insects with flesh eating appetites and an impossibly vast array of poisonous plants. His prospects of ever returning to Earth continued shrinking. He knew they meant only to make him more aware of his surroundings, but the effect was the opposite.

Gerald was terrified.

"Stay on the path and listen to the Naem. They know this jungle," Carter finished as he strapped down the small back on Gerald's back, taking a moment to ensure the weight was distributed properly.

Gerald grunted as the straps tightened. "Are you sure we can't take the truck?"

"You heard O'Hara. It's too loud. We're going to need every advantage we can get. The Fat Man will be heavily guarded and expecting us."

"How can he know? He wasn't home when we got there."

"No, he wasn't. but his security system will have reported the breech to him and possibly identified us," Carter said. "Assume he knows we are here. The Fat Man knows he's being hunted and that makes him very dangerous."

"Shouldn't we call in reinforcements?" Gerald asked.

"We did," O'Hara said from the opposite side of the truck. "Well, the Earth Alliance did. McMasters won't be expecting me, or the Naem."

"You and two Naem don't seem enough to go up against McMasters and win, O'Hara," Gerald said.

A wicked grin was his only response. Gerald held his tongue and reached for his rifle. To his surprise, Carter didn't stop him.

Instead, he asked, "Do you know how to use one of those?"

"Point, click, and shoot."

Carter liked the bravado but gave Gerald a quick lesson anyway. The last thing any of them needed was an accidental discharge resulting in a friendly fire loss. "There. All set. Just remember to keep the safety on until we get into a fight."

"Thank you," Gerald mumbled.

It was the first true act of kindness either man had shown him. He only took a step before Carter grabbed him by the shoulder strap and pulled him close.

"Don't let him fool you. Or me for that matter. We both have separate agendas that don't revolve around you … or your friends. When he says he has reinforcements it's a safe bet to assume he has more than either of us are prepared to deal with."

"How many Naem are there, Carter?" Gerald asked with a whisper.

The Lazarus Man thought for a moment, his eyes locked on the two lanky yet muscular creatures impatiently waiting at the clearing edge. "The last report I read estimated a population of tens of thousands."

Gerald swallowed hard. Just thinking of that many aliens swarming over McMasters' people left his blood chilled. And if they were all loyal to O'Hara … He let the thought die. Time would tell where allegiances lay, and, if his suspicions were correct, there was a massive shake up coming.

"They look impatient," he gestured to the Naem warriors.

Carter agreed and they hurried to catch up with O'Hara as the he entered the jungle.

O'Hara stopped them at the clearing edge. "From here on there is no talking. Sound travels farther at night and no doubt McMasters will have sonic detection equipment positioned around the perimeter, as well as eyes and ears."

"Stay close to me, Gerald. I'll be one step behind you the entire way," Carter assured him. "Trust the Naem. They will get us to the dig site before long."

Trust the Naem.

Stick with me.

Don't let him fool you ...

Gerald's mind was already stretched to the limits and now he was left with minor issues rattling around to further confuse him.

"Let's move, people," O'Hara said and disappeared behind the Naem.

Gerald would never have spotted him if not for the faint glow of a chemlight attached to the top of O'Hara's pack. The dull green glow was just bright enough for him to follow without fear of stepping off the trail.

Shit. I'm going to die.

***

Mr. Shine sat in the cockpit of his private shuttle as it roared across the stars to distant Cestus. The nav computer suggested he would be in flight roughly three hours at sub-light speed. Factor another six for traveling into Cestus' gravity well. Nine hours to finalize his plans for removing Roland McMasters from the problem and claiming the treasure of Karakzaheim for the Lazarus Men.

With the treasure secure, all of his plans would achieve fruition. His fleet would spread across the galaxy in a campaign of conquest. Governments would bow to him or face annihilation. Wealth and anonymity were all well and fine, but it was the lure of power driving him from day to day. He wanted to become the supreme force in the galaxy and maintain control for many long years to come.

Nine hours.

Destiny.

THIRTY-FIVE

2273 A.D.
Deep jungle enroute to Naem ruins

The convoy arrived at the site slightly before dark. It had been an all day trek filled with vehicle breakdowns, security issues, and a host of problems. McMasters grew increasingly silent the closer they got as old memories resurfaced. He'd never been a believer in God, or any other deity. Life was simply what one made of it. He did not believe placing his faith in prayers to the unseen would contribute to his success or result in godly fires funneling down on him from the heavens. That much he knew for certain, but now, as he returned to the scene of a great, inexcusable crime, he couldn't help but wonder if he was wrong. He hoped not. If there was, he surely would hold McMasters accountable for his role in the past.

A quick look around his vehicle interior showed him the others were alert and anxious. His people remained relaxed yet ready to launch into action the instant trouble appeared. Creeps fidgeted with some odd knickknack he'd picked up for the ride, clicking the metal repeatedly in a most annoying fashion. Out of them all, it was Charlotte who interested McMasters the most.

The young archaeologist couldn't take her eyes off the jungle covered ruins of the Naem. He hadn't told her that this was once the heart of their empire. The soul of their people. The very place where he had once come and committed slaughter in the name of a cause he didn't believe in for men he never met. Conquerors often had a way of obfuscating bits of truth to suit their goals. McMasters decided the information wasn't pertinent to helping her find the location of the treasure.

Besides, these were his personal demons. He was often accused of being heartless when it came to business matters and, for the most part, his accusers were right. But if they only knew the tears his heart once bled upon seeing the swath of destruction he'd been an active participant in causing they might change their minds.

There was a time, long before now, when he allowed his feelings to dominate the outcome of his actions. A foolish time. He had since learned to cull those useless feelings and control his appetites. McMasters wanted to dominate. He'd become hardened by the events in this village. Hardened and determined. Still, every once in a while, when he was alone, his thoughts eventually returned to that singular defining moment.

"This is it," he announced as the driver pulled into the center of the ruins, precisely in the middle of the coordinates the key revealed. *The scene of the crime. How long I've avoided returning here*.

"Can we get out?" Charlotte asked with thinly disguised excitement.

"Patience, Charlotte," McMasters cautioned.

"I don't understand."

McMasters indulged her, explaining, "Mr. Edgemeyer must see to security first. This is not friendly territory."

To Edgemeyer, he said, "I want a perimeter established immediately. Lock this area down."

Edgemeyer exited the vehicle without a word.

McMasters scanned what he could see, searching for any signs of disturbance or ambush.

They were alone for now, but time was against him. The wolves nipped at his heels. Soon his foes would arrive.

"Mr. Gholson, take your team and begin seismic monitoring. I want this plateau accurately mapped and ready for us to get into those tunnels within the hour."

"Yes, sir." Gholson pushed his glasses up the bridge of his nose and snatched the small computer case on the way out.

Tianna watched him leave before asking, "Where do you need me?

"See that the workers are unpacked and ready to begin operations. There can be no delays. Not this close."

She nodded and paused just long enough to ensure Charlotte understood the look in her eyes before following the others.

"What about us? What are we supposed to do?" Creeps watched Charlotte suppress a shudder.

McMasters grunted. "I've half a mind to set you loose in the jungle to see how long you last, you impetuous twit. Sit here and mind your tongue. You've already managed to grind on my last nerve."

Rebuked, Creeps settled back into his seat.

"I suppose you can't wait to get a closer look at these ruins?" McMasters returned to Charlotte. He delighted at the way her face lit up at his question.

"You've read my mind," she replied. "But I think I will keep waiting until the area is safe."

"If you insist. The jungle is an ever dangerous place, even for a party as heavily armed as we are. I don't fault your need for caution. Come out at your leisure, but do not take too long. Darkness will be upon us soon. The treasure is very close," McMasters said.

He shut the door behind him.

***

The finality in his tone spoke volumes. Charlotte struggled with her growing concerns. The very thought of studying these ruins, hallowed ground for the Naem, of giving society the opportunity to learn more about this ancient civilization, was almost too much for her. This was an unprecedented opportunity she had only dreamed of. Whatever harm had befallen the Naem was ancient history and, despite her initial reluctance to intrude, Charlotte allowed the pull of rediscovering the past to take over. This was her element.

Charlotte had been in tense situations before. Looters and vandals were a constant threat to archaeologists, especially on lightly populated worlds that had yet to be mined for natural resources or hidden riches. That there were potentially dangerous creatures stalking them from the security of the surrounding jungle took this dig to unexpected levels. She knew McMasters didn't care about archaeology. He just wanted the treasure and would use any means to obtain it. Ultimately, she knew there was no way she'd be able to sit in the airconditioned comfort of the vehicle.

Destiny waited for no one.

***

McMasters exited the truck, setting foot on the killing ground for the first time in decades. He'd always known he'd return here someday. Long had he avoided thinking on how he'd react standing among the rubble of all those souls he'd helped murder. The dust of their bones was beneath his boots. The military proclaimed it a great victory, awarding the senior leaders and several others who had 'distinguished' themselves in combat.

McMasters knew it was all a bad joke. The truth never got out. There was no reason for his unit to massacre these civilians. They did so out of bloodlust, pent-up frustrations, and poor training. Nothing more. Little did anyone know that he was the sole survivor of his unit. Or that he had been the one to orchestrate their demise one at a time. He took simple satisfaction in the knowledge, but he still had far to go before redemption was his. Once his task was complete, he could finally lay the past to rest—he hoped.

"The perimeter is secure," Edgemeyer said, walking up. "I will have the motion sensor array in place and activated within the hour. No one will get in without us knowing."

"Excellent. Are the security teams fully briefed?" McMasters asked.

"Yes, sir."

No further explanation was necessary. McMasters knew Edgemeyer was thorough and efficient in his assigned tasks, especially when it came to providing security.

"Very good. I'll dispatch Tianna to you for additional measures," he said.

Edgemeyer shrugged. "If you say so, but I can handle it."

"I know you can, my boy, but I can't afford to take chances."

McMasters turned and smiled as he watched Charlotte take her first steps into the ruins. She was already rolling up her sleeves.

His life's work was about to reach fruition.

Nothing could stop him now.

The first sign of something going wrong happened shortly after the sun was gone. Jungle nightlife crawled from den and bole, throwing the motion sensors into turmoil. Edgemeyer and Tianna tried removing the natural interference to no avail. They were about to report to McMasters when rifle fire broke out on the far side of camp. Sporadic shots echoed through the ruins before cutting off with unnatural abruptness. Edgemeyer sprinted in the direction of the shots, leaving Tianna in place. She returned to the command tent and the bank of computer screens, hoping to spy whatever had caused the disturbance.

A second bout of gunfire erupted from the opposite direction. Three guns this time, as if the defenders were concentrating fire to suppress a large scale assault. Aerial reconnaissance drones over each of the cardinal directions showed her nothing however, leaving Tianna and the camp effectively blind. This was unacceptable. Her fingers typed furiously, desperate to recalibrate the drones and defense systems to detect other vision spectrums.

Once again, the gunfire ended too quickly to be natural. There was no tapering off. No residual fire as men tried to determine if the moment of danger was passed. Just an abrupt ceasefire suggesting something bad. Unlike before, a high-pitched scream ripped out of the jungle. The cry was picked up by several others from various points around the perimeter. Birds erupted, taking flight. Low hanging branches snapped and broke to the southwest. Tianna drew her handgun and set it on the tabletop for easier access. Should death decide to make a grab for her this night she'd meet it with her own special brand of violence.

"What is going on?" McMasters demanded as he swept into the command station.

The small popup tent she was in was large enough for three tables, each holding an array of computers and monitoring equipment. Light emitted by the low-level lighting bulbs was kept inside the tent by dense fabric, ensuring the command area was well protected against prying eyes. Technicians sat at two of the tables, busy in their work and anxious to avoid their employer's ire. A holographic map depicting progress by the excavation teams covered the far wall.

"Someone answer me," McMasters demanded again.

"I don't know. The sensors are going haywire. We've picked up a mass of heat signatures moving to the north, but the drones have spotted nothing. So far, the gunfire has been concentrated here and here," Tianna paused to point out the incidents on the map.

"Bring up the tactical schematic of the outer perimeter. I want flares illuminating the area continuously for the next thirty minutes. No one, I repeat, no one breaches the perimeter without paying the consequences."

"Yes, sir," she answered with looking up.

"Has there been any positive identification?"

"None yet, but Edgemeyer has gone to the first position. He should be there by now."

"Raise him. We can't commit forces to one particular area without knowing the size of the force," he ordered. "I wan … n …"

Light machinegun fire lit up the eastern approach, cutting off his words. Leaves and small bushes disintegrated under a withering stream of fire. Tianna and McMasters hurried from the command tent and viewed the last stitch of rounds trace into the jungle. The smell of cordite choked the air, hovering in thick clouds billowing out over the ruins. Men ran from one position to another.

Night vision partially distorted, Tianna picked out Edgemeyer's gaunt frame marching through the ruins with undisguised authority. The android carried a rifle and a furious glare. She peered closer, he was dragging something behind him.

"Who did this?" McMasters growled, gesturing at the corpse Edgemeyer deposited at his feet. Broken spear shafts riddled the body.

Edgemeyer gave the body a final look. "Unknown, but I don't believe the numbers are significant. Otherwise they would have swarmed us already."

***

McMasters knelt; the simple act ridiculously difficult due to his immense proportions and shot knees, to examine the killing weapons. He had seen them before—flashes of the past returning to toy with him. The ghosts of the Naem had indeed arisen.

"Why can't we find them, Edgemeyer?" He knew there was no reasonable explanation as to how the Naem were able to stalk close enough to kill without being spotted in return, or how they had arrived her so fast.

"My only guess is that they are moving in small two to three man teams, and at speed. If the jungle was filled with these creatures there'd be more of a physical presence."

"Take care, Edgemeyer. These are Naem spears. The Naem aren't human at all," McMasters muttered.

"I thought you said you killed everyone in this village?" he asked.

"We did, but not the species, as you know. If my guess is correct, they will continue to strike throughout the night. It's an old terror tactic designed to inspire fear."

McMasters glanced at the corpse. Fear was already taking root in his people. All it would take to push them over the edge was a little nudge.

THIRTY-SIX

2273 A.D.
Naem ruins, Cestus III

Creeps had never endured a night so fraught with terror. Every time he drifted off to sleep he was awakened by the sounds of gunfire, or worse. His nerves were beyond frayed. Shadows took on the characteristics of fanged killers. He had no one to turn to. No one to invest his fears in. He began to think he'd made a terrible mistake. If he hadn't betrayed Gerald, he wouldn't be in this terrifying place.

All of the adventures since leaving Oberon City served to worsen his life. He'd only seen the promise of payment for services rendered. McMasters was clearly at wit's end with him, not that he could blame the man. Creeps didn't enjoy being around others of his own quality. He certainly didn't belong around men like McMasters.

He cracked his fingers in an attempt at relieving some of the compounding stress but only achieved a strained sensation that irritated him. Creeps stopped looking for support sometime after midnight. The work crews were either busy setting up camp or in hiding. Only McMasters and Edgemeyer seemed unperturbed. If he'd been thinking clearer, Creeps might have taken comfort from their examples, such as they were.

"Wake up, you useless sack of flesh."

Creeps groaned, a hand reaching for weapons he didn't have. His eyes fluttered rapidly in an attempt at clearing the sleep away to see who his confronter was. His eyelids felt stuck together. Crud caked them shut, reluctant to give up their hold. His body was sore, tired from sitting awkwardly in the back of the truck for so long. The worst part was his bladder felt like it was about to explode.

"I said up, now."

He knew the voice. Edgemeyer. Creeps frowned as the android came into focus. For the moment, his fear of McMasters' killer was more than his fear of the unknown.

"Wha … what is it?" he asked, trying to shake the sleep still gripping his mind.

Edgemeyer remained stoic. "Mr. McMasters wants you."

Creeps slid out of the vehicle and was hit with a wave of humidity that turned his empty stomach. He began to sweat. Tiny biting insects swarmed to his exposed flesh. He knew enough about the Cestus environment to know that many of these bugs carried diseases that had no cures. He should have gotten his money and run the moment they arrived at McMasters' compound. This was intolerable.

The ground was soft but not muddy as he expected. What bothered him was the atmosphere. The very air felt like … like death. The notion was ridiculous. McMasters said his raid happened over forty years ago. There was no way, not with the decomposition rate in the jungle, that any part of those bodies remained. No doubt even the bones had been dragged off and gnawed away by local predators.

He found McMasters standing outside of the command center looking like a battlefield general.

Despite his girth and age, he was a dominating presence, capable of inspiring intense emotion.

McMasters looked down on him with clear disdain. "I have a task for you."

Creeps resisted the urge to run. To steal a vehicle and head back to the relative security of Absolution and hide until he could escape back to Mars. The reality of his current situation was far less forgiving than his frail dreams. His mind screamed for him to remain silent. To keep his mouth shut rather than express his distaste with the situation. Edgemeyer's presence at his back all but forced the words out.

"What is it?" Creeps asked. He couldn't keep the reluctance out of his voice.

McMasters tried not to sneer. "The time has come for you to use your particular skillset. I want you to go with the lead team and find the passage to the treasure chambers."

Creeps made a show of looking around. False bravado gradually returned as he couldn't believe his turn of luck. "Where?"

"Underground, young man. Where else would the Naem have secured their wealth?"

The answer, while obvious, sent chills down his spine. "Me? Underground? I don't think so. It looks to me like you have more than enough people for that job."

"Odd. I don't recall offering you a choice," McMasters said. "Edgemeyer here will see you are outfitted with proper gear. Digital mapping devices will be attached to your harness. Make this quick and I'll consider our arrangement concluded."

"If I don't?" The words were out before he knew what he was saying. He felt Edgemeyer step closer.

"As I said, you have no choice. Do as I say, or your body will be yet another in a long list of victims in this dreadful place. Now go and do not fail me."

He was dismissed with a nonchalant wave, adding insult, and Edgemeyer snatched him by the elbow and half pulled him to where the handful of excavators were already preparing to make the trek underground. Several wore frightened looks, as if they knew this could be a one-way trip. Creeps wasn't afraid of being underground in cramped spaces. That didn't bother him. It was his fear these ruins were haunted robbing him of strength. Knees weak, he struggled into his gear.

The others ignored him, for the most part. He was another inconvenience forced upon them by McMasters. One more life thrown into the grinder that was a steadily expanding empire of naked ambition and uninhibited, though secretive, violence. Creeps wanted to introduce himself. To feel some form of companionship before the mission. Nervous silence told him it would not happen. He was alone, just as he had been since selling out his friends.

When he was finished, Creeps waited for Edgemeyer to inspect him. There could be no chances taken now. No errors to halt progress. Deemed ready, the android led them down to the entrance of an expansive set of tunnels and chambers previously unexplored. The narrow openening beckoned with darkness.

"Go. Report your progress every five minutes," Edgemeyer commanded.

They filed underground without question. Creeps was forced into the middle in the event he decided to bolt.

***

"I should be with them," Charlotte fumed as the last man disappeared underground.

McMasters appreciated her enthusiasm but wasn't willing to risk her expertise. "Not yet."

"You know not one of those men has the proper qualifications to put them in that position."

"Patience, my dear," McMasters insisted. "You'll have ample opportunity to explore. I can't allow you underground until my men have cleared the area of potential traps. The Naem are a most resourceful people. If the treasure of Karakzaheim is here, it will be well guarded."

She edged a little closer to the monitors. "Is that who attacked us last night?"

"Most definitely. This is a sacred site to them after all." He looked around the jungle, as if trying to pick out lurking Naem warriors concealed behind the trees.

Charlotte paced; hands wrung in front of her. "How long will this take? I can't help but feel that time is against us."

"It most assuredly is. We are in the midst of a great conspiracy. A game of impossible angles and with too many threads for even me to keep track of easily. You should be so fortunate to remain ignorant." McMasters folded his hands and resumed his watch on the jungle.

A preemptive expedition led by Edgemeyer produced negative results. If the Naem forces were indeed nearby they remained well hidden. A troubling fact on a good day, but after their harrowing night,

McMasters couldn't help but feel concerned. His security detail suffered two casualties. Both men died from poison tipped spears. There was damage to the surrounding area caused by weapons fire, but they had yet to discover a single drop of blood. Curious.

His thoughts turned to the men burrowing deeper underground. Initial mapping showed the area was a complex maze of winding tunnels and deep pits. Finding the treasure, or at least those suspected places adequate enough to hide it, was no sure thing. He knew many of these treasure expeditions across the galaxy ended in failure or catastrophic loss, their benefactors going bankrupt in the process. While he wasn't in danger of losing his vast fortune, McMasters stood as much of a chance at failure to find the treasure as all of the others.

He idly wondered for a moment what it was like being down in that dank, cramped environment with only your breath for a companion. Were his men choking in the tight atmosphere as much as he was here in the middle of the ruins? Waiting without action, he ultimately decided, was a fruitless endeavor.

"Tianna, has there been any further activity on the perimeter?" he asked.

"None. Not since dawn broke," she answered.

So, they play a game. McMasters began to pace. They were in for a very long day and the promise of an even longer night.

***

Mr. Shine had been on Cestus III once before. In terms of climate, he didn't mind the high humidity or the blanket of sweat coating his waxy flesh the moment he stepped into the open air. There were certainly worse conditions on other planets. No government officials were here to greet him. Nor were there any assistants or forward based agents as he went from the flight line of the small terminal to the set of contractual offices used on an as needed basis. Shine chose to recall the additional firepower he threatened Carter with after deducing the entirety of the Fat Man's plan. Besides, Carter assured him all pertinent information for the coming task would be uploaded and encrypted in one of the computer banks—accessible only to Shine.

The information was there as promised and so it was Shine learned of McMasters' destination and who was accompanying Carter into the jungle ruins. It greatly disturbed him that an agent of the Earth Alliance was working hand-in-hand with one of his best agents. All political machines were corrupt in his experience and the lies the Earth agent no doubt spewed, while sounding enticing, wouldn't serve any point to Shine's plans: Project Daedalus needed to proceed.

He did find the knowledge and use of the local Naem against McMasters interesting, but the Naem presence would present unanticipated problems. He needed to find a quick, logical way to eliminate them without compromising his position. That they were the true inheritors of Karakzaheim made things much more difficult than he wished. Still, they would serve their purpose without knowingly helping his. It was, as in all matters in his experience, a matter of applying the proper manipulation. Once the trigger point was discovered, all else fell into place.

Shine shut down the computer and pulled a small vial of clear liquid from his jacket pocket. He unscrewed the cap and poured the contents on the row of computer banks.

They burst into flames.

THIRTY-SEVEN

2273 A.D.
Naem Ruins, Cestus III

Time underground held little meaning. Each moment spent without the comforting reassurance of the sun was an eternity. Creeps felt his world crash down upon him as the continued to twist in an impossible maze. Why anyone in their right minds would decide to expend so much time and energy in developing such a system was beyond him. Though, to be fair, his was a simplistic life meant to stumble from one moment to the next without pursing much thought on the future. It was the combination of payment and the others in McMasters' employ that kept him going deeper.

Creeps would have run if not for the man with gun directly behind him. Cursing his fate while resigning to it, he kept going. The first tremor was barely noticeable. A few pebbles cascaded down the rough walls. Small clouds of dust puffed up.

He shivered, despite sweating profusely. His skin itched, as if a thousand spiders were crawling over him. A cramp in his right calf nearly toppled him, forcing the group to wait long enough for him to rub it out. He tried taking his time, but the menacing glares of his counterparts forced him to suck it up and keep moving. The only positive thing he discovered was he was not alone with his distaste of the tunnels.

Remote sensors were deployed, small spheres filled with mapping technology. Scientists had been using them for years as humanity continued expanding to new worlds. Two men in front of Creeps monitored the sensors as they relayed real-time data back to the small handheld computer that transmitted to the command center. Everything they saw, McMasters could see as well.

He didn't care about any of that. Instead, Creeps' focus lay in finding the treasure and getting out of the jungle.

Creeps looked over the tech's shoulder, noticing the small pocket of dark mass in the center of the screen. "What's that, right there?"

The tech, clearly irritated, shrugged Creeps off. "I think it's what we're looking for. Now get back and let us do our jobs."

Rebuked, Creeps did what he was told. He followed the group deeper underground to investigate the anomaly. They made it another twenty meters, almost to the massive chamber Creeps had spotted on the monitor, when the floor collapsed beneath them.

***

"Sir! We have a problem," the main computer operator shouted.

Both McMasters and Tianna stared hard. His face twisted upon viewing the clouds of dust billowing on screen.

"It looks like a cave in. We lost the entire advance team," the operator was visibly shaken. His right hand trembled. "They're … they're gone."

"Gone where?" McMasters demanded.

"Sensors indicate a tunnel collapse. There are no life readings."

McMasters drummed his fingers on one forearm. Too much was going wrong. First, the long night which, to be fair to his planning, was at least partially expected. Now four more lives lost. He didn't care for any of them. They were useful tools. Nothing more.

He mused over losing Creeps. The man was naught but dead weight to begin with and Cestus ended a problem he hadn't been looking forward to dealing with. Still, his death was a lesson in greed.

"How far did they get?" he asked.

Tianna jerked in surprise, looking at him with newfound uncertainty. "We just lost four men. I—"

McMasters ignored her concerns, instead focusing on the wall monitors. "They don't matter. How much did they map before they died?"

Close to a kilometer of tunnels were clearly mapped out. There was no telling how much more lay undiscovered, but he felt he had enough basic information to proceed. The treasure would be, in his estimation, near the center of the maze in a large chamber if rumors of size and quantity were to be believed. But where?

He spied the massive compartment at the very end of his team's progress. Several branches split away from the main tunnel, giving additional access points beyond the collapse. There was no way of knowing the structural integrity of these tunnels. The possibility of further collapses or worse remained high. Yet he couldn't take his eyes away from the edge of the chamber.

What secrets did it conceal in the deep dark of the world?

"There. That room. I wat excavation teams to begin digging directly down into it," he said, pointing to the map.

***

Tianna's eyes pinched in concern. Four men had just died and McMasters showed no emotion. She knew he was a hard man but never had she seen him behaving so callously. The notion was disturbing. "How can you be sure the treasure is there?"

"It is."

He turned and walked away, the trail of cigar smoke trailing behind him in the morning air.

"Ma'am?" the operator asked.

"Do it," Tianna seconded. She hurried to catch up to McMasters.

"What was that?" she demanded as she slid in next to him.

He kept walking, regarding her with a scowl. "Questioning me in front of the others now?"

"I'm questioning how your reckless behavior is costing us valuable lives without producing results," she countered. "Our enemies are getting closer, Roland, and we don't have the extended capabilities on hand to fend them off should they arrive before we secure the treasure."

"A handful of lives are insignificant when compared to the mission. Do not doubt now, not when we are at the end of a long journey," McMasters told her. "The treasure is paramount to every other consideration. Am I clear about this?"

"Of course," she said. Tianna ran through various potential scenarios. Ultimately, his way was the only way. That didn't mean she liked it. "How soon do you want us to begin digging?"

"Immediately."

Crews were already several feet deep when more troubles arose. Digging machines were largely ineffective due to the closeness of the ruins and the unstable nature of the ground. Men who were digging remained skittish, fearful of dropping to their deaths. Tianna listened to McMasters vent threats, and when that failed to work, he offered huge bribes to no avail. Regardless of his motivation methods, the men were too frightened to move faster than was deemed safe by the lead engineer.

Also, the men continued to look to the jungle. The events of the night before left them raw and tired. There were whispers of boogeymen and monsters ever out of eyesight. Not even Edgemeyer's predatory movements succeed in convincing the men to work faster.

In the end, it took Tianna's subtle encouragement and quiet threats whispered in the occasional ear to get the dig teams moving again.

Midmorning brought about a renewed threat. Whooping cries rang out around the perimeter. They were close and threatening enough to put Tianna on edge. Bloodthirsty calls taken up by more and more of their unseen antagonists. Weapons were hastily passed out to the work crews. The men had little to no training on how to use them. It took little imagination to see how disastrous this could turn.

A few nervous workers fired off sporadic bursts into the foliage. The roars and taunts intensified. Spears and large stones were launched into the perimeter. Vehicles were dented. Tents ripped. There were no casualties, however. She considered that positive, given the current unraveling of their situation.

Digging slowed substantially as men became more focused on the exterior threat than finding McMasters' treasure. Work practically ground to a standstill.

Trained as a spy and occasional assassin, Tianna's skillsets were useless when confronted by an unseen enemy. No help in the open, she returned to the command center and paced as the reports of movement and incoming projectiles continued filtering in. The need to do something made her muscles jump. She hated standing around while the rest of their group was besieged—her nerves built.

"Ma'am," the main operator called. "We're picking up large bodies of movement coming in from the north, east, and south."

Tianna closed her eyes, wishing it all to go away. "Is there positive identification?"

"Not yet."

She slammed an angry fist into the light metal field table. A stack of datapads bounced and fell to the ground. "Damn it! Find me legitimate targets so I can kill them!"

A handful of drones were launched and sent to the areas with the heaviest concentration of movement. The tips of her fingers blanched white as she gripped the back of the chair in front of her. Fleeting images of shapes came into view. Tall, lanky yet deceptively muscles. Crimson and blue. She bit her bottom lip, drawing blood—

Naem.

Scores of the natives. More than enough to overrun the beleaguered camp and kill everyone within. She snorted. *Fitting, all things considered.*

"Open fire," she said and watched as laser fire and 2.75in rockets slammed into the swirling masses of Naem.

Several bodies dropped. Nowhere near enough to save the camp but enough to enrage the Naem further. Tianna feared all she'd done was provoke what promised to be a violent demise.

***

Gerald's feet were burning. He hadn't ever walked this far. Ill fitting boots produced numerous blisters; small but growing with each passing step. His shoulders ached from the weight of his pack and swaths of his flesh was rubbed raw. He felt blood drip into his shirt. Sweat caked his hands. More than once he dropped his weapon along their route of march, much to the dismay of his companions.

Pure darkness occluded his point of view. It was so dark Gerald could see nothing around him. Only the faint light on the back of O'Hara's pack guided his way. Gerald had never seen such raw darkness before. Everywhere he'd ever been on Earth was marred by light distortion. Even Mars had a bright quality to it. Only in the jungles of Cestus did he find near primordial night. He'd never experience such complete darkness. It frightened the wits out of him.

He couldn't speak. Couldn't explain his fears in order to combat and defeat them. No, all he had were the myriad voices in his mind as opinions and observations clashed. The torment was excruciating. Gerald tried to focus on the end; on finally clearing his name and returning to a normal life. Nothing else mattered. Once they reached McMasters and did what they set out to do it would all be over. Finished. He wasn't foolish enough to believe that, but the lie comforted him as the kilometers strolled by.

Strange sounds reached him over the sound of his own heavy breathing. Unmistakable sounds. Footsteps. Low growling. He figured, hoped, they were additional packs of Naem. Their fierce countenance inspired his strength, despite leaving him to the point of being petrified. They were terrifying to a man who lived in the press of the big city. Yet that terror was subdued by the knowledge that they were temporary allies.

Carter's hand on his shoulder jolted him. His heat hammered, threatening to burst free of his chest.

"Easy, Gerald," Carter whispered in his ear. "We're halting here for five. The Naem don't need to stop, but we do. Drink some water. If you have to take a leak kneel down to reduce the noise impact."

Gerald knew better than to ask why, even though his mind screamed in protest. Ultimately, he decided it wasn't that important. He followed instructions silently. Soon enough this would all be over. A bad dream left to the ever-dimming tide of memory. All he needed to do was keep putting one foot in front of the other for a while longer.

One step at a time.

THIRTY-EIGHT

2273 A.D.
Naem Ruins, Cestus III

Edgemeyer stormed through the ruins. His processors worked rapidly to compensate for the increased activity on the outer perimeter. Everywhere he went workers cowered, desperate to avoid his wrath. Thus far he had failed to find a single living Naem. Compounding his frustrations was the fact that the surviving primitives secured their fallen and slipped away before Edgemeyer was able to arrive on scene. Living and dead disappeared, leaving behind already drying pools of blood.

He growled and turned to stalk the perimeter again.

***

McMasters watched the scene play out as the day progressed. His faith in Edgemeyer's ability to coordinate a static defense coupled with Tianna's natural aggressiveness allowed him to focus on the prize. Dig crews continued to burrow deeper into the sacred ground. How could he have known all those years ago that this was a place of holy worship for the Naem? To a man barely out of his teens, it was just another battlefield. Yet eight of his men had already paid for that ignorance with their lives. Though they were of little consequence so long as he secured the Karakzaheim's treasure. All those years of longing and waiting would be fulfilled the moment he laid eyes on the jewels.

"You didn't have to send him in," Charlotte said from his side. Her arms were crossed. It was clear to him she was still fuming over the deaths of the advance team. Of Creeps.

McMasters winced at the vehemence of her tone but otherwise showed no outward reaction aside from shifting the half-smoked cigar to the opposite side of his mouth. "Necessity dictates here, Ms. Bailey. Creeps did not die in vain."

"Didn't he? What did Creeps do to deserve falling to his death who knows how far underground? Will his body ever be recovered, or is he to remain and join the horde of ghosts already haunting this ground?"

"I am a businessman above all else. Creeps was an asset. An expendable asset I had no qualms against using," he explained. "His death was unfortunate, but as you well know, these endeavors are prone to risk."

"We take precautions to prevent the loss of any life," she defended.

He turned, peering down on her. "What would you have me do?"

She sputtered. "Anything! You can't just send men underground into undiscovered areas when there is technology capable of performing the very same act. Yes, risk is part of this job but those in control have an obligation to ensure their people live."

He wondered how she'd react if he told her the truth about Creeps' inevitable fate. Seeing her anger, watching her twitch from foot to foot as she struggled to control her emotion was as amusing as it was inspiring. No, he decided. Telling her wouldn't serve any purpose aside from turning her against him permanently. McMasters usually had a good sense about people. He ultimately wanted her at his side for the next few years as plans for expansion and potentially funding additional digs entertained him.

"I agree with you. The loss of those four men was regrettable. Their families will be well compensated once we are finished here. You have my word," he said.

Before she could respond, an excited runner hurried up the slope to their position. McMasters motive the runner over.

"Sir! They've broken through the ceiling," the man said, sucking in deep breaths. Nervous excitement rolled across his face.

"At last," McMasters uttered. "Lead on." He glanced back to Charlotte. "Ms. Bailey, if you will accompany me. Our conversation will have to wait until later."

Charlotte almost leapt in front of him, eager to see for herself. The bug had bitten and she was hooked. Years of toil. Research, and disappointment were all so close to ending. Imagining her name in every respected journal, invitations to speak at major events and committees, she felt the crowning achievement of her career within her grasp. It was enough to set aside her anger, for the moment.

The trio walked at a brisk pace, as fast as McMasters' immense frame could manage, to the center of the ruins. Mounds of freshly removed dirt were piled off to the far side, inadvertently providing a natural barrier against Naem aggression. McMasters had no doubt Edgemeyer was already incorporating that into his beleaguered defense scheme. A quick glance around showed him that patrols looked to be all but abandoned at this point as the excitement of possibly finding the treasure spread, which did not make him happy. His military training, long ago it may be, suggested that if the enemy broke through, his people would be overwhelmed with little difficulty.

Forcing aside negative thoughts, McMasters halted at the lip of the massive hole and peered down. The opening was easily capable of fitting several men at once. Sunlight filtered through the canopy but lacked the punch to see down very far. He needed an access system to get his people down to the ground and the treasure out. Provided it was in this chamber. It wasn't yet noon and his nerves were high. Somewhere on Cestus III were a handful of men intent on keeping him from victory. Combined with the calculated Naem aggression, McMasters knew the odds were stacked against him.

The clock was ticking.

Gholson appeared, datapad in hand. "Sir, we've managed to create a wide enough entry point, but haven't proceeded deeper. The ground is extremely loose and we fear losing more equipment to a cave in similar to the one that already occurred."

"Is there any sign of the treasure?" McMasters demanded.

"We haven't been able to determine an accurate location, but the sensors are picking up a massive metal signature not indigenous to the planet's geology," Gholson said.

"Speak plainly."

Gholson's face twisted as he rephrased, "There are many shapes in the center of the chamber that are not organic. This suggests the items were placed there strategically."

McMasters rubbed a bug bite on his chin. "I want people down there immediately. We can afford no more delays."

"But the ground …"

"Is of no consequence to me," McMasters growled. This close to the prize, he wasn't willing to accept any further delay. "Show me."

Gholson took him to the point where the artificial lamps were already dropped in place so the workers could see what they were doing. McMasters was drawn to the piles of crates and boxes heaped in the center. His breath caught. So close. Judging the depth to be well over thirty feet and oppressively dark despite the lights, he failed to make out any specific gold or jewels.

The anticipation was proving too much for him.

"Is this area stable?" he asked.

"Sir, I—"

"I advise against continued use of the machinery," Charlotte interrupted. "With this much of the ground already removed we've weakened the outer crust. Any more digging, at the speed we have moved thus far, could cause a collapse, burying everything you've come for."

"Meaning I won't collect my due," he finished.

Tick-tock.

She shook her head.

McMasters asked her, "Will the current situation sustain body weight?"

"I don't see why not," Charlotte said.

Inwardly, he smiled. "Good. Mr. Gholson, use ropes, ladders, whatever equipment necessary to get teams on the ground. I expect to be touching the first of my treasure within the hour."

"At once, sir." Gholson hurried away to relay orders. He passed a thankful expression to Charlotte as he walked by.

"Is your opinion based on logic or desire?" McMasters asked Charlotte once they were alone.

She jerked at the question as her earlier statements were being twisted and thrown back in her face. Any other time she would have been incensed. "My prognosis is based on how much longer it will take before you lose your temper. You don't seem to understand that digging through ancient sites isn't meant to happen in the space of a single afternoon. Each shovel destroys a piece of the past that could help us develop as a people."

"The development of the human race will happen with or with my interference. I have no care for the Naem. They were worthy enemies but little else. Now they are all that stands between us and the greatest discovery in hundreds of years." He paused. "When men look back on this moment, do you suppose they will lament the desecration of these ruins? Or will they praise a daring group of people who were willing to risk all for the sake of the future?"

Charlotte frowned. "What are you really going to do with this treasure?"

"That is none of your concern," he said a little too fast.

"You're going to keep it!" she guessed.

To which he snapped a laugh. "Of course, I am! You didn't expect me to just hand it over to the local government or feed masses of hungry unfortunates did you? I've spent a lifetime searching for this. By that right alone I have every claim to use the treasure of the famed General Karakzaheim as I see fit."

Charlotte placed her fists on her hips. Uncontrollable rage washed over her. "This treasure belongs in a museum! Or back to the Naem. Not in your bank accounts, Roland McMasters. What gives you the right to rob history?"

He gestured to the circle of armed men around the camp. "They do. Every man here with a gun does. How many people have wasted their lives on foolish quests for treasures that didn't exist? The lost Dutchman's mine, Oak Island, Olympian Trench on Mars, and countless others scattered throughout our history. All of them ended in failure. Nameless men and women searched and searched only to die without finding anything. History is written by those who succeed."

"I refuse to help you anymore," she said defiantly. "This isn't why I came along."

"No. You followed me like a willing puppy. All you cared for was having your name attributed to this find. Consequences be damned. I haven't seen you lift a shovel since we've been here. You, Charlotte Bailey, are little more than a glorified seeker parasite."

"How dare you!" she all but screamed. Her face burned bright red. Tears hinted on the corners of her eyes.

McMasters loomed over her. He jabbed a pudgy finger in her chest and held it there. "One more outburst from you and I'll give you to the Naem. You're here at my request and only through my tolerance do you remain. Rest assured that once my amusement with you ends, you will be sent far, far away. Or perhaps you care to meet an end similar to Creeps?"

So you did have him killed. You cold-blooded bastard. Charlotte pressed her lips shut and walked away before she did anything foolish.

***

"I told you she was more trouble than she was worth," Tianna whispered to Edgemeyer as the young archaeologist stormed off. "You shouldn't have brought her here."

"I did what I was told," Edgemeyer replied. "He wanted her and the other one."

Tianna scowled. She enjoyed her job but found McMasters' mood becoming increasingly erratic. His once sound decisions were being replaced with furtive, spur of the moment ones resulting in the loss of lives. She wasn't about to have her name added to his growing list of casualties.

"I should get rid of her," she said.

"I wouldn't. Mr. McMasters was adamant about delivering her unharmed," Edgemeyer cautioned.

She knew she couldn't count on the android as an ally if things went sideways. He was wholly devoted to McMasters and would act within the limits of his programming to neutralize any subversive attempts on her part. Never one to be without an exit strategy, Tianna was growing uncomfortable with her decision to attach herself to McMasters. The Naem had been unexpected by all but McMasters. His admission during the trip to the ruins, when it already far too late to voice her concern, showed her just how far he was willing to go to achieve his dreams and of the consequences should he fail.

Their position was growing more precarious as the day wore on. It wouldn't be long before the Naem were ready to launch a full offensive. Judging from the violence already displayed, she doubted they were open to taking prisoners—nor could she blame them. McMasters' group was yet another band of reckless humans desecrating one of the Naem's most sacred sites. Vengeance would be terrible, if not swift.

"What are your plans for when they break through your defenses?" she asked.

Edgemeyer regarded the question with suspicion. "When? I don't foresee them doing so. They are savages without technological advances. We will be safe here."

More the fool. "Of course they will," Tianna countered. "We've already lost a fair portion of firepower, to casualties or in the dig. They have us outnumbered twenty to one."

His flat face stared back at her in silence.

Frustrated, Tianna balled her fists and returned to the computers. Some battles weren't worth fighting.

She'd only been seated a few moments before Gholson entered, out of breath and fidgety. "What is it, Gholson?"

He pointed back toward the center of the ruins. "Mr. McMasters has gone down into the chamber."

Son of a bitch! He should have gotten Edgemeyer or me to do that first. What is the fool up to? Incensed, she stalked off toward the hole.

***

Roland McMasters had lived a good life. Not long enough to accomplish all of his plans or dreams, but enough to have left his mark on society long after his demise. It wasn't enough. He was far from ordinary. Nowhere close to normal. He wanted more. He wanted to control the galaxy from behind the scenes. Now, he was close to achieving his final, ultimate victory. His palms were sweaty. His mouth so dry he had trouble swallowing. All due to the crates and covered boxes filling the chamber floor.

"What are you waiting for? Open that box," he demanded, glancing at Charlotte. Childish giddiness laced his voice. "Hurry."

"They could be trapped."

"So?" he blinked.

"So, more people could die for no reason," she replied. "You'll lose who knows how much of this treasure that way. Are you prepared to walk away from here emptyhanded?"

He wasn't. They all knew that. Growing furious with impatience, he pointed to the nearest worker. "Grab that box on the edge and bring it over here."

The man looked from McMasters to Charlotte—the gunshot rang out before she could open her mouth. Blood puffed from his chest as he fell. Charlotte stared at the smoking barrel of a small pistol in McMasters' hand.

Satisfied he now had their full attention, he gestured to the next man, who hurriedly obeyed. A few grunts and tense moments of struggle later and the man had the oblong box safely away from the rest of the pile and at McMasters' feet. His fingers trembled as they pried the ages old lock apart and flipped back the lid. He shied away in anticipation of an explosion that never materialized.

When he found the courage to open his eyes, the worker found the others staring wide-eyed. There, nestled in a forgotten box, were gold and jewels of every color. Some the size of a fist.

They had found the treasure of General Karakzaheim.

THIRTY-NINE

2273 A.D.
Naem Ruins, Cestus III

"Quickly, get these boxes ready to haul to the surface. I want this chamber emptied and onto the trucks immediately," McMasters ordered. "Get everyone not on the perimeter to help. Load now and we inventory later."

"I never believed ..." Charlotte gaped.

McMasters looked smug. "That is why you won't be remembered. No one remembers the doubters."

She didn't have a reply, knowing anything said now would only serve as fuel for his arrogance. Charlotte stepped away from the treasure as men hurriedly began moving boxes and crates into position to be pulled to the surface. A pair of drone lifters, much larger than the defense platforms deployed in the jungle, were flown in and loaded. Charlotte and McMasters boarded the first one and were lifted clear.

The wait wasn't as long as she expected for the first loader filled with treasure to reach the surface. At least a small part of the treasure was above ground for the first time in generations.

As if on cue, Naem warriors rushed the automated gun defense systems. Spears and stones were heaved at the stationary weapons. Naem fell in the storm that followed. For a while it looked as if Edgemeyer's defense grid was going to hold. The initial assault was repulsed as clouds of thick smoke hung over the ruins.

Any hope of salvation evaporated as the perimeter took incoming fire. Small arms and heavy caliber weapons lashed out from the jungle to take down the defense grid. Naem warriors poured through the gaps in unstoppable columns. They killed the unfortunate guards who failed to throw down their weapons in surrender or fall back to better defensible positions in time. Charlotte stared at the scene in horror, even as she reconciled with her part in the story of the treasure.

***

"Fall back to the command center! Protect the command!" Edgemeyer roared and charged into the Naem.

His superhuman strength was equal to that of the native warriors. Bodies collied in a puff of dust and clash of flesh. Fists pummeled. The Naem grunted; Edgemeyer grinned, feeling no pain. Naem bone snapped. Synthetic blood spilled from tears in the android's skin. He gave the Naem an uppercut that drove the warrior back. Dazed, the Naem staggered—Edgemeyer leapt up and wrapped both hands around the Naem's neck and twisted. The audible snap was heard meters away. Edgemeyer dropped the body and move on to the next opponent with robotic precision.

***

From her vantage point in the center of the ruins, Tianna watched as Naem continued swarming out of the jungle. Scores turned into hundreds and more kept coming, making it abundantly apparent that whatever falsehood McMasters once told himself about these primitives were lies. Perhaps, just perhaps, if she gave him over to the Naem they might let the others go. It was evident none of them were going to get out of this debacle alive otherwise.

"Stay here and direct what remains of the defense," she instructed Gholson before hurrying out of the tent.

***

Dawn broke and the exhausted team was still kilometers from the ruins, again prompting Gerald to question the intelligence behind abandoning their vehicle in favor of sneaking up on McMasters. What little he knew of military history suggested that the element of surprise was paramount to tactical success. As civilizations continued to advance technologically that meant fighting at night. It was a far cry from the Middle Ages when men walked into battle in lines or laid siege to stone fortification. Their idiotic trek through the jungle cost them time and energy and amounted to a wasted effort in his mind.

His one solace was he could finally see again and the need for strict noise discipline was reduced. Only the Naem seemed disconcerted by the reduced pace. Though Gerald couldn't help but feel their building aggression. It was as if they knew a great secret the three men didn't. He meant to bring it up with Carter, but their sudden renewed pace and his constant breath as the kept pushing for the top of the plateau helped keep him quiet. It was all he could do just to keep pace.

They halted again two hours after dawn for water.

The Naem growled, arguing with O'Hara. Frustrated, he waved them off and walked back to Carter and Gerald.

"What was that about?" Carter asked.

"They say we are moving too slow. Something about it has already begun," the Earth Alliance agent said.

Carter stiffened.

Gerald was confused. "What's begun?"

"If you listen closely, you can hear the sound of gunfire coming from up ahead," Carter explained.

It was difficult to make out, for the thick canopy and foliage of the jungle muted much of the sounds. But eventually Gerald could hear the telltale pop-pop-pop of weapons fire. A sound he hadn't heard before this adventure began and one he'd never be able to forget. Provided he lived past today.

"What do we do?" he asked. Nerves made his voice crack.

O'Hara hung his head. Sweat dripped from the tip of his nose. "We're almost to the site. If what the Naem are suggesting is true we will arrive well after they attack. We need to pick up the pace and try to salvage this before it gets too far out of control."

Gerald snorted. They'd been out of control for the last few days. Why bother stopping now? Reluctantly, he hefted his pack and stretched. The weight burned as the straps dug into the well-worn groves in his shoulders. "What are we waiting for?"

Carter nodded approvingly. "That's the spirit."

The last stretch of their journey went remarkably fast, much to Gerald's relief. Each step carried him closer to that ultimate showdown with the man responsible for ruining his life. He used it, taking Carter's advice to turn his emotions into raw energy. Anger was often a powerful motivator but only so long as the man didn't allow it to consume him. Once set down that dark path there could be naught but heartache and ruin. Gerald wasn't certain if he had what it took to see this affair through, but if it meant returning to any normalcy of life, he owed it to himself to try.

It wasn't long before they heard the heavy sounds of a fully developed firefight. Weapons fire and the roars of more Naem than he imagined existed filled Gerald's head. He walked past the torn body of a Naem. The warrior's lifeless eyes stared up at him. A reminder of the grim fate awaiting. His stomach turned. A firm hand clutched his shoulder and forced him on.

"Focus on me. There's nothing you can do for the dead," Carter shouted above the report of a heavy weapon.

Gerald hadn't realized he'd stopped.

"Stay behind me," Carter explained. "This is going to get hairy."

Going to? Another time Gerald might have debated that but, as he'd come to learn, listening to those with more experience helped increased the likelihood of a longer lifespan. He dashed in after Carter as they wormed their way through the trees to the clearing edge. Moss covered stone walls broke the otherwise flat landscape. Black smoke curled up from destroyed machines. Tents filled the central space before him. Men in green uniforms ran here and there. Naem warriors sprinted through the ruins in search of vengeance. Gerald didn't pay attention to any of it. His sole thought was of not getting peppered by incoming rounds.

The rate of gunfire had lessened abruptly since the trio made their final push. Broken trees littered the scene. More Naem bodies cluttered the ground. Many more than he wanted to think about. Each time he stepped in a pool of blood is splashed over his boots, staining his pants. He couldn't imagine how anyone might get used to such slaughter.

Carter halted at the outer stone wall and crouched for added protection. Only then did Gerald notice O'Hara was no longer with them.

"Now what?" he asked. Gerald thought it best not to bring up their companion.

Carter watched as Naem warriors swarmed over the defenses and into the ruins. "We wait. I don't want to take the risk of the Naem viewing us as the enemy through all the confusion going on in there."

"What about Charlotte and Creeps?" Gerald blurted. "We can't leave them to die like the others."

"No, we can't, but I have no desires to get killed in the process of searching for them. We wait," he said with finality.

Gerald couldn't sit back and watch his friends get slaughtered. He needed to act. To do anything in the hopes of saving them. But he was no hero and had no experience in these matters.

A thought popped into his head. He didn't know what him want to charge in for the rescue. Knowing Charlotte and Creeps were out here somewhere in this mess, Gerald could not resist the urge to find them. After all, neither would be in this position if not for him. Gerald did the brashest thing in his life. He slipped away from Carter's reach and charged into the ruins on the heels of a small band of Naem.

Charlotte and Creeps were out there, and he was going to find them.

***

O'Hara used the distraction of the battle to abandon Carter. He expected the Lazarus Man was ready to do the same. Their arrangement had been one of convenience. Neither trusted the other and both had orders setting them on a collision course. He harbored no personal animosity against Carter Gaetis and had no desire to see him dead. That's as far as it went. O'Hara appreciated that Carter had taken genuine interest in Gerald's wellbeing though. Men like Gerald were needed in this world.

O'Hara was rethinking his plans as he slid behind a stand of trees thick enough to conceal him. He waited as Carter and Gerald moved out of sight. Satisfied they weren't yet worried about his disappearance, he hurried off to find the Naem guides. He hoped their allegiance would hold a while longer. Proud warrior instincts would keep them at his side until the Fat Man was stopped. The problems would arise once the fighting was ended and there was only the treasure to consider. He wondered if he would be able to abscond with it in one of the Fat Man's trucks while the Naem were still celebrating their victory. The idle thought of being rich tickled him.

His hopes diminished as he watched one of the trucks burning out of control. The Naem were content with the old ways. Spear and flame. They viewed all that man had brought to their world as contamination. How they'd managed to survive this long was beyond him.

Reaching the nearest breech point, O'Hara raised his rifle to the ready position and stalked into the ruins. Bodies and destroyed equipment littered the area. Smoke made it hard to see. He nearly missed the defender with his rifle rising up from a pile of stone. Nearly. O'Hara spun and fired. The man gave a startled groan and fell dead. O'Hara continued moving deeper into the ruins and the fog of battle.

His efforts were rewarded a short time later when he laid eyes on the immense figure of the Fat Man. Roland McMasters stood beside the nearest operable truck, directing his people. A used rifle rested comfortably in his hands. Treasure crates were being hauled from a hole in the ground and loaded onto the truck. How any man could continue working in the midst of such chaos astounded O'Hara.

He made his move.

***

Gerald had never been more terrified in his life. Not even watching Edgemeyer murder his neighbor in his door produced such torment. A Naem approached, noticing his marking as an ally before slipping into the smoke and dust. Gerald decided to follow.

He tripped over a body and fell beside it. Gerald pushed up from the already cooling corpse of one of McMasters' guards. His hand came away slick with blood. Sickened but oddly becoming used to the tragedy, he avoided looking at the man's face and kept going. It was at that moment Gerald realized he didn't know where he was going or what he was looking for. He wanted to find Charlotte and he needed to deal with McMasters. He was blind in the midst of a battle and lacked direction.

The vague possibility of finding either had been a fool's notion—until now. No one in his tiny circle wasted any time theorizing about the treasure. At least not openly to him. Perhaps there was a way to fill his pockets in passing. A reward for the misery they'd all put him through.

Choking on smoke as it passed in front of his face, Gerald waved through it and was met with a sight that made his heart leap. Charlotte was there, crouched down behind a truck being loaded with aged crates. In front of her stood a man of immense proportions. It was his former employer, Roland McMasters. Gerald slipped the heavy pack from his shoulders and clicked the safety off of his weapon. At last, his moment of redemption was at hand. All he had to do was make the shot.

Tucking the stock deep in the pocket of his shoulder like he'd been taught, Gerald raised the barrel.

One quick shot and it would all be over.

His fingertip slipped over the trigger as he closed his left eye. The crosshairs in his scope lined up on McMasters' chest.

One quick shot. That's all he needed.

FORTY

2273 A.D.
Naem Ruins, Cestus III

"Get under the truck," McMasters told Charlotte as they watched the army of the Naem advance through the ruins virtually unopposed.

The outer defenses were shattered. Most of his guards were slain. Those lacking the courage to fight were cut down even as they tried surrendering. The Naem were hungry for retribution.

Charlotte watched as a change came over McMasters. He was no longer the greedy puppet master controlling entire governments. That persona faded; replaced by a solider. Until now McMasters had been the one to order others to do his dirty work. Now … She watched him snatch up a rifle from the back of the truck and begin firing at the Naem. Two dropped before the small group knew what was happening.

"We need to leave!" she screamed over the howls and roars of the Naem.

He shook his head and, unexpectedly, said, "No. This must end here. Today. I've escaped from my past too many times. The moment of reckoning is at last upon me. I hope you survive this, Charlotte Bailey."

He began to walk off before she could protest. A metallic pop pinged over her head. She looked up as paint chips and miniscule shards of metal peeled off of the truck from a small bullet hole. They were being shot at! But the Naem had no weapons other than primitive ones. Her heart sank at the prospect of a new enemy creeping into their midst.

She had to warn him. "Roland! We're being shot at!"

He stopped and turned, mouth open to reply. Blood fountained from his left shoulder, striking her in the face and hands. He staggered, almost falling to his knees.

Charlotte screamed.

***

Carter cursed himself for not following Gerald, but his assignment was higher priority than a man who, by all accounts, was already supposed to be dead. Gerald was never meant to leave Earth, much less the train on Mars. That he continued surviving one impossible scenario after the next was testament to his skill, or just plain dumb luck. Carter was no longer sure which.

"Good luck, Gerald," he whispered as the man disappeared in the wall of smoke. "I hope you find what you're looking for."

Satisfied that he had done enough, Carter shrugged his pack off and double-checked his rifle. The Fat Man was out there and so too was Agent O'Hara. It was a safe assumption that both were now considered hostile. Once again, the Lazarus Man was on his own. It was a comforting thought. Men like Carter Gaetis preferred working alone.

The first Naem attacked him seconds after entering the ruins, confirming his suspicions. He fired a three round burst into the warrior's face, blowing out the back of his head and killing him instantly. Battles were won by men with ruthless composure. Slipping back into that mode was easier than he imagined. Carter was once again a killing machine. But he was not the only one in the ruins.

More Naem bodies dotted the area. Most bore no visible signs of gunshots, meaning they'd been killed by hand. Carter knew of only one man here capable of committing so much carnage—Edgemeyer. Pushing thoughts of the Fat Man and Gerald aside, Carter set off in search of the Fat Man's favorite killer.

No one was safe until Edgemeyer was stopped.

It didn't take long before he came upon his target and a lone Naem warrior locked in single combat. Five bodies were on the ground around them. Carter was appalled. Edgemeyer had accepted some obscene code of Naem honor demanding trial by combat. They readily leaped to their deaths at his bloodstained hands. And for what? There was no amount of honor worth the lives of so many.

Carter had long suspected that Edgemeyer was other than human. Wounded in numerous places, Edgemeyer was beginning to slow. There was a tiny shower of sparks coming from his elbow. *No wonder the bastard has been able to handle these Naem. He's an android.* Carter knew his best chance for victory was by killing Edgemeyer from a distance while he was distracted. Yet as much as he wanted to take the shot, he felt the first inklings of personal revenge spring forth. He wanted a fight. Wanted to beat the android into submission and remove his threat from the galaxy for good.

He never got the chance.

Hard metal pressed against his head. The soft voice following the familiar click of the safety being taken off chilled him. "Drop the gun, Carter."

He closed his eyes, feeling foolish for getting consumed with the action in front of him. Gun on the ground, Carter rose, slowly, and turned with his hands in the air. "Tianna."

"You couldn't just walk away," she chided. "This was never your fight."

"You wouldn't understand," he said.

She snorted. "Try me. I could have killed you on Mars."

"You and I both know you were fortunate to escape me. Twice."

Tianna stepped back, her gun hand wavering slightly. She was unwilling to kill Carter in cold blood. She couldn't deny her attraction to him. The other way they might … She lowered her weapon. The fight was gone from her. "Go, before I regret this."

Carter stepped clear and glanced over his shoulder at her. He was surprised to see the conflict etched in her feature. "Tianna, I …"

She shook her head. She'd seen enough violence and bloodshed. Years of unquestionable loyalty were washed away by the insanity of the last few days. Tianna wanted nothing more than to escape the clutches of the man she once viewed as a father.

Sensing this, Carter lowered his hands and grabbed his rifle off the ground. "Let's not cross paths again."

He hurried away, in search of the Fat Man and his prize. Tianna threw down her weapon and sobbed.

***

The command center was awash in chaos. Computer terminals were frozen from the massive amount of data streaming in. A few of the techs had already fled, abandoning their posts. Gholson stood in the middle with only one other man. The gunfire had died to almost nothing, replaced by the animalistic roar of the Naem. He looked at each screen. Any hope of securing the treasure and heading back to the safety of the compound was gone. Most of McMasters' team was already dead. Their quest was finished.

Gholson's allegiance to Roland McMasters didn't include dying for him. They were well beyond that point now. He gave the command center one last look before quitting. There was no viable scenario in which he saw himself dying. Making a show of cleaning his glasses, Gholson did the only thing he could think of.

"Get out of here while you can," he told the last tech.

Taking his own advice, Gholson slipped through the side flap—

His world evaporated. Those careful constructs of his imagined security washed away the instant he entered the battlefield. The dead were everywhere. Smoke and fires. Gholson felt a trickle of urine run down his leg. His hope faded. Then he spotted McMaster's private transport, it was unguarded and unharmed.

Not believing his luck, Gholson looked around to ensure the area was clear and rushed to the truck. A short time later he was speeding down the plateau and back through the jungle, to Absolution and the next transport off world. He didn't discover the small chest filled with jewels until right before takeoff.

***

Charlotte watched McMasters stumble into the side of the transport truck. A smear of blood marked his falling. The unexpected smile on his face as he gazed into her eyes shocked her.

"Go. Run," he said. His voice was raspy. Blood bubbled on his lips.

She was frozen in place. Charlotte had never watched a man get shot. Never imagined how much anguish and suffering was possible. Overcome by fear, she tried to move. Her legs didn't follow.

"Go!" McMasters insisted.

The crack of his voice sent her into motion. She ran without knowing where she was going or what to do. All that mattered was escaping the sniper trying to kill them. Crimson skinned Naem were everywhere, though no seemed interested in her. Charlotte used that to her advantage and pushed herself harder. She kept her eyes focused ahead, doing her best to avoid looking down at the bodies.

Smoke thick with oil clung to her skin and hair. She choked on it. The uneven ground made it difficult to keep her balance. More than once she stumbled and fell. Her knees were scraped. Elbows bled from cuts. Desperation attempted to take control. Emotionally she was fraught, on the verge of collapse. The glory of finding the treasure of Karakzaheim was suddenly unimportant.

"Charlotte!"

She skidded to a halt and turned at the sound of her name. Her mouth dropped open as her eyes fell on a man she never thought she see again.

***

Gerald pulled the trigger a split-second before being tackled to the ground. He dropped the gun and drove an elbow into his attacker's stomach then pulled free. Light spots burned in his eyes from the impact. When he started to rise, a kick swept out to take his legs from under him, effectively pinning him to the ground.

"Stay down if you know what's good for you," O'Hara growled.

Gerald placed a hand over his throbbing temple. "What the hell?"

"You idiot! Killing McMasters was never part of the plan. What are you trying to do?" the Earth Alliance agent said.

"I'm trying to get even!" Gerald shouted back. "He took my life from me, *Earl*!"

O'Hara shook his head and glanced at the wounded McMasters. "Does going to a prison colony for murder right anything? You're a good man, Gerald. Don't do this. Let me take him into custody. He's more valuable to everyone alive."

"Not to me he's not," Gerald stood defiant.

"Think about what you are about to do," O'Hara countered. "Think about your friends. They're out here somewhere. Do you really want to abandon them to this course?"

Charlotte! He looked up to see her duck out from behind McMasters and bolt back toward the center of the ruins. His face blanched as realization struck. He could have killed her.

"Keep it together," O'Hara said. "This is almost over. Go and get her. Take her out of here while there's still time. Make a new life, Gerald. You deserve it."

He didn't need further encouragement. Gerald hurried after her, his only weapon the small pistol he'd secured on Mars. O'Hara was right. He didn't need to kill McMasters to find fulfillment. The more he thought on it the more he understood this wasn't who he was or what he wanted to become. Best let others handle this unfortunate affair. The number of Naem coursing through the ruins, and O'Hara's willingness to engage him spoke volumes of just how badly the Fat Man was reviled.

Gerald drew his pistol for self-defense as Naem rushed by. He thought one was from their journey through the jungle. The Naem paused a heartbeat to stare at him. Blood dripped from his fangs. The Naem warrior gave a knowing smile and kept moving. Gerald felt sick to his stomach.

Charlotte hadn't gotten very far. When Gerald was close enough he shouted her name.

His heart quivered when she turned. The look on her face told him she thought he was dead, already decomposing on Mars. Or worse.

They rushed toward each other. A host of questions plaguing each. How did she get here? Where was Creeps? None of them were as important as the single most pressing issue he could think of. How do we get back to Absolution, and home?

"I thought you …" she began.

Gerald wanted to laugh. "No. Almost, but no. I … made a friend and managed to escape. Where's Creeps?"

She swallowed the lump in her throat. "Gerald, he betrayed you from the start."

"No. That's impossible." The admission felt like a dagger to his heart. Another betrayal on a growing list.

"It isn't. Creeps was contacted by McMasters once you registered for transport to Mars. McMasters has been tracking you since New York City. Creeps betrayed you for a fee since you first called him," Charlotte explained.

"Where is he now?"

"He died yesterday in a cave in. McMasters sent him underground. I think he wanted Creeps dead," she said.

Gerald frowned, having difficulty processing his emotions. "Tell me more about it later. We need to get out of here. There are too many different factions at work. Are there any vehicles that still work?"

An explosion made them both crouch.

"Just the one with treasure being loaded on it," Charlotte said. "The Naem have destroyed all the rest. How did you get here?"

He shook his head. That was an experience he was not repeating. He hoped there'd be time enough for explanations later. Then he remembered the untouched transport they left back in the jungle. It would be a long, difficult walk … one that might well prove impossible given their conditions, but it was his only bet.

"Come on, I think I can get us out of the ruins," he told her. Gerald grabbed her hand and they headed toward the jungle.

It felt good to feel her hand in his. A comfort in knowing at least a measure of his task was complete. When they rounded a corner where trees had overgrown the path he jerked to a halt. The scene playing out in front of them was almost impossible to comprehend. Edgemeyer was engage in battle with a Naem warrior. Many dead were on the ground around them. Even closer, Tianna had Carter on his knees at gunpoint.

The whole world had gone mad.

***

Whether it was rage or impulse that spurred her actions, she would never know. Charlotte snatched Gerald's pistol and clicked the safety off. She drew a bead on Tianna. Her arm waivered. This was her one opportunity to avenge all the suffering and trouble she had endured since being kidnapped on Mars. A cleansing moment opening the path for her return to academia and the celebrity sure to come from discovering the greatest treasure in modern history. Yet when her mind screamed to pull the trigger, her finger resisted. Pent up frustration and the growing levels of internal disappointment filled her. At last, she cast the weapon to the dirt.

"What was that about?" Gerald asked in dismay as he recognized Tianna Everson.

Charlotte stood her ground. "Nothing. Let's go. I am tired of all this, Gerald. I want to go home."

They froze at the sudden rustling in nearby bushes. Armed warriors emerged, weapons pointed at the pair. Gerald's stomach clenched. *Looks like we're not going home after all.*

***

Crowds of Naem surrounded them. They pushed a bound Tianna and McMasters into the center to stand beside Gerald. Carter appeared not long after, beaten and haggard. Over his shoulder, Gerald could see Edgemeyer's body. The mad killer had finally gotten his due. The only one missing from the reunion was Gholson. O'Hara stood off to the side, guarded by a trio of angry Naem.

"So much for allies, eh *Earl*?" Gerald quipped.

O'Hara stayed quiet. The Naem betrayal of the Earth Alliance was not a surprise. Gerald took in their collection of misfits and wondered what came next. There were no other survivors. All had been killed during the raid. Not that Gerald blamed the Naem. This was their most sacred site, if what he'd learned from O'Hara during their trip out of Absolution was true. Now it belonged to them again.

"My, my," A chilling voiced mocked from behind the tall warriors. "What a pretty sight."

Ranks parted to allow an unassuming, pencil thing man to slip into the circle. Gerald stared at the pale man who commanded the arena. Then it hit him. The voice. He'd seen this face before. On the train from Oberon City to Creighton Colony. His heart thumped.

"Shine."

Mr. Shine removed his wide brimmed hat to see who had addressed him. A wry smile creased his face. "Ah, Mr. LaPlant. I see you have managed to survive all of this."

"With no help from you," Gerald growled.

Carter raised a staying hand. "Gerald, don't."

Shine stepped up to Gerald. "I could have had you killed at a dozen points along your journey. You are alive because I allowed it. You are welcome."

"What of the rest of us?" McMasters asked. His voice was slurred from a quick dose of pain medication. His hands were in cuffed and attached to a chain running to O'Hara. His shoulder was bandaged.

Shine's smile became genuine, yet predatory. "You, my friend, are now property of the Earth Alliance. They've been after you for a very long time. You and Agent O'Hara will be released to Earth Security Forces once we return to Absolution."

McMasters glared venom. "What gives you the authority? This is my world, not yours, Shine. You don't belong here."

"One might argue similar for you, Roland," Shine taunted. "Be that as it may, your little game is at an end. I'm quite afraid you lost."

"But the treasure!"

Shine nodded, enjoying the outburst. "Yes, unfortunately part of my arrangement with the Naem was to leave the treasure with them. Not the outcome I preferred, but it did belong to their greatest hero."

McMasters struggled against his bonds. “You bastard! You wanted this as much as I!”

“Perhaps, but the outer worlds have agreed to compensate me handsomely for turning you in,” Shine explained. “So, you see, I still win.” He paused to take in the motley collection of survivors. “Goodbye, Roland. We shan’t meet again.”

He turned to leave. The tip of his walking stick poking into the soft ground. A chime sang across the area. Several Naem recoiled and readied their weapons. A frown spread across Shine’s face as he reached into his jacket pocket and placed the comms device to his ear. Anger flushed his cheeks. His back stiffened.

“I see,” he said after long moment. “Very well.”

Replacing the device in his pocket, Shine confronted the prisoners. He licked his lips. “It appears this is your lucky day, Agent O’Hara. You are free to go on your own. Cestus government officials have reached an agreement with our friends here. The treasure will return to the Naem with certain conditions. This site will become a sacred historical place for generations to come. McMasters is yours. Carter, it is time we left this wretched place.”

Shine motioned for Carter, who followed obediently.

“What about the rest of us?” Gerald asked.

“I don’t care. Go and live your lives. You will find your name has already been cleared. Either go back to your stagnant life on Earth or forge a new one. Forget you ever heard of us, Mr. LaPlant. Your life will last longer that way,” Shine said.

Gerald watched the most dangerous man in the galaxy disappear back into the jungle where he his transport awaited. The Naem went about returning their treasure to its burial site. A handful of them escorted McMasters away. O'Hara was at his side. Gerald watched Tianna climb into the truck cab, waiting for it to be unloaded so she could drive away.

"I need a vacation," Charlotte said when they were alone.

Gerald nodded. "We both do. Where are we going?"

"Nowhere if you insist on standing in this jungle," O'Hara called from the edge of earshot. "I will take you both at least as far as Earth Alliance space. After that you're on your own, Gerald. I …I am sorry for all of this."

"Save it, O'Hara. You did what you were told and used the rest of us," Gerald replied. "I don't agree, but I think I understand. Just do me one favor."

"That being?"

Gerald's grin turned fierce. "Leave me alone for the rest of our lives."

"I can do that, Gerald. I can do that."

The trio followed the Naem back to the jungle and the way home. Their long ordeal was at last over.

END

The Lazarus Men will return soon in:

Repercussions:
Book 2 of the Lazarus Men Agenda

REPERCUSSIONS

A LAZARUS MEN AGENDA

CHRISTIAN WARREN FREED

2275, a girl walks into a bar....

And is thrust into the adventure of her life. She and a motley assortment of bounty hunters, soldiers, shapeshifters, and academics have been chosen by a mysterious benefactor to be the first to find a long-forgotten jewel. It is a treasure hunt for the ages.

When Mr. Shine, enigmatic leader of the Lazarus Men gets a whiff of it he sends his best agent, Carter Gaetis. Backstabbing, shaky alliances, and the threat of a galaxy wide war fill this fast-paced adventure across the stars. Will any survive the hunt, or will the Lazarus Men get their due?

From award winning author Christian Warren Freed, the Lazarus Men combines the action of James Bond, Science fiction of Total Recall, and the intrigue of the Maltese Falcon.

Other Great Series From
Christian Warren Freed

The wolves are returning to war.

Exiled millennia ago, the dark gods have tirelessly sought to return and bend the world of Malweir to their will. Their agents roam the world in search of weak-willed men. Only through corruption and chaos can their master's return. It begins in the northern kingdom of Delranan the night King Badron's castle is attacked, and his only son murdered and his daughter kidnapped. Angered, he leads his kingdom to war against the neighboring Rogscroft.

A small band of heroes is assembled to find the princess and return her safely, but all is not as it seems. Badron falls under the sway of the Dae'shan, immortal agents of the dark gods, and unwittingly begins the final campaign that will reduce Malweir to willing servants of evil.

Hammers in the Wind is the first of six books in the Northern Crusade series. Combining military fantasy with modern tactics and written on the battlefields of Iraq, this is the ultimate military fantasy.

Law of the Heretic

Immortality Shattered Book 1

CHRISTIAN WARREN FREED

Immortality Shattered Book One.

The Staff of Life has been lost for a thousand years. Imbued with the powers to dominate all life, the Staff can save or ruin the Free Lands. Many have sought out the Staff. All failed. Until now. Betraying his oath and bond, the Black Imelin sets out to find the lost Staff of Life. With it he will bring the Free Lands to their knees. The only thing standing in his path is a young Aron Kryte, a leader of promise and the unknowing heir to the future, if he lives long enough.

Filled with dangers, monsters, and creatures hidden for centuries, Immortality Shattered delivers the same intense action and character driven world building combined with his military experience that fans worldwide have come to enjoy. A small band of heroes assembles but success is far from guaranteed. Life and death hang in the balance and the future is in doubt.

BIO

Christian W. Freed was born in Buffalo, N.Y. more years ago than he would like to remember. After spending more than 20 years in the active-duty US Army he has turned his talents to writing. Since retiring, he has gone on to publish over 30 military fantasy and science fiction novels, as well as his memoirs from his time in Iraq and Afghanistan, a children's book, and a pair of how to books focused on indie authors and the decision-making process for writing a book and what happens after it is published.

His first published book (Hammers in the Wind) has been the #1 free book on Kindle 4 times and he holds a fancy certificate from the L Ron Hubbard Writers of the Future Contest. Ok, so it was for 4th place in one quarter, but it's still recognition from the largest fiction writing contest in the world. And no, he's not a scientologist.

Passionate about history, he combines his knowledge of the past with modern military tactics to create an engaging, quasi-realistic world for the readers. He graduated from Campbell University with a degree in history and a Masters of Arts degree in Digital Communications from the University of North Carolina.

He currently lives outside of Raleigh, N.C. and devotes his time to writing, his family, and their two Bernese Mountain Dogs. If you drive by you might just find him on the porch with a cigar in one hand and a pen in the other.

www.ingramcontent.com/pod-product-compliance
Lightning Source LLC
Chambersburg PA
CBHW010356310726
48979CB00006B/1062

* 9 7 8 1 9 5 7 3 2 6 1 1 5 *